RESTRAINT

THE REVELATION SERIES
VOLUME TWO

D1521893

RANDI COOLEY WILSON

Edited by Kris Kendall at Final-Edits
Proofread by KD Phillips with Indie Solutions by Murphy Rae
Cover Design by Bravebird Publishing
Cover Image by ©Susanitah

Restraint (The Revelation Series, Book #2) | Randi Cooley Wilson
Printed in the United States of America
Second Edition November 2015
ISBN-13: 978-1495429293
ISBN-10: 1495429296
LCCN: 2014906092

ALSO BY
RANDI COOLEY WILSON

THE REVELATION SERIES
REVELATION
RESTRAINT
REDEMPTION
REVOLUTION
RESTORATION

ROYAL PROTECTOR ACADEMY
VERNAL
AEQUUS
NOX

For my daughter, Maddison,
whose favorite realms are filled with unicorns, rainbows
and sparkly fairies.

"Innocence, once lost, can never be regained. Darkness, once gazed upon, can never be lost."
— John Milton, *Paradise Lost*

Contents

1 Innocence Lost

The biting, frigid wind whips around me in an angry whistle. A heartbreaking reminder that even in the tranquility of this moment, death is inevitable. The skies are painted gray, a depressing cue that darkness is on the horizon. My eyes scan the cemetery draped in pure white snow like a lover's embrace. Lifeless trees provide no shelter from the grief this resting place emits. A single tear falls in silence, inching down my crimson cheek. The little bead of water nearly freezes before I wipe it away with my glove-swathed hand.

"I'm so sorry, Aria," I whisper, swallowing the painful lump present in the back of my throat. I just stare with an empty focus at the white marble marker before placing one perfect pink rose on top of the stone.

It lays there, motionless. The delicate and flawless petals are unaffected by the melancholy cold breeze whipping through the peaceful memorial park.

I pull off my glove. The coldness hits my trembling hand as I lift my fingertips to caress the stone engraving.

Arianna "Aria" Donovan
Beloved Daughter, Sister, and Friend
July 20, 1996 – December 29, 2014

"I miss you," I barely choke out. "I can't believe you're gone. How could you have run at Deacon like that?" My voice is lined with sorrow, resentment, and admiration as I whisper to her grave.

I close my eyes, reliving those last moments. Aria's pink pixie hair whooshes by in a rush of air so fast that she's a blur. Deacon's sword enters her stomach then exits out her back. The scarlet liquid drips from her almost lifeless corpse, staining the untainted snow. Her eyes are wide and her pink glossed mouth is open, soundlessly.

She shifts her peaceful chocolate eyes to Asher then me as her essence drains out of them. With difficulty, she swallows and I lean down, pressing my ear to her lips before life leaves her body.

Aria speaks softly, "He's your savior," she forces out, "and you're ours."

Shit. I squeeze my eyes open and then closed, shaking myself out of the mental picture before focusing my gaze on the rose. My final gift to her. Its petals are so vivid and elegant, like Aria.

"How am I supposed to continue on this crazy journey without you?" A strangled laugh falls out of me, as do the tears. I turn away from the grave. I can't look at it, at what I've done to her.

"She would have loved that the rose is pink." Abby appears next to me clasping her hand in mine. A tiny poignant smile crosses her lips and her gaze slides from me to the stone. "By the grace, that girl loved pink. Everything in our college dorm room was a shade of the color."

"She's the only person I know who could pull off pink hair and black combat boots with a frilly sundress and still look like a beautiful doll," I add, my tone solemn.

Abby caresses Aria's name on the grave. "Well, we did always say her real parents were Marilyn Manson and Barbie," she recalls in a thoughtful way.

I inhale a sharp breath and lock my gaze onto the motionless forest behind the cemetery, attempting to keep the tears from falling again, just barely able to hold the heartache at bay.

"How on earth did she get to Deacon so fast?" I ask the stationary trees before turning to Abby. "Her speed was exceptional. What the hell was she thinking?"

Abby faces me, squeezing my hand. "Eve, she loved you. She loved all of us. That girl was the only one I know who unconditionally accepted who and what we are. She knew what our paths were supposed to be. Aria sacrificed her life, so you can complete your ascension and fulfill your destiny. I can't answer the how and why of her actions, but I can promise you her death will not be in vain."

Her reply is more of a vow than a response to my question. I acquiesce with a nod and forgive that she disregarded my inquiry of speed.

Abby tugs on my hand, guiding me toward a black Escalade. "Come on. Michael would like us to get you to England before nightfall."

I numbly follow, allowing her to steer me through the serene park. She clutches my hand as we walk toward a patiently waiting Callan, who's dressed only in his navy blue pea coat, frayed jeans and a pair of boots. *He must be freezing.* Then I remember the coldness doesn't affect them the way it does me.

As we approach, Callan pulls me into a bear hug. "It's going to be all right, Eves. I promise," he speaks in my ear with a quiet tone before opening the door and coaxing me in. "In you go, cutie," he orders, assisting me into the middle bench seat and Abby into the back.

As I climb in, I look up and lock eyes with a pair of beautiful indigo ones, marred by sorrow for both Aria and me. Asher sits without a sound, waiting for me to slide in next to him. His black leather jacket groans as he opens his strong arms.

I fall into them, placing my head on his solid chest. The scent of smoky wood and leather assaults my nose, the calming fragrance that's all Asher St. Michael soothes me.

The dark stubble on his jawline and chin tangles in my hair, comforting me as the protector bond warms me from the inside.

Asher's deep, soothing voice is gentle. "Keegan, we're ready to go."

At his command, I lift my long lashes and notice McKenna's platinum blonde hair, in the front seat next to her mate. A tiny smile brushes over my lips. I'm safe with the London clan of gargoyles, my protectors.

I curl into the shelter of Asher's secure arms, and for a brief moment, shut my eyes, internally saying my final goodbyes to my roommate and friend while Asher holds me possessively.

When my lids reopen, my gaze focuses on pink rose petals floating in the icy wind. Thinking it's a sign from Aria, I glance one last time toward her stone marker while Keegan begins to drive at a slow pace out of the cemetery. My eyes widen when I notice both the headstone and flower have vanished.

In their place, Deacon stands among the destroyed white marble, his hand open as the crushed pink petals drift in the wind, toward me. I sit up and press my forehead and hand to the glass, fixated on him and my heart rate increases, reaching an abnormal pace.

Deacon bestows a sinister smile. As we drive away, he mouths, "It's just beginning."

I retreat from the window in alarm and my body involuntarily shudders at his threat. Asher's eyes snap to the cemetery, but any sign of the half-demon is gone. When he sees nothing, he returns his focus to me and pulls his brows together in concern at my sudden behavior. I take in a deep breath and reposition myself back into the protection of his warm embrace.

"I've got you, siren." His voice has the seal of a promise to it.

My chest swells at his declaration and physical presence. Asher brushes the hair back from my face, entangling his hands in the long, light brown strands while searching my eyes.

I close them, afraid of what he might find. No one should endure living with death hanging over their head everyday…but this is our reality.

A brief time later, we pull up to a small airport located on the outskirts of Boston. It's private and accommodates personal and chartered planes. Keegan slows the Escalade next to a large jet parked in an enormous hanger. There's a crew patiently waiting outside of it for the vehicle to stop.

My eyes slide to Asher in disbelief. "You guys chartered a private jet?" I whisper, stunned.

Asher gives me his signature sexy smirk and leans into my ear, conspiratorially. "Actually, we own the jet. It's a Gulfstream G650," he answers with an air of cockiness.

I roll my eyes. "When you said fly to England, I assumed you meant, you know, actually fly."

Confusion crosses Asher's expression before he breaks into a deep laugh. The sound flows through my skin and rattles my soul. "Wait, you thought we would like, fly-fly you all the way to London, in the freezing cold?" His question's soaked in delight by my misunderstanding of our transcontinental transportation.

I frown at him. "Yes," I admit, feeling a bit foolish for the inaccuracy.

Asher's eyes soften at my admission. "Eve that would be a very uncomfortable flight for you. This will be more restful. There's a bed and bathroom, it's warm and we even have snacks." He cajoles with an adorable wink before opening his door and extending his hand to me so I can exit the bulky SUV.

I place my small hand in his large one begrudgingly, mumbling under my breath, "Is it so unreasonable for me to assume a gargoyle, who has wings, would rather fly himself than on a private jet?"

Asher leans in, his scent engulfing me as he murmurs in my ear, "This gargoyle also has excellent hearing, siren." *Damn gargoyles and their heightened senses.*

He grins and interlaces our fingers, leading me up the stairs to the plane's entrance. Callan and Keegan assist the crew in loading our bags into the cargo area while Abby and McKenna make their way onto the airplane. Everyone's on high alert and anxious. The unease is overwhelming.

I inhale a deep breath and look around the airport once more before climbing up the flight of steps that will lead me to another chapter of this divine path imposed on me. My destiny.

"Come on, siren," Asher encourages before we hike up the ten stairs and step into the aircraft.

As someone who's only flown on commercial planes, I inspect the private jet in awe. Once again I'm reminded of the St. Michael's amassed wealth.

The décor is serene with dark walnut cabinetry, trim, and tables. There are three seating areas covered in cream leather. A table flanked by four chairs, a couch area with a flat screen television and separate seats near the cockpit.

The back of the plane houses a small bedroom with a queen size bed and a petite bathroom complete with a shower, all accented in granite. *Yep, Eve, so out of your league.*

Asher tugs my hand, pulling me out of my astonished gawking. "Let's go sit upfront for a bit, yeah?" he suggests, compelling me forward.

We pass Abby and McKenna on the couch, speaking in hushed tones. Their mates, Asher's brothers, Keegan and Callan, board and take their seats. Once we're all secure, we begin to taxi onto the small runway heading toward the clan's home in England.

I shift my gaze from the heaven-like clouds outside the circular window to Asher, who's sitting across from me. I methodically scan him, taking him in, inch by inch, as he sits with his eyes closed, resting and looking peaceful.

His short, dark brown hair has grown out a bit since we first met. The worry line between his brows seems to have deepened. His long lashes fan over the dark circles under his fatigued eyes and sculpted cheeks.

Those cheeks are home to my favorite part of him, his permanent five o'clock shadow. On most guys, the stubble adds ruggedness. On Asher, it just makes him appear striking and alpha male, like a true gargoyle warrior.

My heart rate intensifies with my gawking. Being this close to my protector always enhances my awareness of him and my body's desire to be in close proximity to his.

Warmth begins to crawl throughout my veins as the bonding energy sets off a dull hum under my skin. I swallow my hormonal want, which is begging me to crawl onto his lap and brush my lips against his soft, pink, full mouth.

Aria's right. *I really need to get laid.* I think to myself before correcting the *'is'* to *'was'*. I'm hit with a sudden burst of sadness at the recollection she's no longer here.

Swallowing my grief, I keep my focus on Asher. He's wearing his usual outfit: a plain white t-shirt, lived-in jeans and black motorcycle boots. The Spiritual Assembly of Protector's mark, a black, shaded Celtic cross tattoo, embellishes the inside of his forearm.

Onyx, his healing stone, is laced throughout his leather bands, which are always securely placed, one on each wrist, helping him to restore health and sustain strength. *God, he's so beautiful.* My lips part with yearning.

Asher's seductive voice drags me out of my hormone-driven ogling. "You should try to get some sleep. We have a six hour flight before we land at Heathrow, and once we do, we'll be a full six hours ahead with the time change," he murmurs groggily.

My gaze catches his before I look away. "I can't. Every time I close my eyes, all I see is Deacon's sword going through Aria's body or the dust of what was left of his brother Kaiden."

His face is sympathetic as he unbuckles himself and crouches in front of me, placing his large, strong hands on my knees. *Oh. My. God.* I really need to concentrate on his voice instead of where his hands are before I embarrass myself and jump him, right here on the plane. Heat inundates my veins and my stomach muscles tighten at his touch, causing me to fidget.

"Stop focusing on your unmerited guilt about Kaiden. You did what we trained you to do. Your actions were simply an act of self-defense. Yes, he was a casualty, but it was either you or him. Your response to his assault was instinctive and essential. He was clearly going to harm you. Killing him was the only way to stop him, siren," he consoles in a gentle manner.

"I know." I sigh. "I just can't help think if I hadn't, Aria would still be here with us. Deacon only murdered her in retaliation for the death of his brother," I answer.

Asher shakes his head from side to side. "You don't know that. Deacon is half-demon. He kills for fun, Eve. Regardless of what happened to Kaiden, he would have attacked you," Asher argues.

I silently hold his stare for a moment. "Tell me you saw how quickly Aria moved in front of me. Ash, that wasn't normal." I breathe out, my eyes pleading with him to see what I saw.

His attention slides to the window with an intense focus on the clouds, as if they hold all the answers. Then, without a sound, he stands, offering his hand to me. My fatigued eyes lift and lock onto his glowing ones.

Asher's expression says more than words can. I place my hand into his and he brings it to his lips, kissing it lightly before guiding me to the back of the plane and into the small bedroom.

Everyone's silent as we pass by. They're guarded. They know Asher and I aren't supposed to have this much contact. We're breaking the rules. But for now, they turn a blind eye in sympathetic understanding.

The moment we're in the room, he closes the door and guides me to the bed. I sit, my eyes never leaving his, or his mine. He bends down, unlaces and pulls off my knee-high boots, one at a time, before standing with me.

I inhale, trying to keep my breath even.

With one hand entwined in mine, Asher uses his free hand to fold down the covers. I slide in and get comfortable. After I'm securely within the warmth of the soft blankets, he tucks me in and lies down on top of them.

Reaching across the bed, he interlaces our fingers. The action nonverbally telling me he fears I'll disappear if he's not touching me.

He gathers me in his arms and kisses the top of my head with a gentle sigh. The small act causes goose bumps to rise on my skin. I close my eyes and continue to focus on controlling my breathing, basking in his closeness.

"Sleep." His voice is just above a whisper and his breath tickles my ear.

"I can't."

"Just close your eyes."

"I'm afraid."

"You're safe, siren. There's nothing to fear," he assures, tightening his hold on me.

"That's not true. I have everything to fear," I argue.

"You're protected. No one can hurt you," he counters.

I close my eyes knowing his words are deceptive but I allow myself to believe, even briefly, that they're true.

"Okay," I concede.

"I'll make all the awful disappear." My protector vows the quiet promise while his fingertips trace random designs on my lower back.

I rest my head on his powerful chest as the echo of his deep breathing lulls me, easing my uncertainties. My hand finds its way over the protector tattoo that binds us through our blood bond. The force hums between us and I float away into a dreamless and visionless sleep.

2 New Realities

Reluctantly, my eyes open, dragging me from my deep sleep into reality. I cling to Asher's peaceful form like a lifeline. Taking advantage of his slumber, I allow myself to watch him while my mind drifts, wondering what it would be like to wake up every morning to his striking face.

Without waking him, I take my fingers and run them over the dark stubble dusting his chin and jawline, cherishing the feel of the prickly hairs. Asher's plump, kissable lips filter air in and out as he dreams. His lids flutter, jolting the long dark lashes before they rest again.

I frown. The truth is, my daydream will never come true. We'll never have peace like this. The realization slices my heart, causing it to bleed out. I release a harsh whimper.

In response, Asher pulls me closer. His breath tickles my hair before he kisses the top of my head again. A tiny smile crosses my lips at the affectionate gesture.

Curling into Asher's side, I vow to relish every moment I can with him. Appreciate every second. Be in the now.

He drops his chin toward me and speaks in a hushed voice. "You sleep okay?"

I nod. "Actually, I did. No visions, nightmares, astral projecting or realm jumping." My response is truthful.

"Good. You needed a peaceful rest," Asher replies.

"You really did make the awful disappear," I whisper.

"You can thank me for my awesomeness later."

I snort. "Don't let this go to your head, gargoyle."

I can feel Asher's face tug into a cocky grin as he tightens his hold on me, enjoying our contact before turning and looking at the clock. He lets out a frustrated growl.

"We've been asleep for a few hours. We're going to land soon. It might be a good idea to get up and grab a quick bite before we reach Heathrow," he suggests.

"All right," I agree, not wanting to let him go. I fear the minute I do, the grief will hit me like a tidal wave.

I begin to sit up but he draws me back to him. I look down at his face, questioning him. I lean on one elbow and lay my other hand on his chest, over the protector tattoo.

I watch his chest rise as he draws in a sharp breath at my touch. His face darkens with something like want.

"Wait," he rasps through a tight jaw, peering up at me from beneath thick lashes.

My eyes scan his with a shared longing and I part my lips as the butterflies in my stomach take flight with anticipation. Asher sits up, moving his seductive lips closer to mine.

"Eve." My name softly rolls off his tongue, like a prayer, causing my entire body to flood with need.

Gentle hands cup my face as his lips brush across mine in a tease. Once. Twice. On the third touch, they firmly press into mine, devouring me.

With every stroke, I cling tighter to Asher's shirt for support. Each caress of his lips causes my blood to rush, filling me with a burning desire, making me feel whole. God, I've never wanted anyone more than him. It's like my soul already knows it's his.

I let out a soft moan at the kiss. The need to be closer to one another overpowers us as he sits up completely, pulling me onto his lap so I'm straddling his legs.

My hands move little by little, under his shirt, feeling his warm skin. He growls at my touch. Asher's thumbs rub the small slit of skin showing between my shirt and pants as our kiss becomes even more fervent.

It's as if we've become one another's oxygen. He tightens his grip on my hips, pulling me closer to him so our stomachs are touching.

My body is about to combust from the zealous emotions running through me. The bond heightens each sensation.

Just as I'm about to pass out from lack of oxygen, Asher slowly pulls away, resting his forehead on mine as we catch our breaths.

"I think...that will...hold me over...for a while," he pants out with each of his breath. "You?"

I shift on his lap and nod once. It's all I can manage. Truthfully, I'll never get enough of Asher. I'll always want more. I swallow hard, pushing down the disappointment that he stopped when he did, and focus on inhaling.

He looks at me apologetically as if he's reading my mind. "If I don't stop now, I won't."

I tip my chin up, watching while he absentmindedly plays with a strand of my hair before leaning over and placing a small kiss on the tip of my nose.

"Your eyes are glowing again." I smile.

"That would be your fault, siren," he offers seductively.

His gaze falls to my lips.

"Don't look at me like that or we will never leave this room." I whine and purposely shift again on his lap, causing a delicious friction between our bodies.

His eyes slide closed and he moans. "I'm in so much trouble. You play dirty," he grunts. "It's all I can do not to throw you down and take you right now."

My eyes widen in surprise. "Asher St. Michael, are you saying my virtue isn't safe near you?"

He looks at me with dark, hooded lids. "Miss Collins, your virtue is the ONLY thing that isn't safe around me."

I offer a sly smirk. "Then I better guard it with my life." I begin to move off his lap.

He releases a raw, throaty sound and holds me in place. "Don't you dare. It's mine, just not today."

Asher watches my reaction for a moment before grabbing my hips and lifting me. He gently places me on the bed and plants the softest kiss on my swollen lips.

"We should meet with the clan. See what the plans are for when we land."

"Okay," I reply with a sad smile.

He just stares at me with an odd expression on his face. "What?"

"You're so fucking beautiful." He brushes my lips one last time with his. I melt into the final kiss.

After we each freshen up, we make our way back to the cabin area where the rest of the family is camped out, snacking and talking.

I head over to the couch and sit next to Abby. She offers me a bright smile, along with a mug of dark chocolate hot cocoa and a bowl of mini marshmallows.

"Thanks," I mumble, nibbling on a marshmallow.

"Were you able to get some rest?" she questions with concern laced in her voice.

"Yeah, a little," I answer.

"Good." She takes my hand and squeezes. "You've got some color back in your face."

Heat rises to my cheeks, knowing the color is from my kissing session with Asher and not the sleep.

Of course, at that moment, Callan lifts his head and looks me over before smiling knowingly. My heart kicks against my rib cage, causing me to feel the way I did the time Callan caught Asher and I in the library, making out.

Sensing my unease, Asher speaks up, changing topics.

"So what's the plan?" He sits down on the other side of me, with his thigh touching mine, sipping on his cocoa. He digs his hand into the bowl of my marshmallows and pops some into his mouth.

He catches my displeased glance and feigns innocence.

"They taste better from your bowl," he points out.

I scoff. Secretly, I love when he eats my food. Smiling like a goofball, I turn back to the group. Callan and Abby return my smile but Keegan and McKenna look between Asher and I with disapproval.

"We should be reaching Heathrow shortly. I have an SUV in the hanger waiting for us. We'll take it to La Gargouille Manor in Wiltshire," Keegan answers.

"Wait, I thought the manor in Massachusetts was named La Gargouille?" I ask, confused.

"Here we go again," McKenna huffs out.

Nice to see our relationship hasn't evolved any over transatlantic waters. I glare at her in annoyance.

"It is, Eves. Our father named both his estates after the legendary dragon," Callan explains, pulling my gaze away from McKenna to him. "The one in England is technically called La Gargouille Manor, Wiltshire."

"Got it." I go to grab more marshmallows but my bowl is empty. I give a spiteful look to Asher. He bats his baby blues and presents me with a full bowl. I take it eagerly and turn so he can't put his dirty mitts in it. His deep laugh causes my stomach muscles to clench.

"Is Michael planning to join us this evening or tomorrow?" McKenna asks Keegan.

At the archangel's name, both Asher and I tense, reminded of our recent warning from Michael reiterating our platonic roles and forewarning us about the consequences of an inappropriate and intimate relationship.

"Tomorrow. He wanted to let Eve get settled before he made an appearance," Keegan replies.

"How far away is your home from the airport?" I inquire in a quick subject switch.

"About one hundred and seventy-four kilometers," Keegan responds without looking at me.

My eyes dart to Abby for help. "Um, I was brought up on the imperial system not the metric system. A little assistance for the American," I tease.

"About one hundred and eight miles," she states, watching my blank face, "or one hour." The exquisite sentinel giggles at my lack of metric unit comprehension.

Damn gargoyles. "Thanks," I say while throwing a piece of marshmallow at her before she returns with her own candy toss. Our momentary food fight is cut short by the in-flight announcement.

"Ladies and gentlemen, we're making our final approach to Heathrow Airport and will begin our descent shortly. In preparation for landing, please make sure your seat belt is securely fastened until we are safely on the ground in London," the pilot says and the crew begins to tidy up the cabin as we all buckle in.

A few moments later, the pilot announces our arrival and the cabin crew opens the door for us to exit the jet. We make our way down the stairs and toward the large Cadillac Escalade with dark tinted windows while Keegan and Callan help load our bags into the vehicle.

From the backseat of the car, I shoot off a quick text to my Aunt Elizabeth letting her know we've arrived safe and sound. I expect her response time will be slow, in part because of the time difference and partially because my quirky aunt just learned how to text on her iPhone a few weeks ago. Asher wore her down until she finally gave in and allowed him to teach her. God bless his patience.

Keegan pulls out of the airport toward Wiltshire and I watch the scenery roll by, taking it in all. This is my first time in England. The weather feels similar to

Massachusetts. Cold, damp, and dreary. Even though the car temperature reads three degrees Celsius, it's actually about thirty-seven degrees Fahrenheit. I draw my body inward, trying to keep warm.

"Cold?" Asher asks, moving closer.

I offer a small smile and slight nod while watching London pass by as we get onto the M5. Part of me is excited to be here. However, the other half is saddened Aria isn't here to experience it with me.

The guilt starts to spread in my chest and my hand massages the area, attempting to ease the ache.

Asher notices my anguish and makes an effort to distract me. "The manor isn't too far from Salisbury where Stonehenge is located. I'll show it to you while you're here."

I force a smile. "That would be cool."

He studies me, our bond alerting him I'm faking contentment. "It'll get easier. The sorrow will lessen with time and you'll begin to heal. I promise."

"I know." I return my gaze to the gray landscape outside the window. "Why are you called the London clan of gargoyles if you live in Wiltshire?" I need to divert my thoughts.

"Our main residence is our building of flats in London."

My eyes shift to him, mouth agape. "You own an entire building of apartments?"

Asher nods once. "Each of us live in our own place. Keegan and Kenna reside on the third floor, Callan and Abby stay on the fourth, and I have my own flat on the fifth. We have a guest dwelling for visiting clans on the second level and the first floor is for Royal Gargoyle

Council of Protectors business. It's mainly an office space with a conference room we use as a general meeting spot."

"Talk about property management," I reply in astonishment. The house in Massachusetts would be more than enough in my book since my aunt's entire home can fit into their kitchen.

Asher just shrugs. "Most of the gargoyles in England prefer to stay close to the city and when my father first relocated from France, he established the clan's base in London, so that's where we ended up living. At that time, each family had their own floor. When our parents didn't return from their trip, we took over the building and separated the flats this way."

I sympathize, knowing from experience how the loss of your parents affects you. I reach my hand out and grasp his, offering him encouragement. He returns the gesture with a genuine smile.

"So how'd you end up in Wiltshire then?"

"We didn't move to Wiltshire until my mother discovered she was pregnant with Callan. Keegan and I were both born in Manhattan, though we spent much of our childhood in and out of London. It was her wish for us to grow up in the country, surrounded by gardens. So when we weren't in New York or traveling, we split our time between London and Wiltshire. Now we just use the manor as a vacation home, or safe haven, if needed."

"How come we don't just stay in London then?" I ask in confusion.

"It's currently not secure to take you to the flat in London," Keegan answers casually, reminding me we're not alone. With Asher, it's like I have tunnel vision.

21

My gaze moves back toward the window and notice we're coming up on another magnificent estate. Asher's hand takes mine. He rubs his thumb in slow circles over my knuckles before tilting his head to me. "Welcome to La Gargouille Manor – Wiltshire."

"Wow," I say breathlessly. "This is…incredible."

"It's a fourteenth century medieval manor. My mother had the interior décor and structure modernized but the exterior and formal Cotswold gardens remain intact and original," Asher explains with pride in his tone.

Keegan stops the Escalade in front of two wrought iron gates, each adorned with the family dragon symbol. It reminds me of the house in the States, oddly setting off a pang of longing to be back there.

As soon as he enters the code and completes the fingerprint scan, the large doors open, allowing us access to the mile-long driveway, lined by strong and exquisite white birch trees.

As we make our way toward the estate, my breath hitches at all the simple but mature beauty boasting from it. The exterior of the manor showcases intricate stonework in various shades of creams and browns, which renders the manor warm and inviting.

Ivy grows on parts of the residence, strategically outlining the windows as if intentionally highlighting them so your eye is directed to that section of the structural design. There are several bay windows in the front, accentuating the multiple gables on the roof. I sigh internally. It's magnificent.

Keegan parks the vehicle near the expansive garage and we all prepare to exit. Asher turns to me, motioning his head toward the monstrosity of a '*vacation*' home. "Come on. I want to show you the inside and introduce you to Fiona," he says with a hint of mystery.

My brows pull together. "Fiona?"

"Our housekeeper. She's a panther shape shifter," Abby throws out with a smirk.

My mouth hangs open, stunned. I need to close it but I can't. "Um, o-okay."

Asher squeezes my hand and grins, clearly amused at my reaction. "She was also our nanny when we were growing up. Since we're not here very often, Fiona lives here and oversees the residence for us. She's a kitten. You'll really like her, siren."

I just nod. No matter how many supernatural creatures I've met over the past few weeks, I'm still processing the fact these legendary beings exist. He laughs at me, plucking me out of the car.

We walk up to the iron door and before Asher can even open it, a short, round, older woman flings it open and snatches Asher in a tight hug, forcing him to let go of my hand and reciprocate her squeeze.

"Hello, luv," she greets with a warm English accent.

The woman backs away and cups his cheeks in a motherly way, dropping her gaze and taking him in.

Asher beams at her. "It's so good to see you, Fiona." His voice is full of admiration and love.

Her yellow-green eyes twinkle at his greeting then move toward me. "Ye must be Eve. 'Tis luvely to make yer acquaintance, dear." She ushers us into the house.

"Thank you," I reply shyly.

I look around and take the manor in. We're in a long, bright entranceway. The walls are a sunshine yellow accented with white crown molding, emphasizing the high ceilings. There are light hardwood floors throughout and multiple stone tables with plants on them.

Asher guides me down the hall and I hear Fiona greet McKenna, Keegan and Abby with just as much fondness.

Once in the foyer, I notice the staircase to the left and an open area to the right, leading to a sunroom, which overlooks the gardens. Contrary to the home in the States, which is made of dark stone and woods, this home is light and airy.

"Fi-Fi," Callan announces like a child who's found his favorite toy. We turn to see him pick up the older woman in an embrace and twirl her around. His eyes light with worship.

"Hello, me baby boy." She pets his cheek after planting a kiss on it and closes the door.

The older woman turns her five-foot self around and plays with her gray haired bun, putting it back in place. I have a hard time imagining her as a panther because she reminds me of Mrs. Potts from *Beauty and the Beast*. Her eyes twinkle at me with delight and I look questioningly to Asher.

"One of Fiona's shape shifting abilities is to read female minds," he explains, amused.

Crap. I smile politely at her and she quirks an eyebrow up. "Now don't ye go tellin' all o' me secrets, lad," she teases and swats Asher with her hand.

He places his hands up in defeat. "I wouldn't dream of it, Fi. Just keeping Eve up to speed."

She narrows her eyes playfully at him. "Well now, are ye all hungry? I have supper waitin' fer ye," she says, her accent heavy.

"That would be delightful. Thanks, Fi," Abby answers.

We're escorted through the bright home and into a burgundy colored dining room. There are two large windows highlighted with silk drapes and a modest fireplace with a gold gilded mirror above it.

Each of us takes a seat at the long wooden table, covered in dishes as Fiona flitters around. She seems happy in her element as she pulls the covers off each platter.

"Fi, you've outdone yourself. This all looks delicious," Callan praises, rubbing his hands together. The gargoyle certainly loves food. I release a soft laugh.

Glowing from the admiration, Fiona walks over to Callan and kisses him on the top of the head. I'm guessing she's the reason Callan is so down-to-earth and loving.

"I made all ye favorites, lad. Cumberland sausage soup, shepherd's pie, roast beef, and Yorkshire puddin' and fer dessert an apple pie with custard." The panther smiles at us excitedly.

"Thanks, Fiona," Abby beams.

"Good." Fiona claps her hands together. "Ye kids eat up. Ye're lookin' too thin," she reprimands as she glares at McKenna. "When ye're all done, we'll have a chat in da sittin' room 'bout the trouble ye're all facin'." She taps Keegan's shoulder then leaves the dining room.

I turn to Abby. "She doesn't join you?"

Abby shakes her head. "No. Fiona likes to 'take care' of us. Always has. She can't sit still. According to her, it makes her nuts."

"Mmmm. By. The. Grace. Eves, you've gotta try the soup. It's the best ever," Callan says, moaning in cuisine ecstasy.

I smile at his foodie enthusiasm. Leave it to Callan to cause my smile to resurface. I sit back and watch everyone eating and joking. I'm once again reminded how lucky I am to be under the protection of this family.

3 Wants and Needs

After the very large dinner and the most delicious dessert I've ever tasted, we make our way into the sitting room with Fiona. Everyone settles in on one of the two plush couches, adorned with silk throw pillows that form an L-shape in front of the fireplace.

Fiona brings in a tray of tea and we each grab a cup, while a healthy fire roars in the brick hearth.

"Eve, dear, please sit wit me, luv." Fiona pats the seat next to her, coaxing me over.

I go willingly, appreciating the kind gesture. I wonder if this is what it would be like to have a grandmother. Both my grandparents died when my mother and father were younger. I guess history repeats itself since both my parents passed away when I was a baby too. My aunt doesn't have any living relatives.

My nose scrunches, remembering Fiona can read minds. *Crap.* My eyes shift to her in embarrassment.

Her response is gentle. "Tis all right, dear. I hope dat ye come ta think 'o me as family." She brushes my cheek affectionately.

"So, you can shape shift into a panther? Forgive me but you seem a little...sweet...for that," I question and Fiona releases a hearty laugh.

"Don't let me soft nature fool ye, child. I can be feral and vicious when need be," she assures.

"Fiona is the alpha female of the Pishyakan Tribe. They're one of the oldest families of werecat shape shifters in the world," Abby explains as her eyes sparkle.

"Dat 'tis correct. My clowder's generations span a long time," Fiona confirms proudly.

"Clowder?" I look to Fiona, unfamiliar with the word.

"A female family of cats is called a clowder. Similar to werewolves who are called a pack," Asher clarifies.

"Are werecats similar to werewolves? I mean, other than shifting into cats versus dogs," I inquire, hopefully not sounding too ignorant.

"Yes and no. In werecat clowders, the females are in charge, specifically in the alpha and beta roles instead of the males. That's why Fiona can only read the minds of women. Other than that, most of the other aspects are the same," Asher answers.

"Werecats think wit der head instead o' der hearts, like those smelly mongrels," Fiona adds, causing me to laugh out loud.

Guess she isn't a dog lover. That makes two of us. My mind momentarily drifts to Leo, Aria's werewolf boyfriend, and I wonder how he's doing without her.

My gaze shifts to Asher then back to Fiona. "Do you have a mate?" I ask.

She dips her head once. "Aye. A long time ago I had a tom. He's no longer wit me." She sighs.

"Tom?" I question.

"A male cat. His name was Barclay. Our daughter, Galena, 'tis my second in command or beta," she continues. "He left us many moons ago. We live nine times longer den humans." The shifter's voice carries an air of sadness.

"Hence the term, nine lives," McKenna interjects with a snort. Holy shit. Did she just attempt a joke?

Fiona pats my hand with fondness. "Enough 'bout me. I am happy ta answer all yer questions lata. Fer now, I want ta know what 'tis going on wit da demons." Her cat eyes lock onto Keegan, waiting for an explanation.

"It seems that the Declan clan of gargoyles is working with Lucifer. Deacon, the leader, has entered into some sort of deal to turn Eve over to the dark army, in exchange for what, we don't know yet. Whatever it is, Lucifer has sent his entire demonic legion after Eve to assist the Declan clan. It's quite a serious situation," Keegan points out in detail.

Fiona nods her head once, pondering this information. "What o' Michael?"

"He is aware," McKenna replies flatly as if bored.

"That's not all." Callan looks to me then back to Fiona. "It seems Gage is also working with the Declan clan," he adds, waiting for her response.

Fiona's eyebrows lift to her forehead. "Are ye sayin' dat Gage Gallagher 'tis cohortin wit da enemy, lad?"

"Yes, ma'am," Asher answers firmly.

"By de grace," Fiona exhales, moving her hand over her heart as if Asher wounded her.

I turn to Fiona. "You know Gage?"

Her shocked expression meets mine. "Know 'em? I practically raised da lad wit dese here hoodlums. 'Twas like part o' da family."

Now it's my turn to be surprised as I transfer my attention to Asher. "Really?"

He shrugs. "We mentioned knowing Gage for a long time."

"I see," I say, slightly put off at this new bit of information he withheld.

"Dat lad 'tis always gettin' himself in ta trouble." She breathes out in disappointment. "Now ye tellin' me he's workin' fer da half-breed?"

"Yes. Still, we're unsure why, Fiona," McKenna informs her.

"Ye're sure da fallen know 'bout Eve?" she questions Keegan.

He nods once. "Editha, the banshee, delivered the message personally."

"By de grace." Fiona blows out on a wave of air.

"I'm afraid there's more. Eve has begun her ascension. Every demon and supernatural creature in the world should be able to detect her existence by now. We felt, with Michael's approval, it best to continue her training here in England under the enchantments while she's still on break from university. There are more of us here to protect her if we need to call in other clans," Asher says.

I sigh. "That, and I turned Kaiden, Deacon's brother, into stone dust before Deacon killed my friend, Aria."

Fiona looks at me with nothing but compassion. She takes my hand in hers, offering comfort. It doesn't make the sting go away.

"What was it you always said, Fiona? In life, sometimes the most courageous thing we do is the unthinkable to prevail in moments of other's cowardliness." Callan looks pointedly at me.

"Aye, 'tis true child. Yer bravery showed in dat moment." Fiona squeezes my hand.

"She did as we trained her and she executed it perfectly," Keegan interjects.

I swallow and turn my gaze onto the fire, choking back the tears. "Tell Aria that."

The room falls silent.

"Michael will be here tomorrow, Fiona," Asher cuts through the silence, altering the subject matter.

"All right. Ye kids go and get yerselves settled. Kenna, be a good lass and show Eve ta her room. 'Tis all tidied up fer her. Breakfast 'tis at eight in da mornin'. Sharp!" Fiona states in a firm tone before bidding us goodnight.

McKenna walks over to me and tilts her head toward the door. "Come on, blood of Eden. I'll show you where you'll be staying."

I follow her up the ten large steps to the second floor before my eyes lift to the landing's skylight, framing the night sky.

McKenna turns to me before following my line of sight to the blackness sprinkled with shimmering stars. "The dark Heavens almost remind you that there's something even greater than us out there."

My eyes fasten on the twinkling fireballs. "It does."

The gorgeous warrior exhales noisily. "I know I haven't been easy on you, but you did good with Kaiden. With focus and hard work, you can do this."

My eyes slowly remove themselves from the night sky and lock onto her sapphire gaze. "Thanks."

She folds her arms over her chest. "Don't allow what happened with Aria to be another distraction."

"Another distraction?" I question, keeping my features void of emotion. "I didn't realize I was unfocused in the first place, McKenna."

"Asher." His name is an accusation on her cool tone.

My mouth turns down. "I see." I just stare at her because she's right. He's all consuming. But is he really a preoccupation that's sidetracking me from the ascension? *Damn her insight.*

McKenna watches me, and for a moment I think I see her face soften before she clears her throat and places her hard mask back on. "Come on. Let's go see your quarters. Try not to get lost."

With that, she's back to business as usual. I brush off the moment and continue to shadow her into a peaceful bedroom. My eyes roam to where the queen bed is positioned. It's tranquil and calm.

"This was Vivian's favorite room," she says softly.

I frown. "Vivian?"

"The guys' mom, Vivian St. Michael. She loved it because it overlooks the gardens," McKenna offers quietly, looking out the window toward the patch of sparse flowers and greenery wrapped in darkness. "It's not much to look at in the winter, but Garrick, Asher's dad, bought the manor because each room has a view of them." As if coming out of a trance, she turns to me, schooling her features. "There's a full bathroom attached and Asher's room is across from this one. Abby and I are down toward the end of the hallway with Keegan and Callan, if you need anything. Fiona is on the lower level."

"Thanks," I reply, mustering up sincerity.

McKenna turns and faces me. "It's been a long day so try giving everyone a reprieve tonight and don't astral project or realm jump." With the snide remark left hanging in the air, she leaves.

I exhale. Surprisingly, it's comforting to have McKenna treat me rudely. It feels normal. My eyes roam around the cozy room. I walk over to the window to view the gardens, but they're blanketed in black. I promise myself to visit them tomorrow. Maybe it will help me feel closer to my aunt. I look over my shoulder, noticing my luggage has been brought up and decide to get organized.

After I unpack and soak in a hot bath, I change into my pajamas, preparing for bed. I plop down on the bed and close my eyes for a brief moment before there's a soft knock. I know it's him before the door even opens. I can feel his presence in every fiber of my body.

"Come in." I acknowledge the knock with a quiet invitation.

Having just showered, Asher walks in with his hair still wet. He's wearing black flannel pajama bottoms and his gray *Property of London* t-shirt. I smile inside knowing it's the shirt he likes me to wear.

"Hey. I just wanted to check in on you to see if you need anything before I go to sleep," he says.

I shake my head. "All set. Thanks though." My voice sounds distant and tired.

He knits his brows. "You okay?"

I keep my eyes fixed on Asher and my mind wanders. Whenever he's around, I seem to get sidetracked. Right now, all I can think about is throwing myself at him. Maybe McKenna is right. What if Asher is too much of a distraction? Scanning his face, I'm reminded that my focus was on him right before Aria ran past me. If I had been concentrating my attention, like McKenna suggested, would Aria still be here?

While lost in my own head, I don't notice that Asher has moved closer and is now sitting on the bed. He leans in and my body instinctively tilts toward him, my veins heating from the bond. *Damn, he smells so good.* My eyes flutter at his scent.

"Talk to me, siren." It's a quiet plea. Those deep layers in his eyes search my face. He moves his right hand over my legs, caging me in with both arms as his breath fans my face.

With a wicked grin, he bends forward and nips at my lower lip. All my previous thoughts escape me, expelled by the feel of his soft lips now caressing mine. The small flame that burns inside me ignites into a full-blown inferno, as is the case whenever he touches me.

I curve further into him and run my hands into his damp hair, tugging him down on top of me. Asher releases a deep, low rumble from the back of his throat. His hands wrap around my waist, guiding me to lie back before positioning himself over me, never parting our lips.

With our bodies pressed against one another, I get lost in the depth of Asher's kiss. His lips move to my neck, dropping the softest kisses in a trail leading to the sensitive area under my ear where he allows his tongue to dart out and meet my skin. I whimper at the sensation.

Warm hands slide under my tank top, caressing my bare stomach. My muscles clench from his touch. I gasp when he presses his lower body into mine. My back arches and my chest pushes into his. His skillful hands continue to explore my body, moving over the swell of my breast. Asher sucks in a sharp breath at the contact when he realizes I'm not wearing a bra.

The loud intake of air brings me back to reality. My mind, which shut off a moment ago, starts to regain focus from the fog. Suddenly, I'm aware we shouldn't be doing this. This proves we distract one another and it's not good.

I stop moving and open my eyes. When I don't respond to his touch, he stills immediately. Asher watches me with concern.

"What is it, siren?" he asks while his hand brushes my cheek.

I close my eyes and try to catch my breath. "I, um…we…we should stop."

Asher studies me for a brief moment before moving off me, pulling us to a sitting position. "Okay." He breathes out in an almost pant, his face void of disappointment or anger.

My body is so riled up it's hard to focus. "I-I'm sorry."

Asher's tone becomes serious. "Don't ever be sorry for stopping. We go at a pace you're comfortable with, yeah?" he says with a small smile, misunderstanding the reason I stopped.

"That's not why." The words sound choppy coming out.

Confusion crosses his face. "Then what's going on?"

My voice is so soft. "I was just thinking, before you came in..." I look away in hesitation.

He takes my chin between his fingers and lifts my face to meet his. "Are you upset because I didn't tell you we grew up with Gage?" Asher's voice is weary.

I lift my brows to my hairline and look at him. "What?"

"I did tell you my family has known him for a long time and he's an old friend."

I close my eyes. "It's fine. I'm not mad about Gage." I pull my chin away.

"Fine?" He plays with the word, unsure what I mean by it. "If you're not upset, then what's going on, Eve?"

I pick pretend lint off my blanket. "It's nothing, really. I guess I'm just tired." *So. Lame. Eve.*

He watches me, waiting to see if I'll cave and tell him all the crazy, ridiculous thoughts and ideas running through my head. I know he can feel my emotions through our bond. I'm already not handling this conversation very well.

Asher sighs when I don't expand. "Okay, your way then, siren. Get some rest." He plants a soft kiss on top of my head before standing and making his way to the door. Before he turns the knob, he stops. My heart is in my throat and I swallow the lump that has formed. "Abby will be guarding you tonight and will alert me if anything happens. She also put up the charms so you're safe and sound," he explains over his shoulder, reassuring us both about my protection.

36

I keep my eyes focused on the wall in front of me, hating what I'm about to do, even if it's necessary. Michael seems adamant that we need to draw professional lines. Perhaps everyone's right. *Just do it, Eve.* Stop being indecisive.

"Michael was right, you know," I blurt out, just above a whisper, before I lose my nerve.

Asher's back is to me but he tenses. "About?" He drops his hand from the doorknob but doesn't turn around.

"Us. Staying away from one another. That we shouldn't breach the oath you took or the reason I was created for selfish reasons," I say, but I don't mean it.

He turns and faces me, crossing his arms and standing tall, like a fierce warrior ready to go into battle. "Is that what you want?" His voice is trained, not giving any emotions away.

I close my eyes. "In the second I hesitated with Deacon, she got by me, Asher. My eyes were on you. Watching yours plead with me not to take Deacon on. In that moment, Aria moved in. If I'd been paying attention to what I was supposed to be focused on, she wouldn't have gotten by me. She'd still be here." I reopen my eyes to catch his, wishing I hadn't.

His face pales. "Are you implying it's my fault she's dead?" he asks with a solemn tone.

I shake my head. "No. I'm saying it's mine. I was distracted, and someone died because of it. All those times you told me you had to put my protection first...well, I get it now." I pause to catch my breath. "I think we should put some space between us for a bit." I regret the words as soon as they fall out.

The striking gargoyle studies me for a moment. "If that's what you truly want, siren, then I will respect your request." His voice is thick.

My eyes shift down. I can't look at him. Though his face is impassible, I know his heart is breaking. I can feel it through our link. "I need to concentrate on the ascension and training. When you're around, I seem to get tunnel vision. We should respect the rules and boundaries that have been set for us," I lie.

Asher stares at me with an unhealthy intensity, like he's trying to read my thoughts and figure out my motives. He prowls to me and I begin to panic inside. If he gets too close, I won't be able to hold my resolve. I tell myself to breathe, not back down. This is necessary.

He stops in front of me, crouching down to meet me at eye level. Without a word, he lifts his hand to a strand of my hair that has fallen out of my ponytail and secures it behind my ear. His hand glides over my cheek in a light caress. It's all I can do not to close my eyes and lean into the sensation, flushing this idea down the toilet.

"Say it," he demands quietly.

My eyes lift and meet his. "Say what?" I whisper.

"Tell me you don't want me and I'll leave," he replies.

"I just need some time to focus on the ascension," I repeat.

He shoots me a look. "That's not what I asked you." His tone is firm.

"What do you want me to say, Asher? I'm asking you for some space to focus. It's simple." I ignore the burn in my throat the words cause.

"I won't allow you to push me away." He growls and grabs my head, forcing me to look directly at him. Slowly, he brushes his lips over mine as a shiver works its way down my spine from the tender kiss. "Say you don't want me. This. Us. It's the only way I'll walk away," he murmurs against my lips.

This is for the best. It's the right thing to do, so I look straight into his eyes as my heart lurches. "I-I don't want you." I barely get the deceitful words out.

His jaw clenches. The tick in his cheek picks up but other than that, he is motionless. "All right. Training starts at nine in the morning. Be downstairs in the gym no later." His voice is void of emotion before he drops his hands to his sides and turns to leave.

"Asher?" I hate that I sound so weak.

He stops but doesn't face me. His shoulders stiffen.

"What we want isn't always what we need." I force back my tears. I fear McKenna is wrong because my body is fighting against this.

Asher snorts. "And sometimes what we need is something we didn't even know we wanted." He yanks the door open in a harsh manner and storms out.

I curl up into the bed, knowing I just made a horrible mistake.

4 Words of Warning

My eyes flicker to the mirror and I scrutinize the stranger staring back at me. An ordinary girl watches my every move with hazel eyes that seem vacant this morning. On the outside, she and I seem similar, but the spark of life her once lively face held, is now dim. I sigh, my reflection mimicking the action.

After I splash my face with soap and water, I run my toothbrush over my teeth and throw on some mascara and my favorite vanilla-coconut lip gloss then make my way down to the kitchen.

The first thing I notice is Fiona singing and flittering away happily by the stove. If possible, her smile gets even brighter when she sees me. It's contagious. I have no choice but to return it with my own small grin.

"Mornin', luv. Ye're da first one awake. Have a seat and I'll bring ye some breakfast," she offers in a cheerful, airy tone while running her palms over her white ruffled apron. A panther, this woman is not. Her eyes widen at my internal dialogue. *Crap.*

Ignoring her reaction, I walk toward the fridge. "That's okay, Fiona. I'm happy to get it."

She waves me off in a maternal fashion. "Nonsense, lass. Sit," she orders and redirects me to the table while pushing on both my shoulders, forcing me into the chair.

Resigned, I stay seated at the large, empty table and Fiona glides around, preparing a plate. My gaze lands on the outside gardens, visible through the four French doors off the breakfast sitting area.

The morning sunlight is filtering through the birch trees, bouncing off what's left of the fall flowers and winter plants. A light layer of fresh snow fell last night and when the sun's rays hit the white powder, it sparkles like diamonds. Everything looks so pure and untouched. Serene.

"The gardens are beautiful, even in the winter. I bet they're spectacular in the spring and summer months." I peer at them longingly, missing my aunt.

Fiona shifts her eyes from me to the grounds and nods. "Aye, 'tis true da gardens are very special indeed. Vivian, da lad's mum, adored them. Aside from da boys, 'twas her pride and joy."

"My aunt Elizabeth would love them. She has an amazing green thumb and affection for flowers and plants," I elucidate, feeling a pang of homesickness.

Fiona places a plate of eggs, hash browns and sausage in front of me with coffee and orange juice. Then she puts hot cinnamon buns on the table next to fresh muffins and fruit. I raise my eyebrows at her as she sits across from me, sipping her Earl Grey tea.

"Yer aunt sounds luvly. She must be special ta ye."

I offer her a genuine smile. "She is."

Asher walks in, and in an instant, our eyes lock. My heart stumbles as my stomach drops and lurches while I relive the stupidity of my actions from last night.

He holds my gaze for a moment, his face softening. Not wanting to get sucked in, I snap my focus to my breakfast.

Fiona notices the obsessive look I'm giving my scrambled eggs and widens her eyes. Her light gray eyebrows pinch together at my odd behavior.

Clearly, I've gone all mental case.

"Morning, Fi." Asher kisses her cheek and offers his breathtaking smile.

"Mornin' darlin'. Sit down and I'll get ye some coffee and make ye a plate," she offers.

"Eve," he says curtly, watching my reaction.

Asher folds his large, intimidating body into a seat directly across from me, even though there are several vacant chairs available. I squirm at his intense gaze, keeping my eyes fixated on my plate as he keeps his on me.

It's like he's trying to see inside my head and figure out my thought process as he places his hands under his chin, scrutinizing me.

We sit in awkward silence while I push around the food on my plate. Fiona finally returns, placing coffee and a breakfast plate in front of Asher as the tension continues to build between us. His eyes never leave my face as they burn into my skin.

Fiona stares at the two of us, hands on her hips. "I don't know what ye did, lad, but whatever 'twas, ye best be fixin' it," she scolds with a no-nonsense tone.

"I didn't do anything, Fi," Asher replies, annoyed. He drops his chin to focus on his plate.

At that, my flight instincts kick in and I stand in an abrupt motion, scraping the chair across the kitchen floor. Fumbling, I clear my plate, dropping it in the sink then turning to the doorway to run upstairs, but not before Fiona blocks my escape route. *Sneaky panther.*

The short, plump woman just stands there. She narrows her gaze at me and places her small hands on her round hips. I swallow, bracing for the lecture.

"Rules are meant ta be broken, if luv's at stake," Fiona reprimands quietly, her eyes unwavering.

I hold her stare for a brief moment before shifting my focus to the wall behind her. "Broken rules equate to nothing but pain and darkness."

Her lips tighten in a straight line. "Stars don't shine wit out da darkness."

Before I can reply, Asher's voice interrupts me. "Training in twenty minutes. If you're late, you'll run," he barks coolly from the table.

With his gargoyle hearing, I'm sure he overheard our exchange.

"I'll be there with five minutes to spare." The sharp note in my tone is not missed and I storm around Fiona, escaping.

ॐक्ष

I make it to the training room with one minute to spare and mentally high five myself. My victory is short lived when I walk in and see Asher already standing there. A severe scowl mars his handsome face. His arms are crossed as he stares at the clock. *What the fuck?*

"You're late." His voice is laced with fury.

"I have a minute," I counter, pointing to the clock.

"Not by my watch. On the treadmill. You're running," he challenges, one eyebrow raised.

I huff and just stand with my hands on my hips like a rebel. "You aren't even wearing a watch," I throw back.

"Keep staring at me like that and for every minute your ass isn't running, I'll add another mile," he spits out, fuming.

Lucky for me, Callan walks in and raises his eyebrows to his hairline. "Lover's quarrel?"

"No!" Asher and I shout at the same time.

Callan puts his hands up in surrender. "For fucks sake, no need to bite a gargoyle's head off."

"Eve's running before she begins training. NOW!" Asher shouts and points to the treadmill.

What is his problem? "Fine." I hop on the treadmill and begin my punishment, seething at his attitude.

"You haven't seen anything yet, sweetheart," he threatens with a cocky air.

He knows I hate it when he calls me sweetheart. He's goading me and I refuse to give into his childish behavior. Instead, I keep my face forward and run while trying to block him out. I apply what I've learned with Michael in my meditation training. I focus all my energy and push the hum of our bond down, locking it away in its own personal compartment of pissed off Eve.

"Are you planning to ride her all day?" Callan questions Asher.

"Do you have something to say about it, brother?" Asher retorts with his arms crossed.

"Nope. Just want to know how today is going to play out. That's all, man." Callan backs off.

"Last night, Eve expressed an interest in focusing on her ascension, so that's what we're going to do. Focus!" Asher states pointedly as he burns holes into my back.

I swallow. *Crap.* It's going to be a long day. After what feels like a lifetime of sprinting, I'm sweating and gasping for air before Asher gives me a reprieve.

"Hand-to-hand with Callan. Get on the mat," Asher demands, pointing to the blue padded area.

I narrow my eyes. "Are you going to order me around all day?" I inquire defiantly.

He stands taller. "Order? No. Help you focus? Yes. On. The. Mat." Asher waits.

I sulk and take my position across from Callan. He's biting his bottom lip in an attempt to hold back a laugh. Clearly, Asher didn't take my request for space last night very well. Well, two can play at this game. I school my features. *I will not give in. I will not give in. I will not give in.* I chant in my head, hoping the more I do it, the more I'll believe it.

"Tough day, cutie?" Callan questions, amused.

"Suck it, Callan," I snip, my grumpiness increasing.

"Less talking, more training," Asher snaps at us.

Callan's eyes glint and his jaw tightens. "Let's get started."

He charges at me and I spin to my right out of his reach only to have my back slammed onto the mat. Pain shoots through my arm as I lay there stunned.

"What the hell, Asher?" Callan scowls, looming over me before he helps me up.

A lopsided smile forms on Asher's beautiful, pouty lips. "Oh, I'm sorry. You're fighting both of us today. Was that not made clear? I'd hate to give off mixed signals."

It's obvious he's not just talking about training.

"No mixed signals here. Intentions are clear," I retort, enraged.

He grins wickedly. "Wonderful. Again then."

We all return to our stances. Asher and Callan come at me simultaneously. I manage to roll my hips and keep my chin down, dodging Callan only to end up getting tackled hard by Asher.

I fall the wrong way on my arm, again. This time, I flinch from the pain. Asher's expression falls slightly at my show of hurt but then pulls back into his hardass façade.

I roll over and groan. "Thanks for the smack down." I inhale to ease the pain.

"Your point has been made, Asher." Callan tries to intervene with a calm tone.

Asher offers me his hand. "Get up."

I stand on my own and throw a nasty smirk at him before getting back into my position.

"Again," he challenges.

"Ash-" Callan gets cut off by Asher's shout.

"Again!" He screams so loud I think they might have heard him in the fae realm.

I exhale loudly, bracing myself for the next hit. But instead of landing on my back, I hear Michael's voice. *Thank God for archangels.*

"It's nice to finally see you taking training seriously, Eve," Michael commends.

At his entrance, Asher and Callan both tilt their head in a slight dip as a show of respect. Oddly, Michael reciprocates only to Asher. The archangel's jade eyes swing over to mine and he politely bows to me. His dark blond hair falls forward at the tilting movement.

"I appreciate the focus," he teases with little humor in his voice as his eyes shift back to Asher in disapproval. Without a doubt, he's still tweaked about walking in on Asher and I lip locking during our last training session.

"Good to see you too, Michael." It comes out snarky.

"That arm is bruising. Perhaps you should put some ice on it," the angel suggests.

I shoot a death glare at Asher. "I'll be fine. Remember, I can heal myself. Must be the archangel spirit in my soul," I snark with sarcastic wit.

Michael just looks at me thoughtfully for a moment. "Right. Well then, I think we've had enough physical teaching for the day. Let's go work on your mental control. On the agenda: astral projecting and realm jumping. Lady Finella awaits us in the Kingdom of the Fae to assist with the realm jumping, so we'll begin there today."

"She isn't done with her training," Asher says, irritated.

"Today's instruction feels more like punishment rather than an exercise in physical strength, Mr. St. Michael." The angel's voice leaves no room for argument.

I watch the gargoyle and archangel in some bizarre paranormal stare down. *My life is so weird.* I step in and turn to face Asher, locking eyes with him. "It's okay. I'll work on the mind control instruction and then we can pick up on the physical training later this afternoon."

"Fine," Asher concedes, grabbing his water bottle and storming out. The sound of the door slamming startles me.

"I'll go talk to him, Eves. You focus on your mental exercises with Michael," Callan offers.

I nod my appreciation and he pats my shoulder before exiting the training room. My eyes travel back to Michael and he smiles at me.

"Shall we?"

"Let's do it."

To be honest, I'm looking forward to seeing Lady Finella again and running away from the Asher drama for a little while.

My eyes open and I'm at peace, thanks in part to the stunning paradise of nature that surrounds me. I inhale a deep breath, enjoying the smell of honeysuckle and lavender. The fragrances signal I have arrived in the Kingdom of the Fae.

"Excellent realm jumping, Eve. Very proficient control," Michael comments from my right.

My eyes roam the woodland area and a sincere grin crosses my lips. I love being in the fae realm. It's so soothing and peaceful with its emerald forest, crystal blue water, and brightly colored flower clusters that look like patchwork along the green grass.

All around the forest, the sprites glow in bright blue, amber and pink hues. The flittering fairies whisper and giggle in a playful and carefree manner.

The warm voice of Lady Finella, Queen of the Fae, wraps around me like a warm blanket. "Welcome, warrior and daughter of Heaven. We are honored to receive you both here," she offers kindly with a slight bow of her head.

I walk over to her and tilt my head before snagging her into a hug. "Hello, Your Grace. It's so nice to see you."

Her beautiful red ringlets cascade around me. The silk strands smell like roses.

Michael saunters over to us, bowing his head in respect at the regal queen. "Lady Finella, as always, it is an honor to see you again. We offer our deepest gratitude to you for allowing us to fine-tune Eve's realm jumping gifts in the safety of your kingdom."

The queen turns to the archangel. "The realm is eternally fortunate to welcome you both."

"I must ask for Your Grace's forgiveness, once again, at the informal way a daughter of Heaven addresses you," he apologizes for my casual greeting.

Lady Finella slides her gaze to me, offering a wink only I'm privy to. "We are very pleased to offer haven to the daughter of Heaven and embraces, if she so wishes," Lady Finella responds in a light, playful tone and I muffle a giggle.

"I have quite enjoyed getting to know Eve this past lunar cycle." Her gold cuffs shine brightly in the realm's sunshine. The runes that run over her arms and legs slither in rapid movement. "I do hope you will be joining me for a light fare and tea at the castle. I am sure the Duchess of Sprites will be very happy to see you again," the regal queen extends her invitation.

"Yes! I can't wait to see Ainsley," I exclaim with abnormal excitement, not ready to return to Asher's brooding.

"Eve and I are most grateful to accompany you for tea, Your Highness," Michael responds properly.

I nod my agreement, grateful to be away from the earth realm. Lady Finella encloses our hands in hers and teleports us all to the Emerald Castle.

Each time I'm here, I'm always in awe of how beautiful the translucent palace is. The see-through walls offer the sensation of being in the forest, while the green tinted glass projects just the right amount of privacy from outside eyes. The openness makes you feel at one with the realm.

Just as we enter the rotunda, the Duchess of Sprites, Ainsley, flitters into the room with a tray. Her amber hue glows bright as she curtsies to both Michael and me before placing the silver platter on the table.

I'm always taken aback at how similar she and Lady Finella look. Both have long, red hair, emerald green eyes and stunning translucent butterfly-like wings.

The only difference, aside from their height and dress color, is the gold runes that run through Lady Finella's beautiful skin. I've repeatedly wondered if they're sisters.

Ainsley presents us with fresh tea and sandwiches made from the herbs and vegetables grown in the fairies' gardens. I can't help but take two, they're that good.

Lady Finella just smiles, amused with me, as a mother would be with her child, before turning her attention to Michael.

"Warrior of Heaven, as you are aware, it is not in my nature to skip pleasantries. Though today, I must be direct

and to the point. I bring news from my assembly with the Royal Supernatural Court," she states in an authoritative manner before sipping her tea.

Michael nods and motions for her to continue. "Of course, Your Grace. Please, we are anxious to hear the information you wish to impart."

Lady Finella places her cup down and gives Michael a pointed look. "I am afraid it is quite serious intelligence. Priestess Arabella has been plagued with countless visions, many of which sorceress Lunette confirmed to be truth. It is with great distress that I advise you and the protectors that the apparitions are in regard to the Declan clan of gargoyles and also the dark army." She sighs sadly before continuing.

I tense at the mention of Deacon's clan.

"Lucifer is moving quickly to ensure Eve does not succeed in her ascension. All five of the supernatural kingdoms have vowed to provide assistance to the Angelic Council and the London clan to assure Eve's well-being and ascension. Sorrowfully, not all supernatural creatures within our realms are loyal so we must be on guard and quite vigilant with whom we entrust Eve's life," she states with a stern look.

"I understand," Michael responds with a very serious tone.

"Eve, Arabella is one of The Seven High Priestesses with the gift of future sight. She's also a member of the Royal Supernatural Court and a very dear friend. The court thought perhaps it might be worthwhile for you to pay her a visit. Now that it appears you have mastered realm jumping, an appointment with her in the Eternal Forest

should be quite an easy journey for you, guided by your protector, of course," Lady Finella explains.

"I'm happy to meet with the priestess," I concur, not admitting my unease.

"I'll discuss it with the London clan and get word to you once they are able to make the journey," Michael adds authoritatively.

"Wonderful. I will speak with the priestess and court and let them know right away of your plans," she counters.

"Lady Finella, it is always an honor when we are in your presence. Your hospitality is most appreciated," Michael offers with a slight bow and they both stand.

Guessing our time here has ended. I stand as well and offer my gratitude.

She turns to me as her face softens. "Batya, it is always a great honor and a most pleasant experience to have you in our kingdom. It is my wish that when your divine task is complete, you enjoy our realm for a longer period of time."

I beam at her. "I would love that. Thank you."

She leans in to embrace me as she whispers in my ear, "Perhaps with your protector." Pulling back, she smirks and winks at me. My heart drops at the suggestion.

"Warrior of Heaven, thank you for gracing us with your presence. Please do share what I've told you at once with Eve's sentinels," the majestic queen asks.

"Of course, Your Grace. Are you ready to return, Eve?" he inquires.

"Yep. Thank you again for everything, Your Highness," I say one final time.

"Until next time, child."

Suddenly, we are returned to the earth realm and the training room where I'm sure I'll be enduring more punishment this afternoon.

Ugh.

Maybe I will just run away to the Fae Kingdom forever.

5 Saraphina

Feathery ice crystals fall in delicate patterns from the puffy storm clouds as I admire the brush strokes of gray that obscure the cool winter sky. I trek my way through the snow-covered gardens.

Bundled up for warmth, I follow the path all the way through the white birch trees toward the lake side of the grounds.

With each step, the sound of crunching snow echoes off the lifeless trees, disturbing the peaceful quiet of nature and marring the untainted soft white blanket. Even in the middle of winter, when the flowers are not in bloom, the garden is picturesque.

Inhaling the frosty air, I allow the coldness to fill my lungs. Though not as lovely as the Kingdom of the Fae, this place has its own natural allure. I can't explain it, but there's something drawing me to the stillness of the sleeping plants, soothing me and providing haven. Perhaps it's just my innate need to be close to nature.

The lightly falling snow surrounds my serene refuge, encompassing me in my own earthly snow globe. I brush off the white marble bench and sit, allowing the bitter chill to seep into my jeans, numbing me. The small lake on the left side of the private grounds is now frozen over with a thin layer of ice.

I shake my head, releasing the tiny white flakes from my damp hair. The frozen droplets of water cling to my strands like a life force. I stop when my body is hit with a flutter of warmth that only he brings.

"One of these days, you're going to freeze to death," Asher says across from me, leaning on a birch tree with his hands in the front pockets of his jeans. A shadow of concern falls over his handsome face.

My body purrs with exhilaration at his proximity. *Crap.* I really need to get my hormones under control. I can feel my eyes soften at the sight of him, but I remind myself to put up my shields.

"Have you come to punish me some more?" I ask in a snarky tone.

The right side of Asher's mouth tilts upward. "No. I won't apologize either. You need to become stronger and more strategic when you fight or you won't last against a demon."

I cock my eyebrow at him. "I lasted against Kaiden."

He pins me with his stare.

Asher's head shakes slowly. "He was a gargoyle and not a very impressive one at that."

"Is that so? You mean it wasn't the impeccable training you and Callan gave me?" I ask, my eyes searching his.

His face is serious before morphing into his panty dropping, come hither look.

Asher bestows his sexy grin. "I am pretty awesome."

My eyes flicker to the lake in an attempt to keep in the emotions that are too close to the surface. Then I return to the deepness of his gaze, yearning to get lost in him.

"I spoke to Tadhg. He said Leo is getting better each day." Asher breaks my reverie.

"That's good. I was worried about him."

An uncomfortable silence lingers between us.

He watches me. "I need to go to London with Keegan and Callan. There's a Spiritual Assembly of Protectors meeting, and Michael and Uriel have requested our attendance. I'm assuming they want to discuss what the Royal Supernatural Court talked about with Lady Finella and provide their approval for our realm jump to the Eternal Forest."

"Okay." I cringe at the sadness in my voice.

The thought of him being away from me makes my anxiety levels rise.

The bond alerts him to my flustered state. "Abby and Kenna will watch over you in my absence. I'll be back as soon as I can," he offers in a soft tone meant to calm me.

I nod, wishing he wouldn't go and then chastising myself for wanting him to stay. I need help.

"While I'm in the council chambers, our link won't be as strong, therefore I won't be able to feel the bond as clearly as I normally do. Do you think, for once, you could do as I ask and stay inside with the girls tonight, so I don't have to worry?" he requests with insistent eyes.

I lift my eyes to his, trying not to lose myself in the deep blue layers. "I can try."

"Not good enough. Do more than try, siren," he counters in a pleading tone.

I swallow the guilt I feel for, once again, making him see me as a nuisance. "Fine."

"Thank you," he replies on an exhale that comes out in a cloud of smoke from the cold air.

More silence.

He stalks over to me and crouches so we're in one another's line of sight. "I'm sorry if it felt I was rough on you during training. It's being done for your protection."

I offer a weak smile. "You were quite the jerk. I get it though." I watch him, watching me.

"I'm also sorry for my behavior toward you. Setting us straight, it was the right thing to do, siren. You're right. We need to focus. I am first and foremost your protector. I appreciate the reminder that it's all I can be," Asher says in a soft, sincere tone.

Crap. What did I do? "Ash—"

He cuts me off. "I took an oath and I intend to see it through without the added consequences of breaking the rules. From now on, I will respect our roles and restrain myself. Consider us protector and charge only. Yeah?" he asks, eyeing me.

My entire body sinks at the consequences of my actions and what he's saying. "And friends," I add, hopeful. This is not what I wanted.

His eyes never leave mine as he nods once, accepting my understanding and approving the *'friend'* title. His hand reaches for my hair, gently brushing the snowflakes off.

"Please come inside where it's warmer."

"Just ten more minutes to get my head clear." It comes out in a mere whisper.

"Five more minutes before I send the girls to come get you," he argues before standing to leave.

"Asher?"

"Yeah?"

"I'm sorry," I offer solemnly.

Asher looks away with pain on his face. "Me too, siren. Me too," he murmurs. "I'll be back in a few hours. Behave, yeah?" He extends his wings and disappears into the sky.

My body completely shuts down in panic at watching him leave like that. *What the hell?* I close my eyes and inhale again, trying to get a grip on my wild emotions. They're all over the place. The moment is broken at the sound of clapping from the wooded area near the lake.

I open my eyes and snap my head toward the forest to see what the intrusion is. On guard, my hands move instinctively toward the daggers I know are sheathed to my legs.

Clap. Clap. Clap.

"Bravo, daughter of Heaven." I barely register a jovial voice.

My eyes land on the ground and take in a small, dwarf-like creature that appears out of the tree line in front of me. My eyes widen. Holy shit, it's a good thing I'm sitting down.

He can't be more than six or seven inches tall, if that, and has a complete look of mischief etched on his face. For a brief moment, I look around, wondering if I've officially lost it and am envisioning things that aren't real.

The small being places his hand over his heart, eyes dreamy. "Young, forbidden love, it's so romantic. Although you and the gargoyle, well that was such a pathetic expression of feelings."

"Who are you?" I demand, proud that my tone sounds strong.

The tiny creature hobbles over to me and bows dramatically. "I am Godry, my lady," the grotesque creature introduces himself in a formal, yet small voice.

"Godry?" I repeat. "What are you, some type of elf or something?" My eyes dart to the woods in search of danger.

He stands tall and narrows his tiny brown eyes at me. "AN ELF?" he shouts, though to me it sounds like a squeak. "Do I look like a fucking elf?" he spits out with disgust.

Oops. I guess my lack of knowledge with regard to supernatural creatures has offended him. "S-sorry, it's just, you're freakishly small. Are you a fairy then?"

His face scrunches as if he smells something rotten. "Do I look like I twinkle and have little wings, you overgrown human imbecile?"

"Hey, watch it!" I warn sternly. "I'm far from being an imbecile, you ugly forest creature."

Godry hobbles closer to me, giving me a better visual of him. He looks like a little old man wearing knight's armor. His ears are long and stick straight out from each side of his head, which is covered by grey straggly hair that falls into his beady brown eyes. I notice the creature has the most disgusting pale-green, wrinkled skin and he's missing a few teeth.

I force down my repulsion and look him in his miniature eyes. "Please, enlighten me as to what you are and why you are here?" I ask with fake sweetness.

He scoffs. "I am a goblin."

"A goblin?" I repeat, unconvinced.

"For the daughter of Heaven, you are impolite and unintelligent," he states snidely.

I tilt my head in a threatening manner, stand and cross my arms. "If I were you, I would be careful not to insult a giant. How easy it would be for me to squish you with my boot," I warn and lift my foot for good measure.

"I'm so scared," he mocks and pretends to shake.

My irritation levels continue to rise at his maddening behavior. I attempt to rein them in. "What's a goblin?"

"Yes, it would seem you are uneducated. What does that fine specimen of gargoyle see in you?" he rambles. His tone disgusted and bored.

"What do you want, little gnome?" I provoke him.

"I'M NOT A GNOME. I'M A GOBLIN," he bellows but it barely registers in my ears.

I exhale a frustrated breath. "Fine, what do you want...goblin?"

"I would be happy to tell you why I'm here, my lady. First, it will cost you. You see, us goblins are known to be a bit greedy. We love money. You show me some and I'll inform you of the why," he states, as if that statement has won me over.

We just stand there staring at one another until finally the fact I can't feel my hands or toes because of the icy weather breaks me and I search my pocket for change. I find a dime and throw it at him. It is almost larger than he is. "Talk, goblin."

"Thank you, my lady. I am Godry of the Quaboag Tribe. I've been sent by Yester Castle to inform you of the dangers of the lake," he says in a formal tone. "Although, to be honest, with your bad attitude, I should let Saraphina devour you."

I prowl at him in agitation. "Who sent you and who is Saraphina?"

"Y-e-s-t-e-r Castle," he repeats slowly as if speaking to a child. "Kenna must want to slit your throat a thousand times a day."

"I've had enough of your mouth." I turn to walk away.

He calls after me. "You know nothing of goblins, do you? So then you have no idea we possess various magical abilities. Keep walking away from me and you'll be waiting, in the form of a frog, for your dark prince to come back. Ironic right? I wonder if Asher would be willing to lip lock with a frog, even for you, Batya."

I release one of my daggers. The metal noisily slides out of the sheath with a whoosh. I spin and point the very tip at his tiny throat. "Who. Is. Saraphina?" I ask in a calm, slow voice while I stalk back toward him.

"The Lady of the Lake. She's a selkie who works for Lucifer." He shrugs, annoyed with our exchange. That makes two of us.

My eyes dart to the frozen lake. "Why were you sent to warn me?"

He sighs. "My tribe owed the London clan a favor. Our Queen, who is also a soothsayer, saw you sitting out here while your protector was called away to the council and felt you should be made aware. I pulled the shortest straw hence my crappy messenger status. Now you know and I need to go back to the castle where it's warm and the demonic creatures I consort with are not as crass as you."

Abruptly, he glows green and vanishes into thin air. *What the hell?* My eyes inspect the gardens but he's definitely gone. I place my dagger in its sheath, ready to go back to the manor when I faintly hear my name on the wind. The sound reminds me of a lover's whisper coming from the lake.

As soon as my name hits my ears, my head fogs and becomes unfocused. My body turns toward the lake of its own accord. I'm not in control of it. My feet and legs begin to move toward the frozen mass of water while my brain is screaming at them to stop.

I reach the lake and the ice begins to shatter like crystal when it hits marble. The large pieces fall away as a stunning woman rises out of the water, rendering me speechless.

She's the epitome of temptation as she seductively moves her body, breaking the water's line. Her ankle length, straight black hair blows in the arctic breeze as her deep chocolate eyes hold mine. I'm unable to look away from her angelic face. The selkie's cheeks turn a shade of peach and her lips part as my eyes roam down her sculptured body.

The long dark stands of hair hang over her naked breasts and float down to her mermaid-like tail, just barely under the water. The skin of her fin is a dark chocolate brown highlighted in purples as the Pisces pelt comes up her right side and drapes over her shoulder like a piece of clothing.

I'm breathless with how exquisite she is.

"Come to me, daughter of Heaven," she purrs while moving closer to the edge of the water, extending her hand for me to take.

My body automatically moves toward the freezing water. My breath increases as my heart rate lurches, pounding inside my chest.

She smiles at me as an unwelcome heat invades my body, setting off a desire sensation. Her stare envelops me, seducing me. Her glance caresses me with slow movements. I gasp at the intimate way she touches me with only her gaze. My head becomes even hazier and it's difficult to think clearly.

"Come, my love. Let me take care of you." She coos and licks her lips.

I move forward in an irrational need to feel her closer to me. The logical part of my brain is screaming danger but it's currently being held captive by my raging desire. My body is begging me to allow her hands to touch me the way her eyes just did.

As if I am a fly trapped in her web, I'm helpless against her advances. Confusion sets in when images of Asher flash through my mind of his strong hands and brooding lips branding every spot on my body.

"Come," she bids again. "I know you want to feel me as I care for you. I can take you places you have never experienced before. Make you feel things," she whispers like a lover.

I release a soft sigh and close my eyes in response. My brain is not functioning properly. It's full of fog and lust for her while images of Asher keep invading my thoughts. It's like my body is confusing her for him. When I open my eyes, she is unhappy, like a shark ready to snap.

"Eve, move away from the water," a masculine voice says in a smooth, seductive tone. I don't want to go to him. I want to go to the beautiful woman standing in front of me and giving me bedroom eyes. *Don't I?*

"Saraphina, release her from the spell at once," the deep voice orders.

"Or what, gargoyle?" She laughs and it sounds like angels singing. I lick my lips in response as she smiles seductively and nods at me in encouragement.

"Or I will kill you myself," the male voice threatens.

She turns her chocolate eyes on the man behind me, attempting to seduce him too, lowering her voice to a sexy octave. "It's a shame, really. You used to be so much more fun. Do you recall all the good times we've had together, lover?"

"Your seduction won't work this time, so save the effort. I'll kindly ask you one more time to release her from the spell before I discharge my powers," he warns sharply.

She pouts and it makes me sad. The need to comfort her overwhelms me until she darts her angry eyes toward me.

Without warning, the chokehold she had on my body is gone. I stumble back, almost landing on the snowy ground before two strong hands wrap around me. As the haze in my brain begins to lift, I start to see and think clearly again.

"Next time she comes to the lake, I will take her to Lucifer," Saraphina threatens then dives into the water, splashing us.

The frigid water increases the coldness running through my bones. My lips chatter from the cold.

A pair of brawny hands grab at me, pulling me away from the lake's edge. "It's all right. I've got you."

The scent of cigarettes and spice hits me.

"Gage?" His name comes out as a choked whimper.

He smirks. "Hello, love."

6 My Soul

My body feels heavy, but it's finally warm. I snuggle deeper into the soft blanket that envelops me. Against my will, my eyes open and I notice the blazing fire. A slight smile crosses my lips, knowing I'm safe. The moment is fleeting as my gaze shifts and land on a large lion tattoo, which is staring back at me as if personified from the lean muscles of the bare back that is home to the animal.

I sit up an inch, holding my breath as the gargoyle turns his amused gaze toward me, offering a charming smile. Shit. Asher is going to kill me, that is, if Gage doesn't first.

"You're up." It isn't a question.

"You're shirtless," I retort.

He looks down before grinning. "Yes, love, I suppose I am. My attire was wet after saving you from being seduced by that nut job of a selkie. No thanks are needed though," he finishes in a light-hearted, sarcastic tenor.

I look around, noticing we're in his concrete loft. "So you kidnapped me and brought me to Paris?"

"Yes." Gage turns back to the fire, blowing out cigarette smoke through parted lips before flicking the remains into the blaze and bringing a short glass to his mouth, swallowing the last sip of its golden contents. "I brought you back to my home," he continues.

"Those things will give you cancer, you know." I point to the now burning stick of nicotine.

He gives me a crooked smile and shrugs. "I'm a gargoyle. We don't get cancer."

I narrow my eyes. "Convenient."

"Would you like some brandy to warm you?" he asks.

"That depends."

"On?"

"On whether or not you're planning to hand me over to Deacon after I drink it." I stare him down.

He holds my eyes, unwavering. "Have some. It will both warm and relax you while I mull it over," he suggests and walks over to a built-in bar. Gage pours the amber liquid half way into a short glass before approaching me with it.

I reach for it and take a small sip. At first, it burns going down my throat but then almost immediately, warmth flows through my veins and suddenly, I'm unexpectedly grateful he found me.

"Aren't you supposed to be at the council meeting?"

His bark is short and boisterous. "No, love. It's a Spiritual Assembly meeting and I'm not a member of that particular assemblage."

I watch him. "You're part of the Secular Set then? No affiliation to either Heaven or Hell?"

"No." Gage feigns disinterest and sits down on a black leather chair positioned across from the couch I'm on.

Damn, he really needs to put a shirt on. His corded stomach muscles are beckoning me to run my hands over them. *Focus, Eve. He's dangerous.*

"No associations then?"

"Relationships and loyalties are messy," he offers, his tone spiteful.

"Why did you save me from the selkie? Aren't you inclined to hand me over to Deacon?" I'm trying to keep the worry out of my voice.

"Inclined?" He plays with the word as if he doesn't understand the meaning. "I don't know, love. I have yet to decide what I'm doing when it comes to you," he claims, more to himself than me.

I swallow my frustration and try to sit up. That's when I realize I'm not wearing any clothing. I grit my teeth and clench my jaw.

"What the hell? Where are my clothes, Gage?" I snap.

His right eyebrow lifts in amusement. "They were drenched and frozen from the snow and the splash Saraphina caused so I'm having them laundered for you."

I snarl my agitation. "So you undressed me?"

He shakes his head. "Love," he replies in a disappointed voice, "I'm more of a gentlemen than that. My housekeeper, Isla, did it before she left. She's also taken care of washing and drying the items for you. They're finishing up the dry cycle as we speak."

"You didn't think to maybe have her throw a t-shirt or something on me?" I ask, annoyed.

He stares at my bare shoulders for the briefest moment. I think I see his face soften with what could be mistaken as want before he schools his features and flicks his aloof eyes to mine.

"You were on the verge of hypothermia. Your body warmed faster without the clothing."

I wrap the blanket tighter around myself. "Well, thank you. For, you know, saving me."

He shrugs. "I'm a gargoyle. It's what we do. We save the human race and all." He waves his hand as if it's an effort to help mankind.

I scoff. "Then why are you so adamant about handing me over to Deacon when he means me harm?"

Gage pauses, looking thoughtful for a moment. "I owe him a favor. It's business, not personal."

"And I'm the favor?" I study his face and body language, trying to figure him out.

He nods once, his face impassible. "Yes."

"So then where is he?" My eyes search the loft.

"As I mentioned, love, I've yet to decide if I'm going to fulfill my obligation or not. I find you very illicit and intriguing. I need some time to decide." Gage's voice sounds far off.

I watch him, reminded of what Fiona said about his past relationship with the London clan. "Asher will figure out I'm here."

"Your protector is with the Spiritual Assembly which means your bond is temporarily on pause, if you will. It's

70

why he didn't save you from Saraphina himself," he points out.

"How did you know where I was?" It comes out harsher than I meant it to.

"I've been following you. Watching from the shadows." He smirks while memories from our last conversation about watching me from the shadows enter my mind. My cheeks flush at the recollection and our intimate dance at Katana, Asher's nightclub.

"Why?" I question sincerely.

He blows out an exaggerated breath. "Why do any of us do what we do, Eve? I have my reasons. None of which I'm interested in sharing with you."

Ouch. I take a larger sip of the brandy. I have a feeling it's going to be a long night and I'll need it. My head starts to ache. I lift my hand to rub my temples, attempting to ease the pressure.

Gage sighs, gets up, and disappears from the room before returning a few moments later with two aspirin.

"The headache is an effect of the selkie's charm wearing off. It will subside in a bit. These should help."

"Is that what she did? She put me under some sort of spell?" I take the aspirin.

"Yes, she enhanced your feelings and twisted them, making you think you felt them for her. It's what selkies do. They have great seductive powers," Gage answers, watching me closely.

My face goes crimson recalling the images of Asher she planted. "What exactly is a selkie?" I inquire, avoiding the current state of my mortification.

"A mythological creature. Although they're often confused with mermaids, they live as seals. Once on land, they can normally shed their skin to become human. Our little Saraphina has been a very naughty selkie and was punished centuries ago. Hence her new title as Lady of the Lake. She is bound to lakes until her sentence has been fulfilled," he explains.

"Sounds lovely. What did she want with me then?"

He smiles but it doesn't reach his eyes. "I suppose what all supernatural creatures want with you, love. Leverage. My guess is she was offered freedom if she handed you over to the dark army."

"She mentioned having known you, in the ah, biblical sense. You really know how to pick girlfriends." My cheeks are burning. I need to learn tact. *Why am I even bringing this up?*

He smirks and the sea green deepens in his eyes. "Saraphina is good at many things, especially in the bedroom."

I swallow the bile threatening to come up. "Would you mind checking on my clothing, please?" I'm suddenly too hot and very aware I'm still naked.

"I would be happy to. Would you like a refill while I'm up?" He points to my glass.

"No, thank you." I really need to keep a clear head around Gage.

He walks down the long hallway and I stand, wrapping myself tightly in the blanket. I make my way to the wall of windows that overlooks the Eiffel Tower then close my eyes.

I try to feel the hum of energy I get from Asher but it's not there. All of a sudden, I'm terrified, cold and alone.

Inhaling a deep breath, I focus my energy and center myself the way Michael showed me, willing my body to reach a hypnotic state. I let my mind wander and focus on my heart, visualizing it. Every beat that it takes, every ounce of blood it pushes through my veins and organs, my body pulls toward the link that connects my heart to Asher's.

All my other thoughts fall away and I focus on my heartbeats as they align with his and my body enters a state of vibration. My soul lifts and I imagine Asher's face, his smile and the five o'clock shadow I love so much.

I move toward his sparkling eyes and concentrate on his heartbeat as my body's soul floats through the astral plane, guiding my spirit toward him.

Within seconds, I notice I'm in a large, circular room. It's similar to a stadium where the seats are in a ring formation and taper off, each step is another row down to a main floor where Michael and another angel are speaking. I can't hear what they're saying. It's like they're on mute.

The ceiling is vaulted and has the most beautiful mural of angels painted on it. Blue and green brush strokes enhance the entire piece. The large hall boasts crisp white walls highlighted with stunning gold gilded moldings. The sanctuary has natural lighting, though I can't tell where it's coming from. Beams of brightness bounce off the gold accents, creating an ethereal setting which appears to glow.

My eyes scan all the people that are seated. It looks like an ancient Greek senate meeting. There must be a thousand men and women in this room. I scan the faces until I see Asher and take in a deep sigh of relief.

As if he senses my presence, Asher's eyes lift and catch mine going completely wide as he stands abruptly and stalks toward me. My heart increases at his proximity. It's like I feel whole again, and safe. My entire body relaxes knowing he's here. He is my oxygen, my lifeline.

Once he reaches me, he takes my elbow and drags me out of two large bullion doors into a white marble hallway that's gleaming with sunlight. *Huh, who knew we could touch in this state.*

"What are you doing here, Eve?" he asks, alert and surprised while he scans my face.

His eyebrows knit together, confused as to how I got here and why I am translucent.

"How come I can hear you but not the others in the room?" I question.

"It's protected by the Angelic Council. Only members can hear the discussion," he replies. "Are you astral projecting?" he whisper shouts in awe.

I nod, chewing the inside of my cheek, unsure if he's upset I'm here or glad to see me. "Yes."

"What's wrong? Are you okay? Where are Abby and Kenna?" he shoots off a mile a minute.

I swallow. If he wasn't mad before, he's going to be really pissed when I explain. "Um, I had a little run in with a goblin and a selkie. I'm okay. Gage saved me and brought me to his loft in Paris, where I am now."

He just stares at me. Mouth agape and face pale. *Crap.* I can't tell if he's angry or about to pass out. Asher exhales, trying to calm himself. I fidget, waiting for the shouting.

"Start. From. The. Beginning," he says too slowly and more for his benefit than mine.

"After you left, Godry came out of the woods," I begin, unsure how much I should tell him.

"Godry? The goblin from Yester Castle?" he confirms, puzzled.

I nod. "Anyway, he said he owed you a favor and since you're here at the meeting, he wanted to warn me about Saraphina. By the way, that little goblin needs some serious lessons in manners. He's extremely rude and tactless. I almost squished the life out of him."

Exhausted, Asher runs his hands over his face and through his hair. "Eve." It comes out as a warning growl. "Focus, please."

"Right, sorry. I was prepared to leave when Saraphina called to me. Apparently, the creepy selkie put some sort of seductive charm on me. I was just about to walk into the frozen water when Gage caught me and pulled me out." I stop and wait for the yelling that surprisingly doesn't come.

Asher just inhales and watches me. Then with great self-control he says, "So, now, you're with Gage?"

"Yes. In Paris, at his loft." I study him, watching me. *Why is he so composed?*

"I'm assuming Saraphina wanted to turn you over to the dark army for her freedom. Is Gage in contact with Deacon?" Asher asks, his voice calm.

Too calm. It's unnerving.

"No. That's just it. He said he owed Deacon a favor but now he isn't sure if he's willing to fulfill it." I pull my brows together. Asher's quiet demenour is freaking me out.

He's still for a moment longer while he contemplates what I've told him. His eyes roam down me and stop on the blanket before his face morphs into fuming anger.

"WHAT. THE. FUCK. EVE. Where are your fucking clothes?" he shouts in a controlled whisper.

Seriously, I've been standing here for like fifteen minutes and he's just now noticing the blanket. I forgot when I project it's in the items I'm wearing.

"Um, they were wet from the snow, so they're being washed and dried," I explain, gauging his reaction.

Asher's eyes narrow at me in fury, but his voice is oddly gentle. "I'm presuming since Gage saved you and is keeping you quietly at his loft, he isn't going to bring Deacon in tonight. That said, for the love of all that is…when you get back, put your fucking clothes back on." He regains control of his temper before continuing. "Then wait for either Abby, Kenna or I to come get you. Understand?" He waits, eyes in slits.

"Yes. Dress and wait," I repeat with a quick nod.

"And by the grace, siren. Do not fucking go anywhere else with that piece of shit! Got it?" he quietly shouts, his eyes wild and raw.

"Yep, crystal clear." I smile, trying to help keep his emotional state even.

"We'll discuss this when I get back from the meeting. Once sworn into the summit, we're not permitted to leave. Under any circumstances." His eyes flicker to the doors then back to me and soften a bit. "If I'm gone too long, they'll come looking for me and notice you're here. Which, by the way, is completely breaking the rules. Also a discussion for later," he scolds.

I cast my eyes down. "I'm sorry. I was just afraid and didn't know what else to do."

Immediately, Asher's entire demeanor changes. The hardness is gone as he pulls me into his arms. "Shit. I'm sorry, siren. Of course, you're frightened. You did the right thing coming to find me. I'll get you out of Gage's place as soon as I can. If what you said is true, then I'm sure he's not going to hurt you. For now, you're safe. That doesn't mean you can let your guard down with him though, Eve. He's in a tenuous state right now and is unpredictable."

I nod, wishing I could inhale his scent to help keep me calm. "I promise to be careful."

"Good girl, thank you. I need to return to the meeting. Are you okay to astral project back?" Asher's hands cup my face, his thumb brushing back and forth across my skin.

"I'm a pro at this now, thanks to Michael." I smirk.

Asher's face scans mine. "I'll see you soon. I promise."

I bury my face in his chest. "Ash?" I murmur.

"Yeah?" he whispers, his chin resting on top of my head.

"You're literally holding my soul in your hands."

My eyes lift to meet his.

He gives me his sexy smile. "There's no place I would rather your soul be, than in my protection." His demeanor is sincere and filled with something else I can't name.

My heart skips a beat at his proclamation and I come to the realization my soul might not be the only thing attached to him.

Randi Cooley Wilson

7 Pendulum

I close my eyes and imagine I'm a glowing white light, tugging on a silver cord attached to my physical body. Gently, I pull and let it guide me back, just as Michael taught me. I return to my physical state, which happens faster than leaving it for some reason.

As soon as my soul hits my body, I stand straighter. I forgot I left myself standing by the windows. I need to remember to position myself more comfortably next time. I stretch my neck from side to side to alleviate some of the pressure the absence caused.

"Welcome back. I trust Asher is alright?" Gage says, standing next to me.

He's holding my clothes and weapons with an unreadable expression marring his lovely face. There's something I see behind his gaze. Anger maybe, but it disappears.

I tilt my head to the side and narrow my eyes. "You didn't think you could kidnap me and I wouldn't reach out to him, did you?"

The calculating gargoyle watches me, a small smile forming on his lips. "I didn't kidnap you. You're free to go any time you'd like, love." He points toward the door before handing my outfit and daggers to me.

"The restroom?"

He motions to the bathroom with his head. "Down the hall, on the right."

"Thanks," I reply quietly and make my way to change back into my jeans and black cotton long sleeved shirt and resheath my weapons. If he meant me harm, why would he return my daggers?

When I return, Gage is sitting at the granite counter in the kitchen with some cheese, crackers and fruit on a platter and two glasses of water, waiting for me to join him. He points to a stool next to him.

"Are you hungry?"

My stomach grumbles, letting me know that I am.

"I guess."

"Take a seat," he orders, imploring obedience. *Why are all gargoyles so damn bossy?*

Sitting, I grab some cheese and begin to nibble on it.

"Why are you being so nice to me?"

He stops eating and focuses on the sink in front of us as if he didn't realize he was being kind toward me.

"I'm not sure."

"Truthful. Weird, but straight forward," I state, confused by his response.

"I take it his highness will be on his way shortly?" he says with little humor.

I glance at him sideways. "If you're referring to Asher, then yes."

The corners of his lips tilt. "The dark prince must have been super pissed you're here with me, love." Gage's eyes roam down my body, causing it to shudder, which catches me off guard. "And unclothed, at that, when you projected."

I groan. "Asher wasn't thrilled, but he did say I was safe with you. Am I?" I send a pointed glance his way.

"For now." He shrugs like it's not a big deal.

I grab a grape and focus on chewing it as we sit in silence for a bit. This is awkward and I'm not sure what to say to Gage. He seems like a nice guy, but his past actions tell a different story.

"You're mastering the astral projection well. Michael is an excellent teacher. It takes great strength to be able to manipulate it the way you have." His tone sounds almost proud that I've controlled the ability.

"I'm lucky he's showing me how to have power over some abilities of the ascension," I reply.

Gage looks at me pensively for a moment. "Does it scare you? Knowing you're the weapon they've created to save humankind?"

My eyes hold his and swallow my grape, hard. For some reason that goes beyond logical interpretation, I feel at ease with Gage. No matter what his threats are, I know he isn't dangerous to me in this moment.

"At first, I wanted no part in it. Now, well, when Deacon killed Aria, it made me realize I have to make that mean something in the grand scheme of things." My answer is painful.

Gage just studies me. "It will. He was wrong to do that. Deacon is half-demon, so there are times he can't control his urges. In that moment though, Aria came out of nowhere, love. Not that I'm defending him but technically he didn't go after her. She jumped in front of you."

"That's what makes it worse," I whisper. "She believed in me enough to sacrifice herself."

"Unfortunately, we don't get second chances with the ones we love, do we?" he says.

I just watch him, ignoring the urge to scream. "Then he desecrated her grave."

Gage stills. "Deacon did?" Appalled, he sighs and turns toward me. "Well, that is disturbing, to say the least. You must've really pissed him off."

I snort. "He's your friend, you would know."

Gage takes my elbow. "Make no mistake, I'm not his friend, nor do I agree with his business practices. I owe him a simple debt of gratitude."

"Okay," I offer weakly, knowing I'm the payment.

"I'm not your friend either, love. The only one I look out for in this world is myself," he adds with a sharp undertone.

"From what I understand, that wasn't always the case. Fiona says you used to be close with the St. Michaels and you were practically family. I was under the impression that Asher, Keegan and Callan were like brothers to you."

Gage exhales an agitated breath. "Yes, when we were mere boys. The world has changed since then, as have I."

"How did you come to owe a stand-up guy like Deacon?" I inquire, taking another grape. Sarcasm drips from my lips along with the juice from the fruit.

"A long time ago, I needed some information and he was able to provide it to me," he admits.

That can't be good. "That's not vague at all."

Gage glances up to see me looking back at him. "Are you asking for my life's story, love?"

I just shrug. "I guess I am. I'm wondering what provokes an outwardly normal guy, with so much to offer, to become indebted to a guy like Deacon. You seem smarter than that."

He turns on the stool, fully facing me, and places a hand on the back of my chair. "Maybe I'm not as normal as you think."

I fix my eyes on his face instead of his bare chest and lift my chin. "I disagree."

He pales and his brows scrunch together. "Perhaps you should ask Asher."

I hold Gage's eyes. "I'm asking you."

Gage just grumbles under his breath. "Look, love, being here, in my home, is not an invitation into my life."

I stand in disappointment. "Understood," I reply and walk back to the couch in front of the fire to get warm. "I'll just sit quietly and wait for Asher to show up and kick your ass."

Gage sighs in defeat, gets up, and takes his place across from me in the leather chair. He just stares at me, as if deciding whether he wants to talk at all.

"The love of my life, my mate, was taken from me in the middle of the night then raped and killed. Her neck was slit from ear to ear before they left her to bleed out. Her lifeless body was positioned in front of my door so I would find her in that state in the morning."

My mouth falls open. "Oh my God, Gage. I'm so sorry."

"Yeah, me too." He gets up and walks to the bar, pouring himself another brandy. With his back to me, he drains the entire glass in one large swallow. I focus on the lion tattoo.

"I don't mean to sound ignorant but I thought you had to pierce the heart of a gargoyle to kill them," I ask, my voice soft, treading on light waters.

Gage turns to me, the vein in his neck pulsing with rage. "She was human."

My mouth is opening and closing like a fish. I need to say something, anything. "Oh, I'm sorry," I offer lamely.

He pours another glass, taking a small sip before settling back into the seat across from me. He frowns before continuing. "There's nothing to be sorry for. It's done. She's dead."

My heart drops. I'm not sure whether to be disgusted by his nonchalance or saddened by the walls he's built because of her death. "Yes, she is. I know what it's like and how difficult it is for you to live with her death hanging over your shoulders each day." Because I do. It's how I'm coping with Aria's passing.

Gage's face flashes with respect and disquiet. "I needed information to find out who killed her and Deacon not only gave me the information, but helped me make it right."

I study him for a moment. "You mean he handed over the demon who killed her?"

"Gargoyle," he corrects coldly.

My eyes widen in shock. "Gargoyle?"

"Lucky for me, gargoyle law states that when one of our kind takes another's life, revenge is warranted, per the holier than thou Royal Gargoyle Council of Protectors decree," he scoffs.

"An eye for an eye?" I'm reminded of Deacon's words during our stand off.

The corner of his mouth rises slowly, unnerving me. "Yes."

"I thought she wasn't a gargoyle?" I mutter, wishing I could take it back once I see his reaction.

Gage leans forward, resting his elbows on his knees. "Camilla was human, however we were mated so she carried my clan mark, the lion tattoo, therefore her life falls under gargoyle law."

"I see." I swallow back the lump forming in my throat. I hadn't realized if a human takes a gargoyle as a mate, they're required to follow their supernatural laws. "She had a pretty name."

"She was from Spain." He leans closer toward me, closing his eyes, his voice soft. "Camilla was beautiful, intelligent and loving. When I close my eyes at night, I can still see her sparkling eyes. My hands can still feel her long hair, which flowed in the wind like silk. She was perfect. She was everything." Gage's eyes reopen and scan mine then, as if burned he gets up, moving with exceptional speed to face the fireplace and lights a cigarette, inhaling the nicotine roughly.

"My love didn't deserve to die such a vile and brutal death. Especially at the hands of my father and the council." Gage rubs his thumb methodically over his bottom lip while exhaling a cloud of smoke.

"Your father?"

He turns and faces me. "Yes. My father was the leader of the Paris clan of gargoyles and second in command to Asher's father, Garrick, on the council. He didn't believe his only son, his male heir, should marry a human let alone one he was charged with protecting. He felt it important I mate with '*our own kind*' as he put it. He was also upset that I broke my protector oath, for which the punishment is stone petrification. So he had Camilla murdered in an attempt to keep me under his control and prevent me from being charged and sentenced by the council."

My eyes shift to the flickering of the fire. "That's awful, Gage." He was her protector?

"Yeah, well, shit happens, love. Deacon knew about my father and provided the information and assistance I needed. In exchange, all he required was a good turn at a time of his choosing."

"So I'm that good turn?" I try not to stammer.

"Yes. He's chosen to cash in the favor by having me deliver you to him," he states as a matter of fact.

I look him in the eyes. "And will you, knowing what my fate is?"

He sighs and turns back to the fire. "I'm unsure."

"If your father's gone, are you not the leader of the Paris clan?" I ask, hoping to keep the subject off him delivering me to Deacon.

Gage shakes his head back and forth vigorously. "No. I walked away from that title when the clan killed my mate. My father may have wielded the sword but it wasn't a solo act. I'm positive he had assistance. There were other gargoyles, and of course, the council. I know they approved her demise in order to avoid sentencing."

I stand and move toward the fire. "Wait, you don't think the St. Michaels had anything to do with her death, do you?"

Gage just stares at me, the lion on his back twitches with his muscles at the mention of Asher's family. He moves closer and brushes the hair off my shoulder. "Garrick St. Michael was not only in charge of the council, but he was also the leader of the gargoyle community. Our king. Did Asher not tell you? He's next in line to the throne. Asher St. Michael is the prince of the gargoyle race."

I suddenly feel as if the wind has been knocked out of me. *What the hell?* How many times have I heard someone refer to Asher as your highness or dark prince? Oh my God. I squeeze my eyes shut and then open them, pinning Gage with my stare.

"You're telling me Asher is slated to become the king of the gargoyle community?" I question in disbelief.

"Yes. He manipulates darkness, hence we call him the dark prince."

"I thought Keegan was older? Wouldn't he be next in line?" I speak softly, stunned.

"No. It doesn't work like that amongst gargoyles. It's the strongest bloodline who rules next."

Holy Shit. "Deacon could have lied to you. I don't believe Asher or his family were part of killing Camilla. Gargoyles are sworn to protect humans," I remind him.

"Love, don't mistake loyalty to mankind as a free get out of jail card. Yes, we are under oath to protect humans but gargoyles, like most supernatural creatures, are not immune to greed. It can breed within our community just like any other," Gage counters, throwing the last of his cigarette into the flames. "I once told you to get all the facts before you choose a side. Even now, knowing he's hidden his title from you, you remain unwavering in your allegiance." His voice holds a hint of sadness.

"That's why you're so angry with Asher and his family? Because you assume Garrick approved Camilla's death, and as the next in line, Asher and his brothers knew about it?"

"It's possible that bloodlines overshadowed alliance," Gage offers. "Her death has certainly led to my distrust of the council."

I exhale my shock. "I don't understand how you just disregard your allegiance to your kin."

"You cannot understand what you don't know, love." Gage's voice is solemn.

"I understand shadows that have a hold on us and skew our beliefs better than you think."

"My shadow left me a long time ago," he states. "With that love, so went my loyalty to one side or another. I trust no side."

"Sounds like you're protecting yourself and putting up guarded walls."

"Perhaps, but my neutral position allows me to be a pendulum, free to swing back and forth to my liking," Gage responds, dropping his voice to a seductive level.

"What about coalitions? Maybe other clans can assist you to discover the true story of what happened to Camilla?" I suggest.

"In the end, my alliances won't make a difference, because like a pendulum, I'll always be weighed down by her ghost. Swinging alone, between sides that have no merit anymore."

Feeling an overwhelming urge to console Gage, I reach out and place my hand on his cheek. "I'm sorry about Camilla, but you're wrong to trust Deacon," I whisper.

He tilts his head into my palm and closes his eyes. "As I said, there is nothing to be sorry for." The enigmatic gargoyle takes my wrist with surprising gentleness and brings it to his nose before inhaling my scent. I still. Without warning, he presses his lips over my pulse as a strangled gasp parts my lips. Gage's gaze lifts and meets mine. He smiles sadly.

"Love?"

"Yes." It comes out breathless.

"Your protector is here."

Randi Cooley Wilson

8 Everything and Anything

As soon as Gage opens the door, Asher storms in like a bat out of hell. His eyes are wild with rage. I stand motionless by the fire, trying to gain control of my erratic heartbeats. To be honest, I've only seen Asher this crazed one other time, at Katana, and it also involved Gage. Crap.

"Asher, so nice of you to join us. Please do come in." Gage's voice drips with disdain as he motions after Asher has already entered the loft without waiting for an invitation.

He prowls toward me, his eyes never wavering. "You're unharmed." It wasn't a question.

Seeing the confusion and worry on his face, I'm rendered speechless and simply nod my agreement. My lack of speech isn't helping Asher's composure.

Meticulously, he scans my body, heating it with his gaze. "I almost beat the door down. Your heart rate was just through the roof. Are you frightened?"

My gaze shifts and lands on Gage. *Crap.* Asher thought my increased heartbeats were caused from fear and not Gage's intimate touch. My mouth is now dry. I just shake my head.

The vein in Asher's neck begins to pulsate. He's mistaken my silence for being afraid as he turns his anger on Gage. "Did you hurt her?"

Gage taunts him with a smirk. "If she said she isn't hurt, then no."

"If you laid a hand on her, I will kill you," Asher spits out, walking toward Gage in a threatening manner.

Gage stands straighter, ready for the attack. "Do your worst, old friend."

Shaking off the crazy in my head, I race over and get between them, facing Asher. "Stop." It comes out as a whispered plea. I place my palms on Asher's chest. "He didn't hurt me, Asher." I look behind me and Gage's face softens.

I swing my gaze back to Asher. His eyes are narrowed, watching the nonverbal interaction between Gage and me.

"We're leaving," he orders coldly as he grabs my wrists and heaves me to him.

Knowing I'm in serious trouble, I try to back away, allowing some space between us.

"Asher—" I begin, but he cuts me off and interlaces one of my hands with his in a vice grip.

"Now, Eve," he snarls before turning his furious stare to Gage. With his free hand, he points a finger at him. "If you come within an inch of her again, I will not hesitate to end your existence." He growls with finality to his tone.

Gage smirks, apparently amused by Asher's demeanor. "That's for Eve to decide, not you. Do I need to remind you that humans have free will, Asher? As much as you hate it, she's her own person and will decide her own path. No matter what crap you are trying to get her to believe or how sound your bond is. She'll make her own decisions. Including those about me," Gage says as if bored with the standoff, but there is an underlining warning to his voice.

"Quí an-mání ú por lem, í ku an-in ú dur," Asher roars.

Gage gives him a pointed look. "Lem-de an-wís dur ú re kat ante ámo ku ulem hiúman, in-saengkt."

Asher yanks my hand forward. "We're leaving now."

"Wait, Asher. Just give me a moment," I plead, trying to pull my hand out of his grasp without success. I turn to Gage. "I'm not sure what you two just spit at one another in your *secret* gargoyle language, but thank you for saving me from Saraphina. I appreciate your protection."

"My pleasure, love," Gage answers.

My eyes slide to Asher's then back to Gage. "Also, thank you for not turning me over to Deacon tonight. I'll remember your kindness."

Gage's eyes grow cold as his light grey wings snap out of his back. "Gres-por ku ágra-lem, rap."

Confused with his sudden change in demeanor and curious as to why he is speaking to me in Garish, I stand there, mouth agape and watching him.

"Let's go," Asher orders, pulling me gently toward the door.

"Gage?" I question in a shaky whisper.

"Leave with your protector." It's all he says before walking down the hallway and slamming a door, shutting me out.

"What the hell just happened?" I ask in puzzlement.

"Nothing that isn't typical Gage behavior."

Asher ushers me out of the loft and back to England.

As soon as we enter the manor, I see the rest of the clan pacing the sitting room and instantly I want to turn around and run right back out. Standing in front of me are four glowering gargoyles with their black wings out, blue eyes glowing and their fists clenched at their sides. *Crap.*

My gaze automatically lands on one really ticked off panther whose mesmerizing eyes are scowling so bright they put the sun to shame.

I take in a deep breath, pondering just how much trouble I'm in this time. If Asher's expression is any indication, I'm screwed. Abby turns and storms toward me.

"Eve! By the grace." She yanks me into a tight hug. "I'm so sorry McKenna and I didn't get to you in time. We rushed to the lake as soon as we heard the ice crack but that manipulative selkie put up spell barriers we couldn't immediately break. By the time I was able to pull the energy to break the enchantment, Gage had already snagged you." Abby blurts out the apology, in what seems like one breath, while tensing her grip on me. "I'm so beyond sorry."

"Let go. I can't breathe," I wheeze out.

"Oops, sorry. I forget you're human sometimes." She releases me and I drag air into my lungs, allowing the blood to rush back through my body.

"Shit, cutie. I'm so glad to see you. We're so very sorry. I assure you it won't happen again," Callan apologies with a bear hug of his own.

"It's not your fault, it's mine," I explain.

"You're damn right it's your fault. You know better than to go anywhere without a protector with you. By the grace, do you always have to make this assignment so fucking difficult?" McKenna's head looks like it might explode off her body.

"Asher was there and I was on the property, McKenna. I had no idea I would get attacked on the grounds. I assumed the charms were up," I shoot back.

"They were. I just didn't extend them to the water. I didn't even consider Saraphina's presence in the lake," Abby steps in, her voice laced with guilt. "They're up now."

"It's all right, baby. You did good," Callan consoles before placing a light kiss to her temple.

"It doesn't matter how it happened. The point is we failed our task of keeping Eve safe. The responsibility falls on all of us, including Asher and myself. There won't be a next time, because we've put precautions in place that will prevent another issue. Your protection is our first priority, Eve," Keegan assures formally.

I swallow, feeling guilty I've caused so much trouble. My gaze shifts to the large black panther silently prowling back and forth in the room. Fiona's eyes lock onto mine and soften for the briefest moment before she ushers the rest of the clan out of the room, leaving only Asher and me.

Sighing, I turn to face him. His expression is guarded and irritated. I hold my hands up in surrender. "Look, I know you're pissed and I'm sorry. I had no idea Gage was around or that Saraphina was in the lake."

In an attempt to avoid, he focuses on the wall behind me. "You're right, Eve. I am mad." He exhales heavily and runs his hands through his hair and over the back of his neck. "Just, not at you. I'm fucking angry with myself and the clan for underestimating both the demonic legion and Gage Gallagher."

"Ash—" I'm cut off before I can finish.

His eyes drop to mine and they're blanketed with regret. "Once again, because my concentration was elsewhere, I didn't pick up on the presence of Godry, Saraphina or Gage. It won't happen again. From this point on, I assure you that my single-mindedness, when it comes to you, will be your safety and my job. Period."

The warning is stern and leaves no room for doubt.

I can't explain why, but at his declaration, I feel my heart shatter into a million tiny fragments. "It's not your fault. I know you would do everything in your power to protect me. You've already proven that to me," I assure.

The intensity in his gaze scares me. "I would. Everything and anything in my power, siren."

"Asher?" I whisper, moving toward him, not wanting this between us.

He doesn't answer. Instead, he turns and walks out of the room without a backwards glance.

"I'm glad ta see ye're all right, lass." Fiona's voice is gentle as it wraps around me.

"Define all right," I state without turning, deflated and focused on where Asher was standing a moment ago.

Fiona is quiet, which forces me to turn around. The stealthy woman moved to the couch where she's sitting elegantly, her eyes twinkling at me.

I swear if she were still shifted, her tail would be swaying and she'd be purring. Amused at my thoughts, she motions to the empty area next to her and I sit. She smiles maternally at me and brushes my hair back like my aunt used to do when I was sick.

"Ye're a strong-willed lass. Ye have ta be. Yer future, 'tis filled with greatness if ye choose ta embrace it," she points out.

"I feel like no matter what I do, I keep making the wrong decisions. No one understands the weight of this. It's not just my life in the balance here. If I choose to trust the wrong people or take the incorrect path, everything could disappear. I can't afford distractions. I did that once and someone I cared very much for died. Maybe...just maybe I'm not the right person to be a redeemer," I tell her, hoping she'll understand.

Fiona turns her focus to the fire, considering my words.

We sit in comfortable silence for a long time before she speaks, breaking my reverie. "A person dat truly luvs ye, lass, will never stop believin' in ye, and will never let ye go, no matter how hard da situation 'tis."

My gaze slides to hers. "That's where you're wrong. Asher doesn't love me. He's bonded to me as my protector and anything he thought he might have felt for me is simply because of the link. Nothing more. He was hired to guard me while I ascend and fulfill my destiny. I'm a job to him." I'm sulking like a child.

She lets out a jolly laugh. "Lass, if I thought fer one second dat ye actually believe dat ta be true, I wouldn't be sittin' here wit ye. Ye're young, and young people say and do foolish things in da name of luv. Dat 'tis da beauty of young luv. Doesn't make it any less true or real. Asher, aye he's complicated, no question. But make no mistake, 'tis dat lad's heart pullin' him ta ye, not da silly bond."

I look down. "I wish I could believe that. Regardless of what we think we might be feeling, we both have a job to do and it's apparent love isn't part of our destiny."

Fiona stands and cups my cheeks affectionately before planting a light kiss on my head. "I wish ye both could see dat ye're each other's destiny." With that, she leaves me to stare into the fire as it lulls me.

I'm standing on the jagged wall of rocks. My white dress flows around my body like cascading water. My bare feet are sore from the sharp edges of the rock formation. I look around in bewilderment. I've had this dream in the past. I know I have. The unmoving trees project their anger at the approach of a stranger, just like before.

The forest's eyes watch me. The dark spirits scrutinize, waiting in anticipation of my arrival. I sense their excitement. Once again, I hear their Welsh murmurs. "Cartref merch Croeso duw," they speak softly. Welcoming me home. This time, I know better. I'm not home.

The gloomy and lifeless castle appears to me. I stare at it in apprehension. My heart pounds with each movement forward. I know what he wants. He wants me. Without me, all is lost for him and his dark army. I scan the forest, aware this time of who he is and the danger I'm in.

I take a step toward the fortress then another and another. Each footstep takes me further and further away from Asher. My eyes close in silent prayer that I'm not too late.

I try to focus on whom I need to save. Beginning my descent down the uneven path, I faintly hear Asher's voice drifting to me, floating like a feather on the air that caresses my soul.

"Come back to me, siren," he whispers on the wind.

"I can't," I answer in a quiet voice, placing my hand over my heart to ease the ache of not being with him.

This is my fate and he can't be part of it. After what happened, I have to protect him and the London clan at all costs.

Focused, I keep moving toward the castle. The voice on the wind reaches me again.

"I will protect you, always," he promises.

I believe him. I know he'll come for me.

I take in a deep breath and reach out my hand as Gage takes it.

"It's time, love. You've chosen."

I jolt awake on the couch, swallowing down my scream and almost falling on the floor in my frantic state. Abby catches me just in the nick of time. My eyes lock onto her but I don't really see her, all I see is blurry water. She carefully takes my shaking hands in hers.

"I've got you, sweetie. It's okay. You're just having a bad dream." She tries to calm me down by brushing the tears off my cheeks. I breathe in deeply, attempting to pull my heart rate back to a normal level.

"It's been a while since I've had one of those," I barely whisper.

"Shh, we're here. It's okay, Eve," she soothes while brushing a hand over my hair.

We're? Out of the corner of my eye, I notice a slight movement in the doorway. Asher's hands are clenched at his sides, his face ashen like he might be sick.

Abby lifts her head, noticing I'm staring at him before he nods at her and walks out of the room. With every step he takes, my heart shatters a little more. All I want is for him to run over here and hold me.

"He isn't upset with you. Ash is struggling with wanting to be the one to console you, Eve. He knows he can't," she says sadly. "You were screaming for him in your sleep."

I close my eyes to gather myself. "I was?"

"This heartbreaking cry," Abby whispers as if in pain.

"Crap."

"Do you want to talk about it? I know this was kind of your thing with Aria, and I'm not trying to replace her, but if you need someone, I'm here. We all are. You're not in this alone." Her voice is sincere.

"It was just a bad dream. I'm all right now." My voice cracks with the lie.

Abby studies me for what feels like forever. When she thinks I've finally calmed down to the point of non-hysteria, she agrees to let me retreat to my room.

As I make my way up the stairs, I faintly hear Asher. "Is she alright?"

"I think so. I'm pretty sure it was just a nightmare," Abby responds in a quiet hush.

"What do you think brought it on? I mean, she was screaming for me like I had been ripped from her arms?" Asher questions. He sounds scared and worried.

I sigh, wishing he would just ask me himself. Not waiting to hear her response, I climb the stairs to my room, exhausted. As I hit the landing, McKenna steps into view.

"We're back to screaming in the middle of the night, are we, blood of Eden?" she snips.

"Go fuck yourself, McKenna." I brush past her and head to my room, not in the mood.

Once in the shower, the heaviness of the day finally takes its toll on me and for the first time in a long time, I begin to cry and not the pretty, delicate, light tears most girls can pull off. I mean full-on-ugly-I-just-won-Miss-America-hiccupping sobs.

I slide down and sit on the shower floor and just let the scalding hot water run over me until I don't have any tears left. At the point I'm sufficiently cried out, I shut off the water and get out of the shower to dry off.

I almost start bawling all over again when I notice Asher left his *Property of London* shirt on the counter. I get into it with my boy shorts and pretend its Asher wrapped around me. Tired, I just want to crawl into my bed and end the madness of the day.

I open the bathroom door to find Asher lying on my bed, waiting for me. His long, muscular legs are crossed,

Randi Cooley Wilson

eyes are closed and his strong hands are resting behind his head. The beautiful gargoyle prince looks so peaceful.

Thinking he's asleep, I take a moment just to breathe him in and my heart clenches. I squeeze my eyes shut, trying to block out the remnants of the nightmare. The need to walk over to him and crawl inside him is all consuming.

As my eyes open, they lock onto his. Neither of us moves. Neither of us speaks. His gaze travels the length of me, landing on his shirt. They darken and my entire body flushes from his perusal.

"You look like shit," he says in typical Asher fashion.

I snort. "Thanks. You sure know how to sweet talk a girl, for being a gargoyle prince and all."

A silent pause falls between us.

"Siren?"

"Your Highness?"

"Gage told you?"

"Yes. Though I can't figure out why you didn't. What's one more secret though, right?"

"With everything else being thrown at you, my title was something the clan felt wasn't important. My status within my community has nothing to do with my protection of you, Eve."

I arch a brow. "And Camilla?"

"I know that Gage blames us for her death. Neither I, nor my brothers had knowledge of his father's plan. If we had, we would have stepped in. I understand he's hurting and doesn't believe that, but I assure you, it's the truth."

I just study him. His face is sincere and in my heart, I know he's telling me the truth.

"Are you okay? I heard you crying."

102

"Fine. Just tired."

Disbelief crosses his face. "And the dream?"

"I don't remember it."

Asher lets out a frustrated exhale. "I felt it, you were terrified. Your soul was calling to me. You were screaming for me, siren."

I swallow hard and feign ignorance. "I didn't mean to scare you."

He stands and groans. "All right, have it your way."

"There is no '*my way*'. I'm okay," I reply heatedly.

Asher just remains in his spot, taking me in before slowly nodding and pushing out a long, drawn breath. "Right now, I'm fighting every thread of my being not to walk over there and yank you into my arms because, siren, I know you're fucking lying to me."

I cross my arms and nod once my comprehension.

"Be sure you're up and dressed early in the morning. We're realm jumping," he adds.

My eyes widen with surprise. "Where?"

"The Eternal Forest. We have an engagement with Priestess Arabella."

"I'll be ready," I confirm.

He pauses before looking at me then the bed. "Do…do you want me to stay?"

Want him to? *Yes.* Need him to? *No.* "No," I answer in an unsure voice.

"I'm across the hall if you change your mind," he offers.

My eyes lock onto his, conveying how much I want to change my mind, to run to him and never let go. However, my mouth has different ideas. "I'll be okay. Thank you."

Asher's quiet, contemplating. For a moment, I think he might say something but he just curtly nods before leaving my room. *Crap.* I have it bad for him, like stalker bad.

I make my way to the bed and crawl in. My pillow still smells like him. I snuggle into it, embracing his scent and the calm it gives me.

9 The Chamber

My hand clutches the silk drape as my vision skims over the Cotsworth gardens. They're completely covered in a new blanket of snow. I lift my eyes to the blue sky, inhaling. The sun is shining this morning and reflecting off the little white, frozen crystals, which gives the illusion of small diamonds embedded in the earth. Everything is so pure and clean, unlike life. The entire world is silent in this moment.

I focus on the lake, shivering at the recollection of Saraphina. My mind wanders to Gage and I catch myself speculating on what he's doing at the moment, as my other hand reaches for the place on my wrist his lips burned. *Focus, Eve.* No more Gage thoughts.

A quiet knock on my door pulls me from my reverie and I release the curtain, allowing it to partially fall back over the window, blocking the lake.

"Come in."

Abby slips into the room, closing the door behind her. She fidgets awkwardly with her hands as she stands across the room from me, assessing me. "Hi. Asher asked me to come in and make sure you're ready for today. See if you need anything."

I offer her a bright smile. "Abby, I promise, I'm okay. Yesterday's events are not your fault. Neither was my nightmare. Please, stop acting like I'm breakable or angry. I'm not either of those things."

"I know." The angelic gargoyle sighs and walks over to the bed. She sits while folding a piece of her red hair behind her ear. "It's just, I'm in charge of the charms and I didn't even consider that Saraphina might be trouncing around the lake. I'm truly sorry, Eve. I dropped the ball on your protection. I swear to you, it won't happen again."

I frown and sit next to her on the bed, taking her hand in mine. "You didn't let me down, Abby. I know all of you would give your life to protect me. Besides, Asher did tell me to go back into the house. Now I know to be a bit more careful around supernatural beings…and lakes."

I let out a slight laugh, causing Abby to smile.

"Are you excited to meet Priestess Arabella?" she asks, sitting up straighter.

"I guess. I've never met a priestess before, let alone one that is revered amongst the supernatural world for her seer abilities."

"She's the most powerful of all the oracles, or foreseers. Kind of like a psychic on crack," Abby explains.

"Great." I grimace. "Hopefully, she won't see anything too depressing."

"Nothing bad will happen. Ash will be with you. So will Callan and me," she says with girlish excitement.

My mood just picked up. "You're coming too?" I question with a spark of hope.

"Asher asked us to join you guys as '*backup*'. Cool, huh?" she states, smiling at me.

"Backup or a buffer?" I retort.

She puckers her brow. "Does it matter?"

"Nope. I'm thrilled you and Callan are coming. Thank you," I smile, giving her a huge hug.

Abby claps her hands like a little girl. "Great. Let's get you changed and then we can head downstairs to begin our realm jump."

I scowl. "What's wrong with what I'm wearing?" I ask defensively, looking at my clothes.

"Nothing, if you're going to class but jeans and a black shirt is not appropriate to meet a high priestess, especially one that sits on the Royal Supernatural Court." Abby moves toward my closet.

Twenty minutes later, and a lot of ducking out of the way of flying clothes, Abby decides she is pleased with my outfit, consisting of a black *Free the People* Elle Lace mini dress and black, open toe, knee boots that tie but have a square heel so I can walk on grass easily. Feeling a little overdressed, I look at myself in the mirror.

The mesh, sleeveless shift with crochet and lace detailing all over it is trimmed with a scalloped lace bottom hem. The entire outfit makes me feel overwhelmed. She adds bangle bracelets because apparently priestesses love jewelry.

"Are you sure I'm not a little overdressed?" I question, throwing her a worried look.

"Eve, you look amazing. Trust me, I know what the appropriate attire is for meeting a priestess," she assures passionately.

It's then I notice she is also wearing a black, sheer lace button down style dress with a high neckline and black, open toe flat sandals that tie up with a ribbon to her ankle.

"I have faith in you," I promise in a hushed voice.

She nods once and grins though it doesn't reach her eyes. Obviously, she's still a bit sensitive about yesterday and doesn't think I fully trust her. I grab her arm, forcing her gaze to meet mine.

"Hey, I entrust my life to you, Abby. You're a great friend and an amazing protector," I say with as much sincerity as one can.

She gauges me for a moment before giving me a genuinely bright smile. "Thanks, Eves. Let's find the guys and go meet the high priestess then. Shall we?"

I muster up as much excitement as I can. "Can't wait." My voice trails off as I follow her out of the room.

As soon as my bottom foot hits the last step, I hear a drawn out whistle. "You ladies look amazing," Callan offers, beaming before heading over to Abby and planting a soft kiss on her lips. *Why does this feel like a double date?*

"Thanks, baby," she replies, taking him in.

Feeling a tinge jealous of their intimacy, I look away only to lock eyes with Asher, as he stands there open-mouthed. His eyes roam the length of my entire body before he noticeably swallows with difficulty. His visual caress burns my skin like flames, marking me as his once again.

Both he and Callan are wearing black dress pants and black dress shoes. Callan is wearing a crisp white button down dress shirt. I guess you dress up to see a priestess. Asher's dress shirt is black with his sleeves rolled to his elbows. I clench my hands at my side, digging my nails into my palms in an effort to curb my desire to touch him.

Predatorily, he stalks over to me, leaning into my space. *God, he smells good.* "You look perfect, siren."

Without thinking, I lick my lips and tilt into him. "Thank you."

"All right, gang. Are we ready to realm jump to the Eternal Forest?" Callan breaks the moment.

Asher's eyes don't leave mine. He holds out his hand, waiting for me to take it. I feel like the gesture means more. Like he's changing the rules somehow with that one simple offer. I slip mine into his as the humming from the bond runs through my veins, causing my eyelids to flutter and my breath to hitch.

"I've got you, siren," he assures me.

"I believe you, pretty boy," I retort.

Asher gives me a beautiful and cocky smirk as he tightens his hold on my hand.

"To the chamber then," Callan says cryptically.

My brows lift and dread consumes me. "Chamber?"

Asher smirks at me and tugs my arm, forcing me to follow him into the library. Once in, the four of us walk over to the back right corner where there is a white granite dragon statue sitting on a black marble table.

Callan begins to unbutton his shirt, and with some assistance from Abby, takes it off. Amused he turns around, facing us so his back is to the dragon.

I pull my eyebrows together in question as Callan smiles and winks at me. "Wait for it, cutie."

The eyes on the statue turn emerald and a green light beams out, scanning the dragon tattoo on his back, which symbolizes the St. Michaels' family crest. Once the statue finishes, Callan puts his shirt on and then speaks in their gargoyle language. "Anvolde lem ansa lók, esh anten skítas de volde lem."

Asher leans in. "It means: The wingless ones cannot speak, and lack the intelligence of the winged ones."

"Charming." My response causes Asher's lips to tilt up.

"We thought it was clever." He gives a cocky smirk.

More like insulting to humans.

I'm about to retort when the wooden slats on the floor spread open, revealing a stone staircase that leads down into a dark tunnel. My eyes slide to Abby and she smiles and nods with encouragement.

As if sensing my unease, Asher presses his chest to my back and guides the hair off my left shoulder, over to my right side, allowing him access to my ear so he can whisper.

"It's a secret chamber we have in each of our homes. Do you recall us telling you that as gargoyles there are times we need to be in stone state?" he inquires. His breath tickles my cheek.

With my eyes fixated on the dark staircase, I nod. My body is frozen in fear, recalling the nightmare that haunted me for months where I was trapped in an underground passage by a demonic belker named Nero. He was an evil spirit created from smoke who tried to kill me before Asher executed him with an Angelic Sword.

"This chamber allows us to go into our stone state, to heal or realm jump under protection since our physical bodies remain. Remember, if we are injured or pierced in the heart during stone state, we are trapped for eternity in stone petrifaction, so this chamber protects us. No one but the London clan can enter or exit. That's all it is, okay?" He waits for confirmation.

I swallow hard and scan Callan, Abby and finally Asher's eyes. "Okay," I manage with shaking hands.

"I'm right here with you, siren," Asher vows.

I grip his hand tighter. "I trust you." I lift my chin.

He smiles, lifts my hand and kisses my fingers. "Good girl. Callan will lead, you follow Abby and I've got your back."

I turn to follow Abby down the flight of stone stairs, into the dark abyss. My hands glide over stone walls. The only light comes from medieval sconces that are lit with flames. A little gothic for my taste but whatever works for the gargoyles. As we make our way further down the stairs, the temperature drops and it becomes damp and smells musty. I force my eyes open and shut, trying to brush off the flashes of my Nero dream.

After what feels like a hundred stairs, the room opens up, becoming brighter and warmer. Even more flames light the tomb. The floor is made of large black marble tiles and the walls are a dark gray stone home to twenty or so alcoves filled with gargoyle statues. Large black candles are lit everywhere.

The wax drips in intricate patterns, flowing like lava onto the stones. Randomly, in the center of the chamber are three large king-sized, four poster beds. Each draped in the most exquisite red, green and black silk fabrics. They're breathtaking.

Noticing my focus, Asher steps in front of me. "Those are our stone state beds. The red is Keegan and Kenna's. The green Callan and Abby's and the black is mine. The silk drapery matches our protector tattoos and healing stones."

Abby pops up next to me. "There are also rubies, emeralds and onyx embedded in each of the posts." Her voice is quiet as if speaking in a church. "This is a peaceful sanctuary for us to come and heal, astral project, or realm jump, and it also serves as a final resting place for many of our ancestors." She points to the statues of different gargoyles.

My eyes roam around the chamber in awe. Creepiness aside, it's actually really beautiful and peaceful. There are three large fireplaces that Callan is lighting before turning toward Asher.

"Why don't Abby and I pull through first to the realm, then you and Eve?"

"Sounds like a good plan," Asher agrees before turning to face me shyly, piquing my interest.

"Um, not to make this stranger than it already is for you, but each bed has been charmed for protection. That means only a gargoyle and their bonded are permitted to sleep in the stone bed that has been created and enchanted for them." His eyes are fixated on the ground.

"Okay," I answer fretfully. Totally not following him.

"Therefore, Abby and Callan have to share their stone state in the emerald bed since they're mated." He stretches his neck to each side. "Ah, because we're blood bonded, we need to share the onyx bed," he explains, indigo eyes meeting mine with a level of nervousness.

"Are you asking me to share your stone state bed, Asher?" I tease, responding to his odd behavior.

Asher swallows with what seems like difficulty. "I guess I am," he replies tensely.

Not understanding why this is a big deal since we've sleep next to one another in beds before, I lightly jab his hand. "It's not a big deal. I totally don't mind," I counter and move toward his bed.

He grabs my arm and spins me around so quickly I get dizzy for a moment. "Wait," he states in a sharp tone. "Only mates share the stone state bed. Once in stone state, you physically and mentally become one with your bonded partner."

"Asher, you're being really cryptic. What are you trying to say?" I prod, trying to make sense of the inarticulate information.

"Let me. Eve, come here for a moment," Abby interrupts and I make my way over to her, confused. She guides me away from the bed and toward a large dragon gargoyle statue. She leans in, giving the impression we're the only two who can hear one another. Though we aren't.

"What's going on, Abby?"

"Okay, don't freak out or anything," she states calmly.

My eyes narrow at her. "Too late." *Why do people say don't freak if they don't want you to freak?*

"The stone state bed for a gargoyle is a very personal haven. A male gargoyle only invites his mate to share the bed with him, usually on the first night of their bonding ceremony to consummate their unification. It's very intimate once in the stone state, and something that is normally only done when two people are bonded forever. How can I put this? It's very similar to you giving Asher your virginity. By inviting you into his stone state bed, he's basically giving you his gargoyle virginity. No one, not even a gargoyle mate, will ever be able to share it with him. Only you." Her eyes plead understanding.

"Do you mean to tell me he will never be allowed to bring his mate into his stone state bed because he's already shared it with me?" I attempt clarification.

"Yes. Even if you are not his forever, the dragon spirits will only allow one," she clarifies sadly.

My eyes shift to Asher. "Holy shit." I look back at Abby. "Why do I have to stay in the chamber? I mean, I understand that you guys do for safety reasons, but can't I realm jump from my bed upstairs?"

"No. To get into the Eternal Forest, a human must be with a supernatural being. In your case, with your bloodline, you must be with your bonded protector while realm jumping and the only safe way to do that is from the chamber."

"Crap." I exhale as the tension in the chamber just skyrocketed tenfold.

"Knowing this, Michael approved this visit to the realm?" I ask, astonished.

"Yes. At the council meeting everyone, including Asher, gave their approval."

"Um, ladies, not to rush this, but we shouldn't keep Priestess Arabella waiting when we're expected. Once in the Eternal Forest, we have quite a bit of a hike before we get to her, meaning we need to start the realm jumping process," Callan informs us.

Abby squeezes my hands reassuringly before walking back to Callan. "Alright, babe. Let's do this. We'll see you guys in the realm," she throws over her shoulder casually while I internally panic.

I turn and watch as Callan plants a very seductive kiss on her lips and helps her into the bed before untying each of the pieces of fabric. The drapes sway out of their ties and close, shielding the inside of the bed from our outside eyes. Callan turns to me and wiggles his brows before climbing in and becoming unseen.

Asher walks over to me and takes my hands, which are shaking. "You don't have to do this, Asher. I didn't realize how significant this would be," I say, choking on my words. *Oh my God.* I sound ridiculous and scared out of my friggin mind.

"Shh-it's okay," he hushes me, leaning his forehead to mine. "Hear me when I say this to you. There is no one in the world, gargoyle or human, I would rather share this with, siren." He pauses and cups my face, forcing me to meet his glowing eyes. "There's no reason to be afraid. I'm honored to share my stone state bed with you, forever," he assures in a soft but firm tone, holding my face tightly.

"Forever is a long time," I whisper, my throat tight.

He gives me his sexy smirk. "Yes. It fucking is."

I let out a strangled laugh as my knees go wobbly on me. "Asher St. Michael, I would be honored to share your stone state bed," I reply, looking him in the eyes.

Asher growls and the soft glow from his eyes burns brighter. "Fuck, that was so hot."

I roll my eyes. "Come on. Abby and Callan are waiting for us."

He blows out a sharp breath. "That just killed it."

I smile at him while he takes my hand and leads me to the bed. His eyes never waver and his hand never drops mine as he begins to untie the silk ribbons keeping the large pieces of fabric open. One by one, they fall, enclosing the bed. I swallow at the intimacy of it all.

Once all the pieces of fabric have fallen, Asher takes the hand that's in his and brings it to his lips, kissing my fingers.

"Is there something special we have to do?" I question with a shaky voice. "I mean, do you just want to sleep with me? I mean take me to bed?" *God, Eve, shut up.*

Asher moves closer to me, brushing the hair off my shoulder. "I could spend eternity lost in the depths of your hazel eyes," he murmurs.

Without thought, I move closer to him. My hands are splayed on his chest, over the protector tattoo as it hums with energy under my touch. I know we're supposed to be showing restraint, but it's so hard when he's this close and smells so good. Asher's right hand comes up and gently brushes my cheek with the back of his knuckles.

"There's nothing more I want than a forever with you, siren." His eyes search mine.

116

My lips part at his declaration. Before I can speak, Asher leans down, kissing me at a painfully slow pace. He pushes all his feelings into the kiss, causing a single tear to escape my eyes, inching its way onto my cheek.

With the pad of his thumb, he brushes it away and helps me step up onto the platform at the end of the bed. I push away the meaning of this moment and how significant it is for him, for us. After this, there is no turning back. It's all or nothing. Everything is about to change.

He releases my hand and moves a piece of the draped fabric to the side, patiently waiting for me to climb onto the mattress. I turn to face him. My pace is slow as I place my palms down on the bed and sit, causing him to inhale sharply. Keeping constant eye contact, I swallow down the fear and move back on the bed so I'm facing him while lying back on my elbows.

With hooded eyes, Asher just looks me over, taking me all in as his lips part. After what feels like an eternity, he unhurriedly moves toward the end of the bed. Releasing the curtain behind him, he climbs over me until we're face-to-face. The weight of his body pressed onto mine causes my skin to go up in flames. My throat goes dry and my breathing becomes erratic. Asher's eyes search mine before he takes my hands in his, interlocking our fingers. He lifts my arms above my head, allowing our combined hands to rest on the pillows that my hair is splayed over.

"Ilem jur pri tú-tim, ew tú-tim pri pos-tim ali ide in-zen, mání, vas-wís, ew ter-ort. Esta-de ai esta Ilem de, Ilem pos-tim in-saengkt pri, tú-tim," he says in his Garish tongue.

"What does that mean?" I ask in a bare whisper.

"Forever," he answers while lowering his lips to mine.

Randi Cooley Wilson

10 The Eternal Forest

I'm floating. That's the only way to describe the feeling I'm experiencing at this moment. It's difficult to tell where Asher begins and I end. We're swirling and morphing into one person. I feel every beat of his heart, each breath he takes, and every single emotion that's running through him. We're becoming one, mind, body, soul and heart. I inhale and let go, leaving my fears behind. He's become the only thing that makes me want to live at all.

Large, warm hands cup my face while a thumb traces my bottom lip. "Open your eyes, siren," Asher commands softly.

I have no choice. My body obeys willingly and my eyes flutter open, pulling into view his beautiful face. My heart skips a beat as I reach for him.

His smile is so bright. "I realize it's a little disorienting. Just trust that I've got you."

As soon as my eyes focus, I notice we're no longer in Asher's bed but lying in dark cerulean moss. My gaze soaks up our surroundings as black trees come into view. This realm is nothing like the Kingdom of the Fae. Where that land is full of bright greens, crystal water and blue skies adorned with colorful pinks and whites, this forest is dark and beautifully haunting.

"Welcome to the Eternal Forest, siren." Asher breathes in my ear, reminding me his body is still touching mine. *Oh my God!*

I take in the shadowy colors of the realm. It's filled with deep blues, dark grays, and midnight blacks. The trees have black bark and are beyond normal levels of what we consider tall. They're maybe over a hundred feet high and have no leaves on them. The tall vegetation crosses at the top, intertwining their branches in an arched canopy, shielding the inky sky. They remind me of the black, leafless decorative trees people put out on Halloween.

The exotic plant life is low to the ground, clinging to the land like a carpet. The bubbling water glows jade with a light layer of smoke coming off the top. The forest floor is composed of black soil sprinkled with dark gray and olive rocks. Surprisingly, it's stunning.

My eyes lock back onto Asher and he begins to stand, holding out his hand for me to take.

"W-what happened? Why do I feel so...?" My voice trails off in search of the right words for the disorientation I'm feeling.

Asher assists me to my feet and brushes the hair away from my face. There is worry and pain in his eyes. Through our bond, I can sense he's scared I will reject him. "It's the bond. We realm jumped together. The first time always leaves you a little out of sorts because," he pauses and exhales, "essentially, we've become one. It will get easier, I promise."

I assess his face, feeling so different. It's like every time I look at him, he's my reason for being. "I'm not going to sugar coat this. That's pretty fucking creepy, pretty boy."

He laughs loudly. "Yeah, siren, it certainly is."

"Finalllllyyyy. What the hell took you two so long?" Callan announces feigning annoyance while he and Abby approach us.

"We're here now," Asher states, interlacing our fingers.

"Good. Let's roll," Callan replies as Abby studies me.

My brows pinch together. "What?"

She muffles a giggle. "Nothing. Let's go meet the priestess." She offers her arm, linking it with mine, pulling me out of Asher's grasp.

"Why do I get the feeling it's not nothing?" I question, allowing her to drag me forward.

She stops and leans in. "All right, don't snap or anything, but your eyes." Abby pauses looking like the cat that swallowed the canary. "They're glowing indigo."

I freeze. "WHAT?" I whisper shout. "I don't have indigo eyes, I have hazel eyes!"

She rolls her eyes before breaking out into giggles. "I know, Eve. That's what is so funny."

"Holy shit! I thought only mated gargoyles have their eyes change to match their partner's color?" I squeak.

"Maybe something happened in the stone state that caused this." The modelesque gargoyle shrugs casually.

Asher comes up behind me, apprehension rolling off him. "What's wrong? I can feel you freaking out twenty realms away."

I turn and shoot daggers at him, hoping he'll notice my new eye color. Asher just smirks at me. His cocky face has a proud look all over it.

"Did you do this on purpose?" I point to my eyes.

He almost looks hurt, almost. "Eve, nothing is permanent. It's simply a side effect of the stone state we're sharing. In this realm, because we jumped together, it marks you as mine for protection reasons. I promise, once we're out of the stone state, your eye color will return."

After a moment, I huff. "Fine. No more marking me without permission. I mean it, Asher."

Asher leans into my space. "Siren, when I do mark you again, I expect you'll be screaming your permission. Perhaps even in the form of: '*OH GOD. YES!*'" he says in a low voice that vibrates through to my soul.

I swallow hard. "Christ." I turn to storm away.

"Oh, and Eve, I promise it will be because you want it." His words cause me to blush.

"Okayyy. Awkwardness now set aside, we're already behind schedule so let's get moving. Unless we want to live out the rest of our days as one of the priestess' white owls," Callan throws out.

"Waiting on you," I retort smarmily and begin walking.

"Ah, siren?" Asher calls out, holding back a laugh.

"What?" I turn and snip, mostly because of the heat in my veins from the idea of Asher marking me, making me his completely. *Damn his dimples.*

Asher points his finger to the left. "We're actually taking that path. The one you're on leads to the trolls and they tend to eat humans."

I cross my arms in irritation before storming off to the other path. "Damn gargoyles," I mutter against the laughter radiating from Callan and Asher.

❧

I'm tired. And hungry. And maybe a little whiny, if I'm being honest. We've been walking for what feels like hours and these heels Abby picked out, not so comfortable. I've lost track of time. It's weird, there are blue beams of what appears to be moonlight coming through the black lifeless trees, but I see no sky or moon. It's like we're shut off from the rest of the world.

"You okay?" Asher asks from behind me.

"Fine."

"Siren?"

"What do you want me to say, Asher? Everything is just dandy. Haven't you heard? I'm a weapon in the war between Heaven and Hell. I can realm jump to creepy dark forests to meet fairies and priestesses. My good friend was killed by a rival gargoyle clan who wanted to hand me over to Lucifer, oh and I'm being protected at the request of an archangel by a legion of gargoyles, one of whom I just shared a very intimate moment with and may or may not be bound to forever simply because I laid on his bed. Way to show restraint!" My voice drips with sarcasm. *Yep, definitely whiny and irritable.*

"Actually, I was just curious if you're okay, meaning are you hungry and do you want a granola bar, but since you seem to have a lot on your mind, I'll just snack on it," he teases while opening the package.

I stop in my tracks and turn to face him. "You aren't going to share?" I question and my stomach rumbles.

His eyebrows lift. "So not only do you want to share my bed, but you also want to share my granola bar?"

I cross my arms. "I don't believe I ever asked to share your bed."

"You said, and I quote, '*I would be honored to share your stone state bed.*' Are you trying to take it back?"

"That's unfair. I said I would be honored to share it. Not will you share it with me."

"Same difference."

"No, it's not." My anger is rising. "Please, I'm begging, just give me a bite of the granola bar."

"Well, since you're begging." His eyes get all smoldering. "With pleasure, siren." Asher moves slowly toward me and my mouth goes dry. As soon as he is in my breathing space, he lifts the bar to my mouth and waits for me to bite it.

I sigh then move forward, placing my mouth over the exposed stick of oatmeal and take a bite, savoring the chocolatey, oatmeal chewiness.

"Was that so hard?" he whispers.

"Are you two going to eye fuck each other the entire hike?" Callan jests and I close my eyes in mortification.

"Callan, boundaries, babe!" Abby exclaims. "That was so crude."

"What?" His eyes go all gooey. "Baby, if I have to watch them do this the entire hike, I'm going to throw up the granola bar I just ate."

Callan laughs as he pulls Abby into an embrace.

She caresses his cheek. "Don't you recall how we couldn't keep our hands off each other the first time we stone slept together?"

Now I'm the one going to puke. *Ugh.*

"We have to make up some time, so let's keep walking," Asher says, his playful demeanor gone as he walks around me, taking the lead and ending the conversation. *Thank you, Asher.*

I narrow my eyes at Callan. "You're mature."

"What?" Callan gives me his best innocent face. "The sexual tension is killing me. Cutie, just sleep with him and get it over with. For all our sakes."

"Callan, that is so inappropriate and none of your business. Sorry, Eve. Come on," Abby apologizes while linking our arms and moving us forward.

"Babyyyy, I was kidding. Technically, she's already slept with him anyway." Callan follows like a scolded puppy dog behind us.

"Is that why I feel all crazy inside?" I ask Abby in a murmur.

"What do you mean?"

"I dunno, forget it."

"No, tell me," she prods.

"Because we're in stone state together, is that why I want to like, um, jump his bones every five seconds?" I look away, my cheeks heating under her gaze.

Abby just looks at me knowingly. "I think it enhances it. Plus, don't forget you're projecting your feelings to him and vice versa. It's like turning up your hormones times a thousand."

"Ugh. Crap." I exhale.

"Would it be so bad? I mean, being mated with Asher?" Abby asks in a serious tone.

"It's not allowed, so I can't even comment on it." It's a weak answer.

"Gargoyles can mate with humans," she reminds me, her tone now stern.

"Yes. But not bonded protectors, Abby. He took an oath. There's also the little detail that he's the next gargoyle king. How would that go over if he took a human mate? Plus, I kind of have a lot on my plate. You know, saving the world and all," I reply dryly.

She snorts. "By the grace, Eve. You're so damn dramatic. Stone state or not, that boy is one hundred percent head over heels for you. His restraint is amazing. What's even more astonishing is yours. Most girls fall over themselves trying to sleep with him and here you are, running in the opposite direction."

"I'm not running," I state, motioning to my *'walking'* feet.

She gives me a pointed look. "You are. You should run to him, not away."

Just as I am about to open my mouth to retort, I trip over a large olive green, scaly rock. Right before I'm about

126

to hit the ground, Abby grabs my arm, preventing me from face planting in the black soil.

"Thanks. I wasn't paying attention." I offer a small smile.

She looks at the rock and then to Asher and Callan.

"It's serpentine."

"What does that mean?" I question.

"It means the soil you see is toxic to many plants. Hence the trees' bark is black and everything looks lifeless around the forest," Callan explains. "It also means we shouldn't drink the water in case asbestos from the mineral has seeped into it."

At that moment, a quiet sound hits my ears, almost as if the twigs are breaking and singeing with heat then turning to ash. I cringe at the sound.

Asher snaps his gaze to me, shock registering on his face. "Did you hear that?"

"Y-yes. Why?" I ask, taken aback at his reaction.

Callan's eyes widen. "She heard the shadow warriors?"

Asher shakes his head. "Impossible. Only supernaturals can hear them."

Abby moves in front of me, protecting me. "It's a side effect of the stone state. Perhaps she's picked up our hearing and sight ability, Ash."

Crap, now I have supersonic hearing.

"What's a shadow warrior?" I question the group before a large hissing sound darts out of the black forest.

"Shadow warriors are an army the priestesses use for protection in the realm. They hide in the shadows, hence the name, unless they sense danger. The top half is a three headed serpent and the bottom half is a man," Callan enlightens.

My eyes bug out of my head and my frightened gaze darts to Asher. "Serpent, as in snake?"

He holds his hands up. "Don't panic. We've got it handled."

"No way. No freakin' way, Asher. I'm terrified of snakes. Like, body completely shutting down scared." My voice quivers.

"Take a breath, cutie. I'm sure they just want to confirm we're not a danger to them, the forest or priestesses," Callan rationalizes as if speaking to a wounded animal.

I shake my head. "No, I can't. I'm like life-will-end afraid of snakes."

Asher walks around Abby to me, not making any sudden moves. "Look at me," he commands. "Eve. Look at me," he states again when I refuse.

He grabs my face firmly in his strong hands. "I will protect you, always."

"I know," I croak out. "But snakes? Asher, I can't!"

Am I panicking irrationally? Yes.

He laughs at me. "There's nothing for you to fear. We've got you, I promise."

My heart rate doesn't slow down but Asher's touch takes some of my anxiety down a notch.

"All right but stay close to me."

He nods once. "Always." Asher dips his chin so he's eye level. "Oh, and this time, Eve, unlike with the barghest, if I tell you to run, you run," Asher throws out.

"Why would I need to run?" I ask worriedly.

Just as the words leave my lips, a large, black figure comes out of the shadows. Six bright white eyes are narrowed at me in anger. My throat goes dry.

"State your business in the Eternal Forest, trespassers," the shadow warrior hisses, his forked tongue darting out. *Oh. My. God.*

"You are in the presence of the London clan. Priestess Arabella has extended an invitation to meet with the daughter of Heaven. As her guardians, we are accompanying her to the temple," Asher states authoritatively.

With one head focused on Abby and Callan, and one directed at Asher, the shadow warrior bends his third head to me, coming within a breath of my face. My body clenches at its proximity. Sensing my unease, Asher grabs my hand and pulls me behind him in a protective stance.

At the movement, the shadow warrior looks displeased.

"I need to read her before I let you pass, dark prince," it hisses.

Asher shuffles on his feet. "Read her eyes only, but do not touch her," he warns. "Guests or not, I will not hesitate to slice your neck open if she is harmed in any way."

"Relax, gargoyle," one of the other heads warns.

Crap, they all freakin' talk.

The large head of the shadow warrior bends within a breath of us before his eyes begin to search mine.

"You may have passage." Then suddenly, all three heads turn in unison and bow to me then to Asher. *Odd.*

"Welcome, daughter of Heaven, and your—" The shadow warrior is cut off by Asher before finishing.

"Protector. I'm Eve's protector," he states flatly.

Weird, what the hell was that about?

"Very well then. You and your sentinels are under our protection while in our realm," the serpent offers.

"T-Thank you," I manage.

The three heads nod once in unison. "You are not far from the Temple of The Seven High Priestesses."

"Many thanks for the passage and protection," Asher offers with a formal and regal tone.

The shadow warrior bows one final time at Asher and I before slithering back into the forest. I let out a loud exhale.

"Good job, Eves. You didn't even pee yourself," Callan quips while laughing hysterically.

"Suck it, Callan."

"You really did great, Eve." Abby beams proudly.

Asher doesn't drop my hand but instead tightens his grip as he pulls me forward, directing me to follow him down the path. "We're almost there. Let's keep moving."

"So, that's not the first time someone has bowed to you in more of a *dark prince* manner. Care to elaborate?" I question.

His focus remains on the path. "They probably just think I'm some spoiled protector because of who my father was."

"I see." I don't believe him.

That's when I get an idea. If we're in stone state, perhaps since we are feeling one another's emotions, I could go into his head and see what he's hiding. Unsure of how to do it, I figure it must be similar to astral projection in the sense of mental focus.

I focus all my energy and then listen to Asher's heartbeat, syncing my pace with his. Allowing my mental focus to float up toward his mind, I see light flashes behind my eyelids and then begin to feel and hear his thoughts.

Without warning, I'm moving rapidly as something sharp hits my back, causing my eyes to pop open and me to lose any connection I had with Asher.

"What the fuck do you think you're doing?" Asher growls out, his irritated breath fanning my face.

Realization hits me. He has me pinned against a tree and seems pretty pissed. He must have felt me prodding in his head.

Confused, I stutter. "I-I was j-just..."

"You were just what? Trying to get into my head, using the stone state to do it because you didn't like my answer?" He seethes. "Don't. Ever. Do. That. Again," he spits out with venom.

Ouch. Before I can even apologize, Asher gently pushes off me, and storms back onto the path.

My eyes dart up to meet Abby's sympathetic ones. She tilts her head in the direction Asher is stomping off in.

"Come on. We're almost there."

"What the hell did I do?" I mutter in disbelief at the anger rolling off Asher.

"Well, for starters, you violated his trust. You don't read someone's thoughts unless you have permission, Eve. Even you must realize that is wrong," she scolds.

"I didn't even think of it that way. I just assumed..." I trail off, feeling guilty. *Damn, she's right. I suck.*

Callan puts his arm around my shoulder. "Abs, why don't you go get Ash to cool off while I chat with Eves for a second." Abby nods and runs to catch up with Asher.

"He didn't mean to be cruel. I think we all forget sometimes that you're human and don't always understand the ramifications of your actions, even Asher. Gargoyles only allow their mates access to their minds. It's very private. Once you open that connection, it can't be closed. If he allowed you in, no matter how much he wants to, cutie, and believe me he wants to, that door can't be closed. Your bond would be tighter, forever. As it is, he already feels as though he's increasing the link between you two and the more secure it becomes, the less likely it can ever be severed. Do you understand what I'm saying?" Callan inquires.

"He doesn't want me for forever?" I ask, swallowing the feeling of dread crawling its way inside my heart.

Callan's brows lift in surprise. "Is that what you want, Eves? Asher forever?"

I sigh. My eyes fixate on Asher's back. "I'm whole when he's near and empty when he's gone. I've felt this way even without the stone state. But all this self-control we have to show, it's wearing on me."

Callan draws me in and kisses my temple. "I know, cutie. Him too. Him too."

We come to an opening in the forest with a huge white marble Grecian Temple. There are four large stairs leading to the entrance. Urns lit with fire are sprinkled throughout the statue-like building.

"Welcome to the Temple of The Seven High Priestesses," Callan announces.

It's at that moment I see sparks of white light behind my eyelids, causing an excruciatingly sharp pain in my head. As if watching an out of focus movie, flashes of images keep moving too fast in my mind, making me nauseous. The force of the pain and the movement of the imagery cause my knees to buckle. I squeeze my eyes shut, attempting to ease the ache. Callan catches me before I fall to the ground.

Holding me, I listen to the painful screams of someone, only to realize it's me who's screaming, as if I'm being stabbed in the head by a thousand knives.

"Give her to me. NOW!" Asher orders.

With great care, I'm moved from Callan's arms into Asher's and he rocks me. "Sshh, I've got you, siren." He strokes my hair. "Do you feel my calming energies? Focus on that energy running through you, yeah?"

At his command, I feel the warmth and calm that Asher's pushing into me.

"It hurts." I whimper.

"I know. I'm sorry, siren." His voice is laced with pain as he tries to comfort me.

It's then the white light consumes me and I feel nothing but peace.

Randi Cooley Wilson

11 Priestess Arabella

I'm standing in a temple. It's so bright I have to force my eyes not to squint. The walls, floor and ceiling are made of a smooth, pallid white marble. I spin around, trying to figure out where I am. Over my right shoulder, I realize someone is standing behind me, shielded by a black hooded cloak. I turn to face the concealed being. It's as though they materialized out of thin air.

"Who are you?" I ask, dropping my gaze to a pair of bare feet.

Silence.

"Where are Asher and the others?" I attempt again.

Silence.

The sound of flapping wings shatters the quiet. I turn to see a large, majestic owl glide into the mausoleum and land on one of the columns near the cloaked creature. Its striking white plumes are a stark contrast to its pitch black eyes that, at the moment, appear to be assessing me. Then it lets out a low-pitched hoot that carries on the silent air.

At the sound the bird is making, the cloaked figure disappears and a white light hits my body with such force I stumble back.

"Eve." Asher's voice sounds scared. "Come on, siren. Answer me."

I shift my eyes to his and blink slowly, realizing I'm outside the temple and in his arms.

"Welcome back, cutie." Callan smiles from over Asher's shoulder.

"What just happened?" I ask with a slight panic to my voice.

"You went into a trance state, fully awake but motionless in his arms." An accented voice from behind us answers my question. Asher helps me up and we all turn toward the temple entrance.

Standing on the last step of the temple is the most beautiful young Indian woman. Her eyes are deep amber with flecks of honey, a shade I've never seen before.

"Priestess Arabella," Asher states and he takes one knee. Callan and Abby follow suit. I stand there, stunned and recovering.

She twists her wrists so her palms face toward the skies and lifts them in an upward motion, signaling for the clan to rise.

"May I present Eve Collins, Priestess," Asher introduces in a quick manner.

The priestess lifts her honey eyes to me and bows her head. "Daughter of Heaven." Her long, straight, thick brunette hair falls forward.

Arabella's crimson and gold-jeweled headpiece dangles in the middle of her forehead. When she returns to her full height, I notice her entire body is decorated in ruby and gold jewelry.

A heavy-looking choker rests around her neckline, matching a pair of chandelier earrings that hang from each lobe. Multiple gold bangle and cuff bracelets adorn her wrists and several ankle bracelets and toe rings decorate her bare feet.

The beautiful woman is dressed in a scarlet and gold sari that highlights her taut, bare stomach. Her golden skin gives off a slight glow. She's absolutely lovely.

I smile and offer a slight wave since the gargoyles seem to have left out high priestess etiquette in my training.

"Welcome, guests, to The Eternal Forest and The Temple of The Seven High Priestesses. I'm certain your journey was extensive and you all could use rest and refreshments. Please, come." She motions at us to follow her up the stairs and into the temple.

Once inside, I realize we're in a room identical to where I just observed the owl. As we walk through it, Priestess Arabella rotates her head in my direction, dipping her chin and speaking to me in a low voice.

A rueful look flashes over her face. "I do apologize for the reverie. This temple is sacred ground. Very few are permitted to enter. I had no choice but to pull you into a trance state in order for Krea to assess you."

"Krea?" I repeat.

She smiles. "My owl." As soon as she enlightens me, the white bird joins her, resting on her shoulder. I swear the creature tipped its head at me in acknowledgement.

"White owls have been companions of The Seven High Priestesses for many centuries," Abby clarifies.

"They are quietly intelligent and extremely loyal attendants," the priestess finishes.

Tongue-tied, I just smile politely and nod. Absorbing everything, the owl just watches me in an unsettling manner. Actually, the creature's behavior is starting to freak me out, so I move closer to Asher. He snags my hand in his but doesn't make eye contact.

We enter a white and gold chamber inside the temple. It has four large Greek columns, one at each corner that runs from floor to ceiling. In the middle of the room is a circular pool with steam coming off the top of the jade water. Hanging from the ceiling, in various patterns, is white sheer fabric, swaying every so often. The floor is covered with large silk pillows and crystals are randomly placed throughout the hall.

Six bare foot individuals enter the chamber. They're all wearing black cloaks, their hoods pulled to conceal every part of them. They're holding plates of fruit and bread and carrying pitchers of water.

Priestess Arabella motions toward the comfortable floor cushions. "Please, rest. It is our privilege to offer the daughter of Heaven and her protectors refreshment while we convene."

We follow Arabella's lead and all take seats while the covered individuals present the trays to us, placing them in the middle of our circle before they quietly leave.

138

Asher sits so close to me, for a moment I think he might sit on my lap. His hand rests on my lower back, protectively. The contact doesn't go unnoticed by the priestess.

"Eve, I do hope you are not frightened by the veiled priestesses. It is customary for us to conceal our identities from those we do not know. Our seer and foreseer gifts are quite sought after and often place us in grave danger. In the wrong hands, knowledge of our identities puts our lives in peril," she explains.

"I understand. So they are the other six priestesses?" I confirm.

"Yes. Since I hold a seat on the Royal Supernatural Court, my identity is known amongst the mystical world therefore allowing me to present myself to you," Arabella clarifies with a warm smile.

"Priestess Arabella, the queen of the Fae realm informed Michael you've had some visions with regard to the Declan clan and dark army we should be made aware of," Callan points out.

"It is true. Myself, and Marguerite, the eldest priestess, have both opened our powers of knowing. Our clairvoyant sight has manifested immeasurable dangers and betrayals. I do hope my dear friend Lady Finella also made clear that sorceress Lunette confirmed the accuracy of the predictions."

Asher nods curtly. "She did."

Arabella releases a heavy breath. "We perceive the demonic legion is strategically working to ensure Eve does not succeed in her ascension. Lucifer is planning to wage war, even if he gains possession of Eve. It is our belief he has shown great patience all this time, and has been making deals with the supernatural world through the Declan clan to ensure their assistance in preparation for the end of days."

"Shit," I blurt out, covering my mouth quickly in embarrassment.

Abby snaps her head at me and widens her eyes in warning. I mouth an "I'm sorry" to her.

"Fear not, daughter of Heaven. We've also seen that you will ascend, furthering the evolution of human consciousness and souls. You will harness divine forces along with positive intention to help influence the course of reality in ways that serve the greatest good," Arabella assures.

The temple falls silent for a moment before Asher speaks. "Thank you, Priestess. We are grateful for your insight."

She motions her head once. "Whatever we can do to assist, we shall. Understand that." Arabella turns her attention to me. "Eve, while you are here, it would be my great honor to read you, if you will allow it."

"Read me?" I question.

"A simple process. I take your hand and use my gift of foresight to interpret your path."

"Okay." My answer is unsure.

"I am grateful. Please." She reaches for me. Her palm is flat, facing toward the sky to indicate I should place my hand on hers.

I swallow my fear and rest my palm face down on hers. I can feel Asher's stare on the side of my face, but I can't look at him. I'm too anxious.

Priestess Arabella closes her eyes for what seems like an eternity before opening them. When she does, her amber eyes have turned a freaky shade of light honey. I fight the urge to pull my hand away.

"I have seen your past, present and future, daughter of Heaven. Trust your instincts. The world has many secrets to be unlocked. Do not take the less obvious path, as that is the route favored. Your future is not what is being presented to you as truth." She closes her eyes again and drops her hand from mine. When she reopens them, they're back to their normal color but her face is masked in concern.

Unsure of what to say, I just place my hand back in my lap and shift my gaze to Asher. Before he lifts his to mine,

Arabella speaks again. "I wish to read both you and your protector. It's of great importance I read you at the same time due to the bond." Her voice is firm and urgent.

Asher shifts uncomfortably and I squirm. I risk a glance at Callan and Abby. Both have paled and their eyes are too wide. *Crap.* This can't be good. Asher nods his consent and I have no choice but to follow his lead.

Once again, Arabella places both palms up and closes her eyes. Asher and I rest our palms on hers. Both of us look straight ahead, motionless. I don't even think either of us is breathing.

Arabella's eyes open and she looks in between us in a trance state. "Restraint." It's the only word that falls from her lips before the tension in the chamber rises, suffocating me. The word comes out loud, sending a chill down my spine. From my peripheral vision, I see Asher swallow hard. "Restraint is good, but redemption is better. Forever has happened," she says, confusing us. "Emotions must be kept in check through times of transition. You must constantly be aware of one another's purpose and the motives of others. One of you will embrace change, while the other will fear it. The gift of healing has been transferred, as will others."

She opens her eyes and her face softens. I pull my hand away before Asher snaps his back. Neither of us speaks.

"Thank you for granting me the privilege of reading you both," the high priestess says while bowing toward us. "The Eternal Forest Realm and The Seven High Priestesses offer our cooperation and support to you in any way we can." She stands, as do Abby and Callan.

Realizing we're both just sitting, Asher and I jolt up. Asher finds his voice first.

"Thank you, High Priestess, for your hospitality and insight." He smiles, but it's forced.

"It was nice meeting you," I offer lamely.

"I bid you all a safe journey back." Arabella elegantly glides out of the room.

The four of us just stand there in awkward silence. Feeling self-conscious, I go to say something but Callan beats me to it. "We should start back to the gateway."

"Yes. The gateway...let's go," Abby agrees, her voice a little too perky.

My glance slides over to Asher. His jaw is ticking in rapid motion. With arms folded, his muscles are wound so tight they're jumping under the skin.

I turn and follow Callan and Abby. The entire hike back is silent. Asher and Callan walk ahead of Abby and I the whole time. He never looks back. He never speaks. He never attempts physical contact. To say I feel ill at ease would be an understatement. Even Abby, who's usually chatty, is quiet.

Once we reach the area in the forest where we first arrived, Callan turns to us, offering a small smile. "Abby, we'll head back first and see you guys in a bit." He reaches out his hand and she takes it and they make their way into the dense vegetation.

I finally muster up enough bravery to look at Asher. His face is ashen and his eyes are looking everywhere but at me. His demeanor is rigid and aloof.

"Um, how do we get back?" I ask, chewing on the inside of my cheek.

His eyes finally land on me. "The same way we came. We will need to merge mentally so we can return. It's easiest to do in a comfortable position." The answer is laced with annoyance.

"Okay. Show me," I state with a little force in my voice.

He fidgets. "It's best if we sit and face one another."

I tilt my head toward the cerulean moss. "Here?"

"Yes."

I sit. Then he sits. Fuck, this is uncomfortable.

"Asher, if we need to merge spiritually, maybe you should tell me what is going on," I suggest.

"Not now, Eve. It's not the time," he states in a final manner.

I narrow my eyes. "Fine."

"It will be easier if you sit on my lap and place your legs over mine," Asher says as he wraps his long fingers around my waist, pulling me forward so I'm draped over him. He sits crossed-legged, my thighs hugging his before he repositions them around his waist and brings my arms up around his neck.

His large hands press on my back, forcing me closer so our chests are touching. Anyone who saw us would think we are lovers fully entwined with one another. The intensity of the moment makes my heart stumble.

Asher's expression darkens as he gazes into my eyes.

"Ready?" His voice is thick.

I nod, not trusting my own voice.

He begins to move his lips toward mine and my breath hitches. "Ash?"

"We need to come together emotionally, so you'll just have to trust me, siren. No matter what else we're experiencing in this moment, we have to be one another's sole focus."

"All right," I whisper, feeling like we're plunging into dark waters.

Asher shifts closer. His hands lift and tangle in my hair, tugging once so my head tips toward his, the gesture commanding. He never breaks our intense eye contact. My breathing picks up and Asher bites his lip.

In a slow, methodic movement, he leans forward and places a gentle kiss on the left side of my mouth then lightly brushes my lips with his as he moves to the right side, mirroring the action. My heart races as my eyes close in pleasure.

"Look at me, siren," he demands, forcing my eyes open.

Staring into the depths of his blue gaze, I feel almost dizzy. His tongue darts out and runs over my bottom lip then the top, causing my lips to part. Asher sucks in a ragged breath as he bends forward and nips my bottom lip, pulling it toward him before allowing his tongue to soothe the pricking sensation his teeth caused.

Finally, his lips press into mine, causing a raw and sexy sound to rumble from his chest. My hands clench the front of his shirt, pulling him closer. He yanks my hair back hard, forcing my mouth to allow him access. His lips are demanding and bruising, searing me with unspoken passion.

This kiss is different from the others we've shared. It's more intimate. A seal of desire that's uniting us. The swirling feeling returns, like we're morphing into one. Marking me. I close my eyes for a moment and when I reopen them, we're back in his stone state bed.

My heart drops, not wanting this kiss to end. Once we're out of the chamber, it will be over. Asher pulls away, leaving only a small slit of air between us before he opens his eyes and stares directly into mine, penetrating each layer. His lips part on a quick, shallow inhale.

"Siren?" It comes out breathy and unsure. My only answer is to shift on his lap as my body brushes against his arousal. "Fuck. If you do that again, I'm going to throw you down right here," he warns, his voice rough and his hands tight around my waist.

Keeping my eyes fixated on his, I move my hips once more. At the bold move, any shred of self-control Asher was holding onto disappears. In one smooth, quick move, he lays me down on my back, pressing me into the mattress and covers my body with his.

A strangled gasp escapes my lips.

With his face hovering centimeters above mine, he takes his right hand and runs it down the length of my bare leg then back up as he hitches it over his hip. My fingers grab onto his shoulders, pulling him closer as his hand continues to climb under the hem of my dress and over my hipbone, simultaneously rocking his lower body into me, causing a spark of heat to ignite.

My eyes roll back at the movement. "Oh. My. God. Asher," I pant. He lowers his head to the crook of my neck, biting and sucking the spot just under my ear. After each painful bite, his tongue soothes the sting.

I dig my fingers deeper into his broad shoulders, grabbing at the cotton material and his fingers find their way between my legs, caressing me over the lace of my panties. At his touch, I release a soft whimper.

"Shit, you're drenched," he says as he lifts his head and scans my face. Watching me, his middle finger runs up and then down over the barrier in a slow rhythm. With each stroke, my body arches into his.

In response, Asher lets out a deep growl, bends down and takes my lips forcefully as his fingers find the edge of the fabric, pushing the material to the side. Without breaking contact with my mouth, he continues to caress and tease me without the lace obstacle, causing me to gasp against his lips.

My hips tilt forward with the pressure of his fingers as they slowly find their way inside of me, while his thumb teases my nerve endings. I shudder as an intense ache builds inside me.

I open my eyes to find his are squeezed shut. "You feel so fucking good, siren."

I'm not sure how much time has past. All I can focus on are his skillful motions.

"Asher." I don't recognize my needy voice. "Please." I'm not even sure what I'm asking for.

"I've got you. Let go, siren." At his command, I let out a muted scream, arching into him while at the same time clinging onto his shoulders. My body trembles as pleasure runs through me.

Asher is motionless, watching me as I come down from my moment of bliss. Once the last of my shudders run through me, he removes his hand and pushes the lace cloth back with a pleased groan. Slowly, he begins to lift off me, sitting on his heels and pulling me up with him.

Once we're both sitting up, he repositions the bottom of my dress, covering me. He's oddly quiet. *Shouldn't someone speak?* I go to open my mouth but before I can say anything, Asher runs the pad of his thumb over my swollen lips.

"Shit, Eve. I'm so sorry. I lost control...I shouldn't have let it go that far. Are you okay?" His voice is filled with concern. I nod. It's all I can manage right now. "There are some things I need to discuss with Michael and Keegan that are urgent. We should go," he says, pulling me off the bed and guiding me toward the stone staircase. *Um, okay?*

Confused, I silently follow him. I should be elated right now. Instead, I just feel cold and empty. He's withdrawn and I think I might have lost him for good this time.

12 London

I'm on edge. Asher has been held up in the library behind closed doors with Keegan, Callan and Michael since we left the chamber. Leaving me alone with my thoughts and the evil clock I've been watching with an unhealthy obsession for what feels like days. I sigh and put my head in my hands. My brain is on overload. Come to think of it, why am I not in the library with them? I know the discussion is about me.

I need to pull it together. My constant overthinking is going to land me in a mental facility if I don't stop. All I can focus on is the one word Priestess Arabella spoke. *Restraint.* What's wrong with Asher and I that not even twenty minutes later, we were in his bed showing the complete opposite? *God, you're so stupid, Eve.* The heat in my cheeks rises as images of what I just experienced with Asher run through my head. How it felt to have him that close to me, only to be rejected and mortified, again, by someone who's supposed to be protecting me. Awesome.

"How long has she been like this?" Abby's voice filters through my scattered synapses.

"About an hour," McKenna answers.

"Poor lass. Dat lad has her all wound up," Fiona replies.

"Has she been talking to herself the entire time?" Abby asks with concern.

"Aye, more like mumblin' and pacin'," Fiona replies.

"For fucks sake, knock it off. You're making me motion sick with all the jittery movement," McKenna yells at me.

"KENNA! Watch ye language, lass," Fiona scolds.

"I'm just saying, how bad could her reading have been that she's this jumpy?" McKenna reasons.

"It wasn't great," Abby mumbles.

I stop walking back and forth and lift my gaze to them. They're all standing in the doorway like a group of mother hens. Staring at me as if my head is about to explode at any moment.

"Hello, luv. Welcome back. Can I get ye sum cocoa?" Fiona asks kindly.

"Um, okay," I reply, just wanting them to leave.

"Splendid. I'll be back in a jiff." The panther shifter prowls away toward the kitchen.

"TALK!" McKenna demands as she crosses the threshold into the sitting room.

"About what, McKenna?" I retort.

"Well, maybe you could tell us how you're feeling about Asher transferring his gift of healing to you? Especially since we all thought it was something Michael passed along," Abby pushes.

McKenna's jaw drops. "Are you serious?"

Abby's eyes dart to her quickly and then back to me. "Well?"

I sigh. "Well, what?"

Abby plops down on the couch. "Well, how does that make you feel?" she repeats slowly.

I shrug. "I'm not sure. I think Asher is pretty pissed off about it. Like he's mad I acquired his gift or something," I comment offhandedly.

"Nonsense. Just means dat da bond 'tis stronger now." Fiona places a tray of mugs and scones on the coffee table before sitting next to Abby.

"Does no one care that a stronger bond is actually a bad thing?" McKenna offers. "It means they're getting too close. They aren't even mated and now they're exchanging abilities?"

"Thanks for stating the obvious, McKenna." I scowl.

Her eyes narrow at me. "Someone has to, blood of Eden."

"I think Asher seemed more upset about you looting around in his head than the gift transfer," Abby blurts out.

McKenna's face grows hard as she snaps her head to Abby. "By the grace," she snarls.

"Yes, yes. We get it, McKenna. Put your claws back in." I huff.

"At least your eye color is back to normal," Abby offers in consolation. *Oh my God, would she just stop talking.*

McKenna throws her hands up in the air. "Did she get the mate mark too? For fucks sake."

"Tsk. Kenna, language, lass," Fiona warns again.

"No. She doesn't have my mark." Asher's cool voice drifts into the room from the doorway.

My heart jumps against my ribcage at the sound of his deep voice. He looks pissed off. His jaw is tight, body stiff, and hands are clenching by his side.

Keegan and Callan saunter in, forcing Asher to move into the room. "Where's Michael?" McKenna asks.

"He was called back," Keegan states, pulling McKenna's back toward his chest and resting his chin on her head.

Asher's eyes widen in panic before he takes five long strides so he's standing directly in front of me, blocking me from the group. His hand comes up with lightning speed as he brings some of my hair forward, covering my neck.

My eyebrows drag together in confusion before I realize he's concealing the spot he was biting and sucking on earlier. My face flushes bright red and he turns his entire body away from me. *Could I be anymore mortified?*

"We're leaving for London," Asher states matter-of-factly to the group.

"Why?" Abby questions as she and Fiona stand.

"We need to meet with some of the other clans, baby," Callan answers.

"The priestess was certain Lucifer is making side deals with members of the supernatural world through the Declan clan. In order to find out who and what those deals are, we'll need to bring in other families to help us. More bodies mean additional protection for Eve while we strategize a defense," Keegan explains.

Fiona sighs heavily.

"It's just for a bit while we get all our intel in place. We'll be back as soon as we can, Fi." Callan grabs her hand and squeezes.

"Aye 'tis okay." She pats his hand. "Let me pack some snacks for ye ta take." She leaves and heads to the kitchen.

"We should get our stuff together. I'd like to be there by nightfall so we can begin to request meetings with the other clans first thing in the morning," Keegan says.

"Let's do it then. Eve, do you need any help?" Abby asks.

"No, thanks." My voice sounds small.

Seconds later we all head upstairs. I'm just placing the last items in my bag when there's a soft knock at the door. I close my eyes and inhale, knowing Asher's on the other side. I push down my nerves and prepare for the awkward talk.

My hand pauses on the doorknob for a brief moment before I yank it open. Lifting my head, I take in Asher. He looks exhausted and at the same time, so spectacular.

"Hi," he says quietly.

"Hi," I repeat.

"I just wanted to see if you needed anything before we head out."

I shake my head. "All good." I keep my voice light.

"Okay then. See you downstairs in a bit." He turns to leave. *Super awkward.*

"Yep." I begin to shut the door but he puts up his hand and stops the movement.

"May I come in?" His voice is thick.

I sigh and open the door, signaling for him to enter with a quick flick of my hand. His scent tickles my nose as he walks by me. I turn and shut the door.

"Ash, I'm not in the mood for a lecture."

All of the sudden, my back is pressed against the door. Asher's body firmly holds mine in place and I let out a soft gasp. His warm breath dances across my cheek. He takes my face in his hands as he leans his forehead against mine.

In a low whisper, he says, "I'm so fucking sorry, siren."

"W-What?" I ask, trying to regain control of my senses.

"I apologize," he repeats.

"For what?" I was expecting a lecture, not an apology.

He pushes off me and moves toward the window, blowing out a long breath. "Everything."

"Um, apology accepted?"

He chuckles. "Was that a question or statement?"

"I'm not sure. I'm at a loss here, Asher."

I give up trying to figure him out.

He turns those deep blue irises directly at me. "Keegan wants to be at our flats shortly. Do you want me to bring that down for you?" he inquires, pointing to my bag.

I nod. *What the hell is going on?*

He grabs the bag and throws it over his shoulder. "I'll see you downstairs." With that, he walks toward the door.

Still in shock, I move just enough that he can open the door and leave.

"What the fuck?" I ask the empty room.

After composing myself, I head downstairs where everyone is already saying their goodbyes to Fiona and heading out toward the Escalade. She hugs each one and promises to see them soon.

"Eve, darlin'." She motions me over and embraces me in a tight squeeze. "I'll see ye soon, luv. Ye behave ye'reself and don't ye be lettin' these gargoyles run over ye."

"I promise."

She pats my cheek affectionately before whispering, "Remember, stars don't shine without darkness." She winks and heads toward Asher.

I walk out the door and hop in the vehicle.

A soft nudge awakens me from my deep slumber. Lifting my head and realize we're in London. I slept the entire ride. Keegan pulls up to a tall building and drives the car into an underground garage then parks next to a few other expensive looking vehicles.

"All right, kids. We're home," he announces.

We each get out and grab our bags before heading to an elevator that I assume takes us up to the flats. I notice Abby only pressed floors three, four and five. Recalling that Asher said the guest flat was on floor two, I turn to him. He ignores me and faces forward. *Swell.* More awkwardness.

Callan and Abby exit on the third floor, offering weak smiles before declaring they'll see us in the morning. Keegan and Kenna get off on the fourth, mumbling their good nights.

Once Asher and I are alone, he finally decides to speak. "I thought it would be better if you stayed in the guest room in my flat. But if you'd feel more comfortable, I can arrange the second floor residence in the morning."

"It's fine," I concede, not really wanting to stay by myself in an apartment.

The door to the elevator opens into a small, light gray hallway. We follow the dark hardwood floors to the black lacquer door. Asher places his hand on the imprint pad, unlocking it. He pushes it open and allows me to enter first.

The entry has the same light gray walls as the exterior hallway. To my right is a long wall with an alcove at the end, which showcases a gargoyle statue on top of a marble counter.

Asher signals for me to walk through the arched open doorway into a small but cozy sitting area. The walls are cream and the furniture is light gray. Floor-to-ceiling windows make up one of the walls and are outlined with gray silk drapes. It's warm. Very Asher.

"All the windows in the flat overlook Hyde Park," he points out. "Follow me. I'll show you the rest of my place."

He walks me around to the modern kitchen. It is small but has a seating area and dark wood cabinets topped with white marble countertops. All the appliances are stainless steel. It feels very masculine.

We head down the hallway past the laundry and bathroom areas then to the guest bedroom equipped with a full bath. I drop my bag on the bed before Asher continues across the hall to the master bedroom where he drops his stuff onto the floor and leads us back out to a suken living room that simply takes my breath away.

There's a glass chandelier that takes up the entire ceiling hanging over two large couches that are double the length of a normal sofa.

However, the most amazing part of this room is the two-tier windows on all three walls that give the impression the night sky goes on forever. My eyes drop from the height to a terrace that wraps around the windowed walls. The main patio overlooks the park and houses an outdoor furniture set and fire pit.

"This is incredible, Asher." I mean it. It's stunning.

"My dad loved open spaces so he bought this building, which used to have ten floors, and made each unit a doubled ceiling. Then he made sure each room had at least three walls of windows if it structurally could," he answers with pride in his voice.

"It's a wonder you ever leave it," I say sincerely.

He's just watching me, his face unreadable. "Are you hungry? I can fix us a bite and we can relax. Unless you're tired and want to go to sleep?"

I look at the clock on the wall. "It's only six. Dinner would be great," I reply, holding back my laugh.

This is weird. Normally, there are other people in a house with us. The two of us, like this, especially after this afternoon...well, it's unnerving.

"I'm just going to take a quick shower, unless you need some help?" I offer.

"I've got it covered. There are fresh towels in your bathroom. Let me know if you need anything else." He heads toward the kitchen.

I make my way back into the guest room. With the heavy drapes and bedding, it feels like an elegant hotel room. I go into the full bath and see the soaking tub and change my mind. A nice bubble bath would be amazing right now. I notice all the brands of toiletries I use are already stocked. *Damn that gargoyle.*

Twenty minutes later, I hear Asher outside the bathroom door. "You okay in there?"

"Yeah. Sorry, I didn't realize I was in here so long. I'll be out in a minute."

He chuckles. "Take your time."

I get out of the tub, dry off, lotion up, blow-dry and brush my hair, put on my vanilla-coconut gloss and throw on my tank top and shorts before heading out to see what Asher's cooked up.

Stepping into the main living area, I stop in my tracks. Asher's sitting on the couch wearing only black pajama bottoms. The tables are full of take-out containers. The smell of curry wafts up to my nose as he lifts his head and meets my gaze.

"I hope you don't mind but I thought we could just do take-out and watch some movies tonight. You know, just have a normal-type evening."

I try not to cry. This is exactly what I need, normal.

"This is perfect, Ash."

That earns me his signature sexy smile.

"Well, I never said I wasn't perfect, siren."

I roll my eyes and plop down on the couch next to him.

"What did you order?"

"There's this amazing Indian restaurant down the street so I had them deliver some of my favorite dishes. I took a stab at what you might want." He hands me a fork and motions for me to dig in.

Restraint

"Did you order biryani?" It's my favorite.

"I did. There's also tandoori chicken, samosa, chole-bhature, malai kofta, dal makhani, and naan. Want a beer?" he asks, getting up.

"Holy crap, Asher. That's a ton of food, but I think I love you," I blurt out. *Oh shit.*

Silence. "I was...hungry." There's an edge to his voice.

I need to find a rock to crawl under.

A few moments later, he returns with two glasses and hands one to me. "Thanks. I-I didn't mean what I...I just meant that...what are we watching?" I chicken out.

"Anything you'd like," he replies, ignoring my lack of clarity.

I grab a piece of flatbread and dip it into the tandoori sauce. "Comedy?"

"American Pie marathon?"

I nod my agreement and he grabs the remote as we settle in for a relaxing, ordinary evening.

Halfway through American Wedding, I fall asleep. I know this because I just woke up in desperate need of water. My mouth is dry from all the curry we ate. I look around the dark room and realize I'm in the guest bed. Asher must have carried me in here. *Crap.*

I throw off the silky sheets and swing my legs over the side of the bed, preparing myself to head to the kitchen in search of water. After snagging a bottle from the fridge, I go into the sunken living room. Everything is dark but the lights of London are twinkling around Hyde Park and I'm mesmerized.

I sit on the couch and bask in the dark abyss that is the night sky. These windows are really amazing. Asher's dad knew what he was doing. It's like the London clan of gargoyles can watch over the entire city and its people. Protecting them.

"Siren?"

I turn my head and notice Asher looking adorable and sleepy. His hair is all messy and his indigo eyes are drowsy as he rubs them. I push down the urge to jump him.

I hold up my water bottle. "Sorry, I was thirsty. I didn't mean to wake you."

He moves to the couch and sits down. "You didn't. I was having trouble sleeping."

Asher grabs my water bottle and chugs it.

"Help yourself."

"I did." He smirks cockily.

We're silent for a moment before he speaks. "I'm sorry for snapping at you when we were in the Eternal Forest. You, trying to search my thoughts, it caught me off guard. I didn't mean to act like a jackass."

I wave my hand in dismissal. "It's fine."

He sighs. "No, Eve, it's not. I forget that sometimes you don't understand how things work in my world. Mind sharing is something that's only done between mates. That said, I should have explained that to you, not gotten pissy."

My eyes shift to him. "I get it."

He holds my gaze for a moment. "I'm also sorry for freaking out when Priestess Arabella told us I'm the reason you can heal yourself and not Michael. I was completely blindsided on that one." He exhales a sharp breath. "You have no idea what I felt in that moment."

I scan his face, my voice barely above a whisper. "Tell me."

He just stares at me. "Transferring abilities means our link is getting stronger, and truthfully, that fucking freaks me out, siren."

My heart clenches at his words. I move my hand toward his face and cup his stubbly cheek. Asher closes his eyes and leans into my touch before jumping off the couch so fast I have to blink a few times to absorb what I witnessed.

Standing a safe distance away, by the glass doors that lead to the patio, he rubs his face in frustration before pushing his hands through his hair.

"I should be able to exhibit more self-control when it comes to you. When we came out of the stone state, what I did wasn't fair. I don't regret it, but I shouldn't have let it happen." He turns to me. The moonlight bouncing off his face shows it's marred in pain. "It's just, when I'm with you…you make me feel things." He pauses before pinning me with an intense stare. "I thought you were an amazing creature before we…but what you are is far more enchanting." Unexpectedly, he turns and leaves.

I swallow the unmerited hurt and sink into the couch, alone in the moonlight.

Randi Cooley Wilson

13 Introductions

There's a painfully bright light behind my eyelids and my face is warm, too warm. I groan and throw the furry blanket I'm under over my head, relieved for the darkness it provides. Just as I start to fall back to sleep, I hear a light rumbling from behind me.

Curious, I toss the covers back off and open my eyes. Crap. I fell asleep in the sunken living room last night. The sunshine is pouring in from all three walls of glass. Ugh. I thought it rained in London all the time.

"Not a morning person, siren?" Asher's deep voice penetrates my sleepy fog.

I growl and throw the blanket off then stand, stretching. The smell of coffee forces me to turn around. Asher is standing there looking all bed headed and delicious. Damn him. He smirks knowingly.

Holding his mug out to me, he asks, "Coffee?"

"Yes. Please," I whine.

He chuckles, moving toward the kitchen. I follow him, not caring how my hair looks or that I haven't brushed my teeth yet. I sit on a stool at the island and he places a cup in front of me.

I lift it to my lips and moan in pleasure. "Oh. My. God. Asher." My eyes close. When they reopen, Asher is leaning against the counter, ankles crossed, coffee mug stopped right before his lips and an odd expression plastered on his face.

"What?" I ask, wiping my face, thinking I have sleep drool on it.

He swallows hard. "Um, I need to go. I mean, go shower. Yeah, shower." He scatters out of the kitchen, quickly. *Okay*.

After making myself some breakfast and cleaning up the dishes, I head toward the guestroom to shower and dress. As I enter the hallway, I notice Asher's bedroom door is ajar. Inquisitiveness gets the best of me as my eyes shift to the open slit. I see Asher sitting at his desk wearing only jeans.

His bare chest glistens with drops of water from his shower. The tattoos stare back at me as if they want me to trace them with my tongue. I snap my eyes shut. *Eve, focus!* I walk quickly to my room and clean up with the coldest water I have ever used.

I throw on my jeans, knee-high boots and black cotton shirt, pulling my thumbs through the holes in the sleeves before putting on the necklace Asher he had my aunt design it for me at Christmas, a silver feather lying on its side.

I brush out my long, light brown hair, throw on some make-up and my favorite gloss and meet up with Asher in the living room. He's put on a white t-shirt with his jeans and motorcycle boots. Leather bands are secured on each wrist.

"Keegan would like us to go down to flat one. Some of the other clans are starting to trickle in and we need to be there to greet them," he explains.

"Okay." I chew the inside of my cheek. At my nervous habit, he stalks over to me and rubs my bottom lip with his thumb, stopping the addiction.

Dipping his chin, he gives me his *'it's going to be all right'* face. "You'll be fine, siren." He grabs my hand and tugs me toward the door, stopping right before he opens it.

Asher turns his head to me, and smiles smugly before chuckling at my shyness. As soon as he opens the door, a black blur jumps at him. It's squealing and forces him to release my hand. Whatever it was, bound in so hard it pushed Asher against the wall.

Panicked, I unsheath my daggers, ready to attack. Then I hear it speak and my stomach drops.

"Asher, baby, I've missed you so much." A female voice drifts over to me.

Pulling myself together, I register a petite girl draped over my protector. Her waist-length, shiny, stick straight, black hair dangles over his hands, which are wrapped around her body. My eyes roam upward, from the side. All I see is hair and then her tongue down Asher's throat.

My blood begins to boil at the site and Asher quickly comes to his senses, pushing her away.

As if in a daze, he shakes his head. "Morgana?"

Her brown eyes look up at him through dark, long lashes as she bites her red lips with her perfectly white teeth. *Ugh, I hate her already.*

"Miss me?" she coos.

At that, I clear my throat. Rather angrily. This seems to snap Asher out of his fog because he shoots me a look with wide eyes then shifts his vision to my daggers and then back to Morgana.

"Um, sure. It's surprising to see you again."

Really? That's the best he can do.

She scrunched up her nose. "You mean, a pleasant surprise, right?" Her red nails run over his chest. At the gesture, he peels her off of him and moves toward me, signaling for me to unweapon myself.

I arch a brow. "Er, Eve, this is Morgana. She's with the Manhattan clan. Morgana, this is Eve Collins, my current assignment." *Ouch.* My current assignment. Insulting.

She snorts. "The human created by Heaven?"

"The one and only," I reply coolly.

Morgana takes a warrior stance. "You don't look like anything special."

I let my eyes scan her from the bottom up. "Neither do you," I counter.

Asher lets out an awkward breath. "We should get down to the flat to meet with everyone."

None of us move. "Okay, then." Asher walks out the door toward the elevator. Leaving the drop-dead gorgeous gargoyle and me in a stare off.

She huffs then brushes past me after him. I roll my eyes and follow them, clenching my hands around my crossed arms tightly so I won't claw her eyes out.

We walk into the first floor loft and everything is dark gray and black. The walls, the floors, even the modern leather furniture. Though the layout is similar to Asher's, this floor feels more like headquarters than a home. Where the sunken room is in Asher's place there is a conference room, currently filled with people.

As soon as Callan sees me, he rushes over, but not before his eyes widen in shock when he sees Morgana attached to Asher's side like velcro.

"Hey, cutie." He pulls me into a bear hug and bends down, whispering. "All okay?"

I plaster on a fake smile and nod. I notice McKenna snag Morgana into a big hug. Of course they're friends.

Callan wraps his arm around my shoulder and walks me into the room. Silence falls over the room and everyone stops what they're doing and stares at me. Abby moves to my other side and I shift on my feet uncomfortably.

"If you all would kindly take a seat, we can begin," Keegan states.

"Eves, you can sit between Abby and me," Callan offers.

"She will sit by me," Asher says, his voice full of authority. Very prince-like.

Callan gives him a pointed look then slides his eyes to Morgana and back to me. "All right."

Asher moves toward me and places his hand on the small of my back. I move away without looking or speaking at him, choosing the seat between Callan and Abby.

He's forced to take the last open seat between Morgana and McKenna. I smile to myself before I look up and see his pissed off face. I throw an angry smirk at him and in return he narrows his eyes at me.

Childish? Yes. Deserved? Absolutely.

Pleased with his seat choice, Morgana smiles and looks up at him like a puppy dog. *Bitch.*

Keegan begins. "I'd like to start by welcoming and thanking each clan for joining us today. We know how busy everyone is and we're grateful you've taken time to assist us with our latest assignment."

Callan interrupts, "And newest family member."

At his added statement, my heart soars.

"I'd like you to meet Eve Collins, daughter of Heaven. She's under the protection of the London clan." Keegan introduces me from the head of the glass table and my cheeks tint pink. "Asher is her protector."

At the declaration, Morgana snorts. *What the fuck is this gargoyle's problem?*

A heavy-set, older bald man stands. Half of his face is hidden behind a long and thick red beard. His bright green eyes twinkle warmly at me and his round cheeks lift, enhancing the freckles that span the entirety of his face.

He bows to me. "Dia duit, daughter of Heaven. I am Angus, head of da Irish clan, and Abby's uncle." Angus's voice is gruff and heavily accented. He motions to his left. "My second in command, my son, Thomas."

At the introduction, a tall, lanky thirty-something guy stands. His hair is short and reddish blond, the same color as his petite beard. He's wearing black jeans, a black hooded sweatshirt and a leather jacket over the sweatshirt.

"Eve." He nods toward me and I smile.

The young Irishman sits and another older gentleman stands. This one reminds me of a Viking. His long gray beard and mustache hit the middle of his broad chest. He's huge and muscular like a wrestler. He has blue eyes that match McKenna's sapphire ones.

"I am Griffin, or 'Griff' as me friends call me, ledah of da Scottish clan and McKenna's kin. Me second en command, Sean." His deep brogue booms.

Sean stands. He is really tall and also very muscular. He has his hair shaved on each side of his head and a dirty-blond braid in the middle of his head that continues down his back that contains the rest of his hair.

He too bows to me. "Nice tae meit ye, Eve."

I smile again and wave in return.

Finally, an incredibly, hot and young, maybe late-twenties, African-American guy stands and turns his brown eyes to me. This guy could be a model. He's so beautiful. Brown eyes twinkle brightly and he offers me his hand.

"Hi, Eve. I'm Marcus, leader of the Manhattan clan."

"Nice to meet you." I like him instantly.

"My second in command, Morgana." She waves wickedly at me and I shift my focus back to Marcus.

He surprises me by offering an apologetic smile.

Asher begins to explain what Priestess Arabella told us with regard to the demonic legion and the Declan clan. Plans are divised for how to recruit informants and weed out those working with Deacon.

Callan leans into my ear conspiratorially. "Eves, stop drooling over Marcus. You aren't his type."

"What do you mean?" I whisper back.

"I think Asher or I tend to be more of what Marcus prefers in a mate." His eyes twinkle with amusement.

"Oh." I Marcus's brown irises as he winks.

Damn gargoyles.

After being briefed and enduring a few hours of strategizing, we're all taking a break while munching on the pizza Abby ordered. Of course, Morgana hasn't left Asher's side. I internally cringe at her desperation.

I scrunch my napkin up heatedly. "How could he not tell me he had a girlfriend?"

Abby's eyes widen. "You mean Morgana? Eve, she isn't his girlfriend."

"Mate-to-be?" I ask.

Abby shakes her head. "Eww, no. They have a history but it's been over for forever now."

I cross my arms. "That's not what it looked like when she jumped him at his front door."

Abby laughs. "Well, she is a lover of the dramatics. She's really close to McKenna."

"Of course she is." I sigh.

I look up to see Asher watching me. Something flashes across his face that I can't quite place. His indigo slits just stare at me as he begins to stalk at me, his eyes never leaving mine.

My hands close into angry fists and I take a step back, needing to retreat. He stops within a breath of me, the tip of his nose brushing mine. My breathing has ceased as his gaze holds mine, searching.

In a low voice, he bends near my ear. "Are you jealous, siren?" *Crap.* He heard Abby and me.

I bark out a short laugh. "No."

His head cocks to one side as a smug smile appears on his lips. "Really?"

"Yes." My hands become numb from how hard I'm clenching them.

He reaches for me and I sidestep his grasp. The last thing I want or need is his touch. He straightens and glances at me, perturbed. Good, he should be.

"You should get back to your girlfriend." I look over his shoulder at Morgana. She's shooting daggers my way. "Although, she might not be so understanding about what happened between us during your last stone state."

Asher's expression hardens. "Come. With. Me." He growls and grabs my elbow, dragging me from the room, down the hall and out the door toward the elevator.

He doesn't speak the entire time. He just pulls me like a rag doll behind him, up the elevator to the fifth floor, through the hallway, slamming the door shut behind us.

Roughly, he pushes me against the wall. He lifts his hands and pins them on either side of me, caging me in as his lips descend on mine in a punishing and painful expression of his sentiments. The length of his muscular body presses against me as his knee finds its way in between my legs.

After a mind blowing, long kiss, he snaps his head back only to move his lips forward again, nipping at my bottom lip. This time, he doesn't soothe the pain he's causing.

Asher moves his hands from the wall to the sides of my head, holding me in place so I'm forced to look at him. His breath on my lips and his voice is horse.

"Let me be very clear about something, siren. She means nothing to me. *You.* Mean. EVERYTHING!" he bites out each word.

That's the second time in about a minute he's taken my breath away. I just stare at him, stunned, while we catch our breaths and he tries to rein in his emotions.

I close my eyes and move my head up and down. "I believe you." I pant across his lips.

I feel him slowly relax. His hands loosely tangle in the hair at each side of my face while his thumb rests on my swollen lips. I latch onto his arms and allow my tongue to dart out and lick his thumb.

Swallowing, he bends his finger so it's in my mouth, allowing me to close my lips around it. Twirling my tongue over the tip and sucking it. Asher lets out a primal rumble.

A knock at the door ceases my motions.

"Asher? It's Marcus. I need to speak with you."

Asher closes his eyes before he lets out a long breath.

"Fuckkkkk."

I gently bite the tip of his finger, causing the blue hue of his eyes to darken. "Do that again, siren, and I will be forced to take you right here against the wall."

I smile, knowing he wouldn't do that but pleased with myself for having that effect on him.

"Don't think I won't," he teases and I release his finger.

I chew the inside of my cheek as he backs away, causing him to smirk knowing where my thoughts are.

Shooting me one final sexy look, he opens the door and greets Marcus. "Hey, man. Come on in."

Marcus swaggers in and they do some sort of male fist pump greeting before he nods to me.

"I came to apologize for Morgana's behavior earlier. She can be, spirited. I've reined her in though. She shouldn't give you any more trouble while we're here," he tells Asher.

"Thanks. I appreciate that, Marcus. She simply needs to remember her place," Asher states clearly.

Marcus turns his attention toward me. "Hey! How are you getting along with our resident brooding gargoyle prince? Let me know if he doesn't treat you right and I'll put in an assignment change for your protection."

"Over my dead body," Asher says in a harsh tone.

At the sharpness in his voice, both Marcus and I snap our heads to him.

"I was just kidding, man. Take it down a notch. It's not like I'm hitting on your mate or anything." Marcus chuckles, watching Asher's reaction closely.

I choke on my breath. "I'm just gonna let you guys talk." I point in the direction of the door, needing to escape. "It was nice to meet you, Marcus. Hopefully we'll see one another again."

He lifts his chin to me with curious eyes. "You too, Eve," he replies and strolls into the living room, out of site.

I turn to leave but not before Asher catches my waist and pulls me back against his hard chest. "I promise we'll pick up where we left off earlier. I'm intrigued by what else your tongue can do," he whispers seductively.

My entire body flushes at his statement.

Randi Cooley Wilson

14 Dimia

After an endless amount of arguing, I manage to convince Abby to take me out of the building. I want to get some groceries and do a little sightseeing since I've been in England for a while and have yet to actually see anything.

Callan approves the excursion as long as I stick to Abby like glue and promise to adorn myself with my daggers. I'm ready to go and waiting while Callan gives us our last minute warnings before planting a juicy wet kiss on his mate. Gross.

"Get a room, would you?" I jest.

Callan gives me a pointed glance. "Listen, cutie, as it is, Asher is going to have my ass in a sling for allowing this little outing. Who knows how long it will be before my lips will be able to kiss my girl after Asher's fists get a hold of them. I suggest you start kissing my ass for sneaking you out."

I roll my eyes. "We'll be fine."

Callan laughs. "Famous last words." He turns to Abby. "Be safe, baby." He kisses her temple.

She nods and drags me out the front door. "If we don't escape now, he'll change his mind. Just walk, quickly. Don't look back at his puppy dog eyes."

I giggle. "Okay. Okay."

"Alright, the first place we're going is Harvey Nichols," Abby informs me.

"Sounds good." Shopping isn't my thing but I'm just happy to be getting out of the flat.

"Then a visit to Louboutin and finally Whole Foods for groceries." She continues planning her strategic attack. "Oh, and we need to head to Rococo. Callan loves their chocolates and if he's going to be getting his ass kicked by Asher, we should bring him a peace offering."

"Agreed. Should we get something for Asher too? A bribe?" I question.

"Maybe we should head to Alfred Dunhill since Asher likes their cologne, Black."

My eyes meet hers. "Maybe this is a bad idea."

"Stop. Let's just go have some fun. You remember what fun is right? Two college girls, hanging out, not worrying about anything other than what they're doing in the moment," Abby says.

I smile. "You're right. What could possibly put a damper on this outing?"

Four hours of bra and panty shopping with Abby. That's what could put a damper on this outing. Not to mention, Abby dropped an obscene amount of money on the half dozen or so items she forced me to buy.

After the intimates' agony, she moved me onto shoe, chocolate and cologne torment. The good news though, each store will deliver our purchases right to the flat so I don't have to carry bags around with me. Yippee. Yep, it's been like that today.

Finally, after quite a bit of whining, we're walking home from picking up a few groceries. I inhale, enjoying the cool fresh air. Allowing myself to bask in the feeling of doing something ordinary. In this moment, I can pretend I'm just on vacation as a normal college student.

"Is it getting easier?" Abby asks, breaking my reverie.

"What?" I give a sideways glance.

"The ascension. Aria. Living with gargoyles. Take your pick," she laughs.

I'm silent for a moment. "I miss her every day. Time's starting to heal the void, but I don't think it will ever be painless." I shrug. "The ascension is slow going, so it's been a little bit easier to swallow." I sigh. "You gargoyles, on the other hand, are a fucking nightmare," I tease, bumping her shoulder with mine.

We both start laughing as we walk through the garage toward the elevator. Before I can hit the button a female voice startles us. "I would have to agree, daughter of Heaven. The London clan is a fucking nightmare to deal with."

Abby and I turn around and place the grocery bags by our feet. I speak in a loud, menacing voice, hoping Asher or one of the other St. Michaels will hear us.

"Who are you?" I ask the tall, skinny, older woman standing in front of us with deep black-brown eyes and short grey hair cut in an elegant bob.

"Dimia. Deacon and Kaiden's mother, and Lucifer's playmate," Abby answers for her.

At that introduction, Dimia's eyes grow black with fury. "Mate. I am his mate."

Abby lets out a short laugh. "Right. Sorry, she's ONE of Lucifer's mates," she taunts.

Dimia flashes her coal irises at me and gives me a creepy smile. "So, you're what all the fuss is about? Why my son is in war mode? And why my other son no longer exists?"

I cross my arms and tilt my chin up. "Yes."

The side of her mouth tips up, the smile not reaching her eyes as she begins to chant in Latin. I can't make out what she's saying, but Abby stills. Well, shit. That can't be good.

"Dimia." Abby gives a loud warning.

"It's futile to try and get the others to help you. I've broken your enchantment and put up a barrier shield," she explains with her eyes in slits.

"Shit," Abby exclaims.

Dimia turns her attention to me. "I suspect you have the daggers on you that killed my son. I look forward to using them to return the favor," she states coolly.

"As you are aware, Royal Gargoyle Council of Protector laws state you are not allowed to harm a human," Abby counters with force.

"I am aware of the rules," the woman spits with evil dripping from her lips.

Without warning, I see Keegan and McKenna appear behind Dimia. I can feel Asher behind me and I'm guessing Callan is next to him. McKenna looks furious and worried at the same time. Keegan is pale, but calm and in control as he scans me for any sign of trauma.

"Dimia. What can we do for you?" Keegan asks, composed.

"Well, Keegan dear, you see, your human killed my son. I'm very torn up about it. The only thing that will ease my broken heart is to have her heart beating in my hand," she answers with an even voice and without turning to face him.

"Not going to happen," Asher rebukes.

"Oh, it will, dark prince. You see, my son will hand her over to Lucifer or there will be war. Either way, Deacon wins. In the meantime, I plan on taking her heart the way she did mine when she destroyed Kaiden," Dimia spits out with hatred laced in her voice.

From my peripheral vision, I see Abby close her eyes, attempting to wield energy. Having no idea what she's planning, I decide it's best to take out my daggers. The metal clinks with my movement and I hear Asher hit the invisible barrier behind me. He says my name in a warning.

This time, I don't look at him. Unlike the situation with Aria, I keep my focus on Dimia as she steps toward me, chanting under her breath in Latin. I can't make out the words but it sounds like she's creating a spell. My eyes shift to Abby, pleading with her in my head to hurry.

Over Dimia's shoulder, I see Keegan pull out a sword. McKenna's eyes never leave me. Both have their wings out. I can only assume Asher and Callan do as well.

Suddenly, my arms rise of their own accord and release my daggers before they hit the pavement with a clatter and slide across the concrete to Dimia. She watches me with an ominous smile on her face and picks them up.

"You're no match for demonic magic, little girl."

"You want me? Come get me," I taunt, trying to buy Abby a few more seconds.

Dimia narrows her almost black eyes at me. "Tsk. So quick to threaten." She taps one of my daggers on her lip in contemplation. "I'm assuming, since you're human, you have affection for all of them." She waves the dagger around toward the clan.

"Your point?" I demand.

She laughs wickedly before dropping her voice to a low, evil tone. "I wonder, daughter of Heaven, which one will survive? Which one holds your heart strings around their finger?"

Just then, Abby produces a loud sonic boom, which has us all turning away, covering our ears and squinting our eyes. The sound shatters the barrier and the rest of the clan comes running towards us.

Once the sound waves have ended, I stand, opening my eyes to witness Dimia within a breath of Abby. My dagger is pointed at Abby's chest. Everyone stills. Two steps, and the dagger will pierce Abby's heart, turning her to stone.

Abby swallows as Dimia turns her threatening smile toward me. She whispers harshly, "Which one, little girl?"

I panic. Without thinking, I run in front of Abby as Dimia lunges for her, only to be pushed out of the way a millisecond later by a large body. I hit the ground hard and snap my head up. Just in time to see Dimia thrust my dagger into Asher's heart. His eyes are furious as crimson liquid trickles down the front of his white t-shirt, tainting its pure color.

"An eye for an eye, little girl. You took someone I love, so I took your heart away. I sensed your love for your protector, a gift of mine. My son will be back to give you to Lucifer," she warns before Keegan plunges Asher's Angelic Sword into her back. The weapon rips through her heart and protrudes out the front of her chest.

Dimia's face disfigures in shock as she slowly begins to turn into crumbling stone while the light breeze from the garage opening blows away the dust remains.

Asher's knees and palms hit the floor in slow motion and I crawl over to him, whispering his name, over and over again. *Oh God. This can't be happening.* I tell myself he's fine and if I just keep saying his name, it will all be okay.

I make it to him and grab his body. With a moan, he rolls onto his back, lying on the concrete. His black wings are lifeless. Asher's breathing is labored and his face ashen.

His lips are white as his eyes meet mine. I can tell he's in excruciating pain as he lifts his hands to my cheeks, pulling me down to his face. He exhales and with his last breath says, "You okay, siren?"

A loud and painful whimper comes from my throat. "Yes. Please stay with me," I beg in a hysterical voice while fisting his t-shirt. "I need you. Don't leave me." My tears drip on his face as his eyes roll back then close and his body goes limp.

"No. No. No. Asher? Ash? Come on, pretty boy. Come back to me. Asher?" I say over and over again. In desperation, I lay myself on top of his chest and begin to bawl uncontrollably as my heart shatters and my body shakes violently.

"Eves," Callan kneels down next to me. "Eves, we need to move him okay? I need you to let him go." Callan speaks softly while placing his hands on top of mine in an attempt to get me to release my hold on Asher's shirt.

My head snaps up at him. "No," I bark firmly and a deep pain rises in my throat.

Abby's tear stained face comes into view next to Callan. "Sweetie, you need to let Keegan and Callan tend to him. I promise you won't be far from him."

I shake my head wildly. "I can't."

Callan and Abby look at one another before McKenna squats in front of me, taking my face gently in her palms.

"Eve. Look at me," she commands.

I don't. I can't get my body to stop shaking, or my emotions controlled enough to focus.

McKenna's voice is even and calm. "Eve. I said, look. At. Me."

I lift my eyes and meet her compelling ones. "Good girl. Now listen very carefully to what I have to say. Asher is hurt. We need to get him back to Wiltshire and get him in the chamber immediately so he can begin to heal. Do you understand me?"

I hold her eyes. "W-What?" It comes out in between sobbing breaths.

"He is hurt. See." She guides my face down with her hands to look at Asher and then with great care, lifts it back up to meet her gaze once again. "He's not stone, Eve. But he's injured. He needs to be placed in stone state to heal. That requires Keegan and Callan to move him. You have to let go so they can do that. Once he's in his stone state bed, we will let you be by his side during his healing sleep. Do you understand me?"

Slowly it begins to sink in. He didn't turn to stone. She pierced his heart and he's still here. *Oh. My. God.* Once I fully absorb what she's saying, I move my head up and down adamantly. Still cupping my face and maintaining eye contact, she stands us both up and moves us away from Asher.

"Take him," she orders in a firm voice, still focusing on me.

My eyes flick down to his lifeless body. "Look at me," McKenna commands, causing my gaze to snap back to her. "We're going to fix him. You need to be strong, Eve. For him."

I nod. Keegan kneels next to Asher. "Abby, you and I will take him back to the manor and get him sorted out. Callan, you and Kenna follow with Eve in the Escalade."

Abby moves toward Asher. Keegan lifts him with ease, bringing him to the gargage opening and shoots up into the air, disappearing with Abby following.

Once they're out of sight, McKenna drops her hands from my face. "All right. Let's take a breath and get into the car. We'll explain everything once we're on our way to Wiltshire. Callan, stay here with Eve while I bring the vehicle around."

As McKenna leaves, Callan walks up to me and wipes my tears away with his thumbs, which only brings more tears. The tender gesture reminds me of something Asher would do. He pulls me into an embrace as I quietly sob into his chest. "I know, cutie. I know."

The entire drive back to Wiltshire, I cling to Callan in the backseat while McKenna drives. Once I've managed to get my emotions somewhat in check, I swallow the painful lump in my throat.

"Explain why he didn't turn to stone," I say on a choke.

Callan shifts me up off his shoulder so he can look at me, but not before McKenna meets his gaze in the rearview mirror. He nods at her before speaking in a low voice.

"Gargoyles, like demons and angels, don't have a soul. We're created for a specific purpose. To protect. Once our purpose is over, we cease to exist. In order for Asher's soulless body to accept your pure blood, he also had to be injected with demon, dark blood, for balance. Therefore, like half-demon, half-gargoyles, he can only cease to exist or be turned into stone petrifaction by the Angelic Sword or while in stone state," Callan explains in a low, soothing tone.

I close my eyes and inhale. "So, that's what he meant when he said there is only darkness behind his eyes."

Confusion flitters across Callan's face. "When did he say that?"

184

"Never mind." I brush it off, figuring Asher doesn't want me sharing that. "So he'll heal and be okay?"

"Yes. But it will take a while. He'll most likely be in stone state for a few days," he explains.

"I don't care." A sob escapes me. "I just want him back," I whisper.

Callan snags me in his arms. "He'll come back to you. I swear, cutie."

The minute we pull up to the manor, I have the car door open and I'm running into the house with Callan and McKenna at my heels. I sprint into the library and wait for them to catch up. Callan takes off his shirt and stands in front of the dragon statue so it can scan his tattoo. Once the floorboards open, I take off down the stone stairs.

I enter the chamber to see Keegan, Abby and Fiona standing around Asher's stone state bed. The black silk fabric is pulled down, concealing him.

Keegan walks over to me, and in an odd showing of emotion, places his hands on my arms. "He's sleeping. Fiona cleaned him up and dressed the wound. Now we wait." I swear his voice cracked a bit.

"I don't want to leave him alone."

"Eve, I understand, but his wound was deep. I'm not sure how long he will need to fully heal," Keegan says in a gentle tone.

I raise my gaze stubbornly at him. "I don't care. I want to be by his side the entire time. When he wakes up, I need to be the first thing he sees."

Keegan shifts his eyes to McKenna who is standing next to me. Something passes between them and his expression softens. "All right. I'll make a deal with you.

You allow Fiona and Abby to get you cleaned up and you can stay with him when you're not sleeping, eating or training."

My eyes begin to water. "Deal."

Keegan nods once. "Deal."

"Come, luv. Let's get ye all tidied up." Fiona takes my arm gently.

"I'd like to see him before I do," I state, my voice timid.

Fiona eyeballs my blood stained shirt, untamed hair, blood shot swollen eyes and dirt covered arms and hands before flicking her cat eyes to Keegan.

He sighs his agreement and she steps aside.

Abby moves one of the black fabric pieces to the side and my gaze roams over Asher's still body, now completely clean. He looks so peaceful when he's sleeping. I let out a shaky breath and force back the tears. He's okay. I tell myself over and over again.

I walk over and allow the palm of my hand to caress the stubble on his jawline. Leaning down, I place a small kiss on his cheek and whisper in his ear. "I would give up everything for just another moment with you."

Fiona leads me out of the chamber with Abby and, to my surprise, McKenna in tow. They bring me to my room in the manor. Fiona starts the shower while Abby pulls out some pajamas and places them on the counter. McKenna sits on the bed, observing me from a distance. I just stand there watching, my body numb from tonight's events.

As soon as the water is to Fiona's liking, she motions for me to get in before allowing me privacy. I automatically undress and slide into the warm stream. After a bit, I dry off and get into my tank top and flannel pajama bottoms. Abby enters and brushes and blows out my hair while I focus on breathing and keeping my emotions in check.

Once pulled together, McKenna moves closer to me, looking me in the eye. She stands tall and pushes her shoulders back before clearing her throat. "No matter what happens, we will take care of you and protect you, always."

My water-filled eyes flick to hers.

"Thank you," I whisper.

She offers a small smile before it slips. "Come on. I'll take you back to him."

I inhale, and swallow the tears before they leak out. Standing taller, I follow McKenna, allowing her to lead me back to Asher.

Randi Cooley Wilson

15 Stone State

I brush a piece of the black silk curtain aside and examine the bed. Memories of the last time Asher and I were in here infuse my mind. I close my eyes and immerse myself in the flashes of Asher's face as he watched me come down from my blissful state. A small smile touches my lips at the memory.

With great care not to disturb him, I crawl onto the bed and hover over his face, taking in his good looks. I lean down and brush my lips against his unmoving ones, silently thanking whomever will listen that he's still alive before I position myself under the covers. Needing to feel him, I curl into his side, hugging his arm. I could swear I heard him sigh in contentment.

I close my eyes and drift asleep.

"Open your eyes, siren." Asher's voice rattles me.

"Asher?" I murmur, stunned.

He chuckles. "Who else would it be?"

At the sound of his laughter, I open my eyes to see him positioned above me. Eyes twinkling as he bites his lip.

Shocked at the sight of him, my hands cup his face.

"Oh. My. God. Asher."

He lets out a low grunt. "It's so fucking hot when you say that." He briefly closes his eyes. When they reopen, the blue hue is darker.

A tear escapes my eye as he follows it, pulling his brows together. "I never thought I would see you again," I choke out.

He brushes the damp bead away with his thumb. "Don't ever think that. I will always come for you."

"Is this real? Am I dreaming?" My voice is barely above a whisper.

His mouth tilts in a mischievous smile. "Are you telling me that you dream of me?"

I roll my eyes. "Hardly."

He raises his brows. "Hardly, huh? I guess we'll have to change that."

Watching me, he leans into my neck as his lips graze my skin. I sigh at the contact. The tip of his tongue flicks over my pulse as my body jerks from the touch. He releases an appreciative sound in response.

In a muted whisper, he says, "Prepare yourself, siren. I'm about to take your breath away."

My mouth goes dry and I wet my lips. Inch by slow inch, his lips close the distance between us. The first stroke causes a pulse to shoot through each corner of my body. He tilts his head, deepening the kiss as my heart begins to pound with each caress.

I try to hold back the rest of the tears that are threatening to come. I never thought I would feel his lips move against mine again. Sensing the change in my emotions, Asher stills and lifts his head.

His eyes lock onto mine.

"What's wrong?" His knuckle brushes my cheek.

"I'm in deep with you," I admit quietly.

He doesn't react, just watches me with an intense stare. "When I wake up, I plan to bury myself so deep inside of you that I might never find my way out."

Before I could think about my actions, I lift my hands to his face and run them over his jawline and then entangle them in his hair, pulling him back to me. I lift my lips as he fuses his to mine. A small moan escapes me as he presses his body firmly against mine, pinning me in place. His knee bends in between my legs, forcing mine to fall open.

Wait. What did he say?

"Asher?" I breathe out against his lips.

"Siren?" He pants.

"Wait. Wait a second." I push against his chest to get his attention.

He lifts his head, concern marring his face. "What's wrong?"

My eyes dart to where my hand is over his heart. Where the protector mark is. Where Dimia stabbed him. "You said, when I wake up. What's going on? Where are we?"

He follows my line of vision to my hand resting over his heart. "Don't freak out."

My eyes snap back to his. "Asher."

"We're in stone state. Dream walking," he replies, watching my reaction.

I sit up, forcing him to sit back on his heels.

"So this isn't real?"

"No, Eve, it's very real. When you and I are in stone state, our bond allows us to reach out and interact with one another mentally when we aren't able to physically. Everything that happens here is actual, I swear to you." All I see is honesty in his eyes.

I fist his shirt in my hands. "I need you. Wake up, please."

His face softens as he rubs my arms up and down in a soothing motion. "Soon. I swear. I'm okay, just healing. Dimia pierced me pretty far with the dagger."

My eyes glisten with tears. "Why did you push me out of the way? You would be okay if you just let me jump in front of Abby."

A growl resonates out of his throat. "It's my job to protect you. No matter what the end result. You're my first priority, Eve. I will protect you, always."

"I thought you were dead. My heart..." I place my hand over my heart and rub the ache.

He takes my chin between his fingers and lifts my head. "Hey, I'M OKAY. Just healing. When I wake up, I'll be better than I was before, I promise."

"Callan told me about the demon blood," I say with caution.

His face unreadable, he nods once. "We'll have that conversation once I've fully recovered."

"Can I stay here with you in the dream walk until you wake up?"

"Not for much longer. It takes energy for me to heal and to dream walk. If I stay in this state, I can't focus that strength into healing," he answers with sadness.

My eyes widen in panic. "What the hell, Asher! Then I need to leave so you can heal."

He chuckles. "I wanted to see you and assure you I am okay." He swallows and looks away. "I heard you screaming for me after I was wounded. It nearly killed me. Even though my eyes are closed, I can hear." His eyes lock into mine. "I heard every one of your cries, every plea, everything."

"Then you know I need you. Let me leave so you can heal," I demand with strength in my tone.

He nods his head in agreement before pulling me to him and kissing my lips with unspoken words.

I pull away a bit. "Oh. My. God. Asher, you were going to sleep with me in a dream walk?"

He bestows his sexy smirk. "Siren, we're already sleeping together." All of a sudden, his face gets serious. "When you give me that gift, I plan on both of us being awake to enjoy it."

I blush. His thumb brushes across the coloring. "I love when you blush. It's so fucking adorable."

I narrow my eyes at him. "All right, gargoyle. I should go. How do we do this?"

"We'll snuggle and fall asleep. You'll wake up when you're ready and so will I."

I just stare at him. "I'm scared you won't wake up."

He takes my cheeks in his palms. "I swear to you, I will." Then he places one last kiss on my lips before pulling me into his arms and I inhale him.

"I'll be the first thing you see when you awake," I vow against his neck.

He chuckles. "I should hope so. When I do, I'll have lots of energy to burn in this big bed," he jokes before dropping his voice to a low, seductive tone. "Plus, I'm still very anxious to see what else that sharp tongue of yours can do."

I groan in embarrassment and hide my face in his side.

"Oh. My. God. Asher."

"I love when you say that, it's so fucking hot," he teases again. "Do me a favor and don't tell the clan that I can hear them. I'd like to see what they have to say, yeah?"

He drops a kiss on the top of my head. Before I can reply, I jolt awake and look to my left to see Asher's sleeping body.

"Do you see now why I told you to be strong?" McKenna's voice hits me from the end of the bed. She narrows her eyes at me. "Don't pretend you didn't dream walk. I'm mated, remember."

"How long was I out for?" I ignore her accurate assessment.

"About ten hours."

"Really?"

"Yep. Keegan sent me down here. He wants you to get up, eat breakfast, shower and meet him in the training room. You can come back later tonight after you take care of yourself," she orders.

"Take care of myself?" I repeat, not understanding why it's a priority.

"I know he can hear me, so heed my warning, blood of Eden. He needs you to be strong for him, to help him heal.

You flourish off of one another's abilities. He's given you the gift of healing, so when you're near him, you pass on some of your healing abilities to him. The more you do it, the faster he'll recover. But you need to be sure you're healthy. Rested. Fed. Strong. Do you understand?"

I push my shoulders back. "Yes."

"Good. Now, I'm on babysitting duty. I have a lot to say without him mouthing off to me. So for fucks sake, get going before I have to deal with Keegan this morning," she snips. *Nice to see the old McKenna is back.*

I make my way to the stairs and stop before I begin to climb them. I turn around one last time.

"McKenna?"

"What?" she barks, annoyed that I'm bothering her.

"Thank you."

Her lips tilt into a tight smile. "Well, someone had to snap your sorry ass out of it."

I grin back. "I'm glad it was you."

As I ascend the stairs, I feel ten pounds lighter.

"We're still not friends." She calls out to me.

"We'll see," I sing and head to start my day.

Once upstairs, Fiona steps in my path. "Mornin', luv. How's da lad doin'?"

I smile. "Good. He's healing."

She assesses me. "I trust ye visit with him 'twas nice?"

I arch a brow at her. "Yes, Fi." *Does everyone know?*

She claps her hands together. "Delightful. Come and get ye some breakfast before dose der animals eat me outta me supply."

Fiona pushes me toward the kitchen and forces me down by my shoulders into a chair before placing a small buffet in front of me.

Callan comes in, followed by Abby and Keegan. They all plop down around me and start digging in.

"How is he?" Callan asks, giving me a side-glance.

"Same," I offer with a casual shrug.

He smirks. Damn gargoyle already knows I'm able to dream walk. Keegan pulls out a piece of paper and slides it over to me. "What's this?" I question.

Keegan grins. "Read it."

I open the letter and skim it. "Is this a joke?"

Callan claps his hands together once then rubs them in pleasure. "Nope."

"In the event I no longer am capable of protecting Eve Collins, she is still to be put through twelve hours of training each day?" I look around at the group.

They're all holding back laughs. "That's what he wrote." Keegan points to the paper.

I narrow my eyes. "You mean to tell me Asher left instructions for you in case something happened to him and one of those line items is for me to continue to train?"

"I believe that is what the letter states. See, he signed, dated and time stamped it here." Callan points to those items.

"You all suck. So while he gets to sleep the day away, I have to train with you?" I pout.

"Not just us. Tadhg is back too!" Abby squeals.

My shoulders sag. "Awesome."

After breakfast, a quick shower and a brief check-in on Asher, I head to the training room.

"Hello, Eve," Tadhg greets me with a big hug. "How's he doin'?"

"Getting stronger. How's Leo?"

"Same. 'Tis hard on 'em," Tadhg offers. "He's missin' da lass sumtin' fierce."

I swallow down the reminder of Aria and how this mess has caused so much heartache.

"All right, cutie, get your ass on the treadmill," Callan teases. He's clearly enjoying himself.

I scowl at him. "Fine."

After warming up, Callan leads me to the mat where Keegan and Tadhg are both waiting. "Weapons training today, Eve." Keegan flips his wrists. Lying in each palm are my daggers, the ones that pierced Asher's heart.

I shrink away.

Keegan frowns, eyeing me as I back away.

His hands hang in the air. "Eve?"

I force myself to swallow. "I...I c-can't."

Tadhg steps forward. "Eve, lass. 'Tis okay. 'Tis hard. Asher wants ye ta practice wit dem."

My hands start to shake. "I'm not ready."

Callan gets closer. "You need to face it head on, cutie."

I close my eyes to keep my breathing in check. "No. I'm not ready," I repeat.

Callan shifts his worried gaze to Keegan who drops his hands and walks the weapons back to a table behind him, placing them down.

"Eve, 'tis okay, luv. Not taday." Tadhg bends so he's eye-to-eye with me.

I can't catch my breath to answer him. Instead, I offer a curt nod as a sudden sharp sting hits my chest above my heart, causing me to cry out in pain.

Callan runs over. "Eves?"

I drop to my knees, my heart clenching itself into a knot. All the blood drains from Callan's face as I try to pull in oxygen. The pain travels from my heart to each limb in a punishing manner.

"Asher," I manage to get out.

Keegan picks me up and turns to Callan "Let's get her down to Asher. Something's not right."

Callan takes a step back, allowing Keegan to pass with me to the chamber. As soon as we enter the room, Fiona runs over. She must have been with Asher while I was upstairs.

"By de grace, what 'tis wrong?" she inquires.

Keegan places me on the bed beside Asher. He takes in a deep breath then releases it through his nose. "We're not sure."

As soon as I lay down, the pain subsides. I signal to Keegan I'm okay and try to keep my expression neutral as he steps back and I close the curtain.

Feeling better, I exhale before turning to Asher. Whatever happened, I know he felt it or sent it to me. "I'm here, pretty boy," I say, caressing his cheek.

At my announcement, warmth starts to fill my veins. I know he's pushing it to me. I smile and snuggle into Asher's side. "I'm okay. Keegan wanted me to use the daggers and I wasn't ready. That's all. I swear I'm alright."

"Eves. You okay?" Callan asks through the silk fabric.

"Fine. I just want to spend some time alone with Asher."

Callan pauses then agrees. I listen for their footsteps as they retreat. "I'm going to close my eyes but don't pull me into the dream walk. I want you to use the energy to heal. I promise I'm alright," I say to Asher's sleeping form.

I slip out of my sneakers and throw them off the bed, repositioning myself back into his side. I close my eyes and let slumber pull me under in contentment.

"You have a listening problem," I state heatedly.

Asher just stares down at me, his eyes gleaming with anger. "What the fuck happened? I felt you panic all of the sudden. Are you hurt?"

"Did you make that stinging sensation over my heart, where you got stabbed, so I would know to come to you?" I accuse.

He cocks his head to the side as a smile forms on his lips. "Did it work?"

I throw my hands up in frustration. "Yes, it worked, you ass. And it was painful."

A curious expression settles on his striking face. "Oops, sorry. I just meant for you to feel a twinge so you'd know I wanted you."

"Well, here I am."

His gaze drifts up me slowly. "Yes, here you are, siren."

"Snap out of it. I told you not to pull me in, because I'm fine. I don't want you wasting energy on this," I bark.

"Talk to me." His voice is edged in concern.

"Keegan wanted me to use the daggers. I wasn't ready."

He glances down at me, his brows knit in confusion.

"That's it?"

"Yes, that is it. I don't want to pick up something that hurt you." My gaze shifts to his heart.

"When I wake up, we'll do it together," he says without hesitation.

I swallow hard. "Okay. Then wake up already," I demand.

He laughs then bites down on his lower lip as his eyes pierce mine. He inches closer and lowers his voice. "Kiss me and I'll wake up."

I narrow my eyes. "Seriously? Who are you, *Sleeping Beauty*?"

His grin spreads. "I want you to kiss me, siren. You've never done it."

"I've kissed you before."

"No. I've kissed you and you've kissed me back," he argues.

I groan into the pillow. "Fine. If I kiss you, will you stop wasting energy?"

"Depends."

"On?"

His eyes dip down and run the length of me before returning to mine. "On how good of a kiss it is. Convince me you want me to wake up."

"Fine. Take off your shirt and lay down," I instruct.

Asher throws me a wink and a smile. "Kinky, siren. I like it," he teases while pulling off his shirt then lays back.

Swallowing my nerves, I straddle him and his gaze clouds with desire. Slowly, I lean in so my mouth is a breath away from his lips. My fingers travel across his jaw, down his throat and over his bare chest, leaving a trail of goose bumps on his skin.

His eyes close in pleasure. "Open your eyes, Ash." He does, watching my every move through hooded lids.

I leisurely dip my head and place a path of light kisses down his neck, causing him to moan.

Once I reach his chest, he fists his hands in my hair as I move my lips over the place where he was stabbed, right through the protector tattoo. My heart clenches at the realization. It's already healed but there's a small scar in between the dragon and fire.

I lift my gaze and peer at him through my lashes. His serious stare drops to my lips as I let them fall little by little onto the wound, kissing it. I push everything I feel for him into the touch. The hands tangled in my hair tighten at the intensity of the contact.

I let my tongue dart out, tasting him then outlining the protector tattoo with it before returning my lips to kiss the scar. After a few moments of allowing my mouth to press on his tattoo, Asher tugs my hair, forcing my head up and bringing me forward to kiss his lips. Devouring me with so much pressure, I swear he's trying to breathe me in.

The kiss lasts forever, yet not long enough. He pulls away panting. "No one has ever, ever, fucking kissed me so sensually before. Best. Kiss. Ever."

"Yeah?"

"Yeah."

"Good. Now let me go back and you wake up."

"Done." He pulls me into his side and curls his body around mine kissing the top of my head. "See you soon, siren."

Randi Cooley Wilson

16 Flames

I'm not sure what I was expecting when I woke up, but to be truthful, I didn't really anticipate Asher's blue irises watching me. At the awareness he's awake, I bolt straight up and literally jump on him. I wrap my arms and legs around his muscular body so tightly if I don't let up, we might morph into one person.

"Holy shit, you really are Sleeping Beauty," I whisper, stunned.

He chuckles. "Well, thank goodness I found my princess then." After the words leave his mouth, he stills for a brief moment.

Unsure of what happened, I pull back and scan his face, letting my hands roam over it, memorizing each line and plane. "It's so good to see you awake again. I didn't think..." My throat tightens, and I let my voice trail off.

Asher leans forward and places a searing kiss on my lips. "I'll always come back to you, siren."

The declaration causes my heart to take flight and I squeeze him even harder. "So much for us showing restraint." I groan.

Asher shrugs casually. "Restraint is overrated. Kissing you is much more fun," he retorts, wiggling his eyebrows.

"Fun, but against the rules," I remind him.

He looks behind me for what feels like forever before speaking. "I don't care right now. I'm done trying to stay away."

I smile. "Good, because I'm yours if you'll have me."

His rumble is deep. "Oh, I'll have you alright."

I giggle at his playfulness as he leans in, kissing me one more time before we hear Callan.

"Eves? Hey listen, we need you to come upstairs. Gage is here, and he has news."

Asher and I both freeze. For Gage to come here, something bad must be happening.

"I'll be right there," I answer, my eyes locked with Asher's.

"All right. We're in the sitting room. Oh, and bring the gargoyle you're lip locking with. We miss the bastard," he teases and the pink tint forms on my cheeks.

"How does he know?" I inquire in a low voice, unable to mask my mortification.

Asher laughs. "It's a gargoyle thing. Come on, siren. Let's go see what Gage wants." His name rolls with disgust off Asher's lips.

I get off the bed and watch Asher stand up.

"Wait." I panic.

"What?"

"Are you okay? I mean…should you be standing?"

His eyes twinkle. "Siren, I've just spent like three days in stone state. I could build a house with all the energy I have now. I'm good, I swear. Better than before."

I stare at his chest. "The scar? Is it permanent?"

He wraps his arms around my waist. "Yes. Just like you. Forever."

I scan his face. Crap, I'm in so much trouble.

"Forever?"

He dips his chin and brushes the hair off my face with his hands. "It's your mark. Each time I look at it, it will remind me how grateful I am that you're safe."

My knees go weak. "If you keep saying things like that to me, we may never leave this chamber."

A raw sound grumbles in his chest as he catches my lips with his. Branding me, marking me as his. "I warned you already, the only thing that isn't safe around me is your virtue."

I lace my fingers with his, tugging him toward the stone stairs. "Let's go see what Gage wants." My nerves start to go crazy once we reach the last step. I haven't seen Gage since he saved me from Saraphina.

Once in the library, Asher closes the chamber opening before he lets go of my hand to greet Callan and Keegan.

Callan walks up to Asher and embraces him tightly.

"It's good to see you up, man."

"It's good to be up," Asher responds.

Keegan does the same, only his hug is stiff as he pats Asher on the back. "You okay, brother?"

Asher blows out a breath, nodding. "I'm fine and ready to see what Gage Gallagher wants." At the mention of Gage's name, I feel my knees tremble, and I know I need to sit down.

"He's waiting with the ladies," Callan rubs his jawline.

Asher shifts his eyes to me and reaches out his hand. I squirm as my gaze darts from him to Callan then Keegan before placing my hand in his.

"I'm formally making the clan aware that Eve is mine. I'd like to keep it between the four of us until we get things worked out with Michael and the ascension. But make no mistake, she belongs to me and is privy to all that comes with the designation."

At his proclamation, my entire body glows with hope and a shiver of excitement runs down my spine.

"As if this is breaking news?" Callan laughs to himself.

With a curt nod, Keegan motions for us to head toward the sitting room. Once in the hallway, we see McKenna, guarding the door. She stands straighter when she sees us.

"It's good to see you awake, Ash."

He pulls her into a hug and whispers his gratitude to her. For what, I didn't hear. At his words, she fidgets uncomfortably and steps away, schooling her face.

"The traitor is in with Abby."

The five of us enter only to have Abby throw herself at Asher in a deep embrace. "It's so good to see you. Thank you for saving me," she sighs before releasing him and pecking his cheek with a light kiss then winking at me.

Gage is standing near the fireplace with his back to us. He's dressed in his usual black attire. At the commotion, he turns and locks eyes with me. A sensation I can't describe overwhelms me and I inhale sharply.

Asher must have interpreted my emotions as anxiety because he pulls me behind him in a protective stance.

"Gage." Asher's tone is inhospitable.

"Keegan, Callan and Asher." Gage greets them before turning to me. "Love." At his voice, my stomach does a nosedive.

Keegan steps forward and a low growling sound of disapproval releases from deep within his chest. "Protocol states that when greeting your pri-" Asher interrupts his directive.

"What do you want, Gage?" Asher's voice is cold and distant.

"Nice to see you too, Your Highness." Gage smirks, amused at the jab. "I'm here with a warning."

Callan scoffs. "Why?"

Gage trains his eyes on me as Asher steps into his line of sight, blocking me from view. "Lucifer is unhappy that one of you killed Dimia, his favorite mate. The pain and utter devastation caused by the death of one's mate pushes one to do the unthinkable."

At his words, I hold my breath. He continues. "He was on a war path before in order to gain control over the supernatural world. Now, it's completely spiraling out of control."

"Why are you telling us this?" Asher's demeanor is cool and aloof.

Gage smiles but it's not friendly as he levels his stare at Asher. "I owe Deacon a favor for Camilla. I intend to pay him back. The rest of the drama doesn't interest me. Your clan's actions in London have set off a full-blown war. Lucifer has stepped up his deadlines and the dark army's efforts, placing your beautiful charge in even greater danger. Your kin killed a gargoyle and demon mate."

"Shit." Callan blows out on an exhale.

"Not only is the underworld gunning for Eve but they'll see to it that she suffers, for your actions. They'll make sure you all do. You have no idea the level of evil you're dealing with or what kind of flood gates Dimia's death has opened." Gage's words are firm. "I suggest you get your end game together, old friend. Heed my warning. It's the only one you'll get from me."

Asher bristles at his last statement. Gage walks right past us to the door. Before he exits, he throws over his shoulder, "We're even now, prince. Consider my debt to you paid." Then he vanishes.

It feels like everyone exhales at the same time. Asher slides his glance to me. "We've got this. Don't worry." I stand tall, trying to emanate strength and not show my fear.

Holy shit, I'm fucked.

Keegan steps to Asher's side. "We should head back to London and regroup with the other clans, as well as Michael."

"It might also be time to bring the councils in," Callan suggests.

"Agreed," Asher replies.

"Let's do this," Callan exclaims and we all make our way to the Escalade.

Asher leans into my ear and drops his voice to a low murmur. "Listen, don't get pissed, but I think it's best if you wait at my place with Abby and Kenna. We'll most likely be meeting with the other clans, Michael, and key members from both the Angelic Council and the Royal Council of Protectors when we return. I'd rather them not pick up on any signals we might inadvertently give off that we're more than a protector and charge."

I snap my eyes from the rolling scenery to his face. "Shouldn't I be involved in these meetings if they're about me?"

He shakes his head. "Strategy." He twists his body towards me and picks up a strand of my hair, playing with it. "You're mine, siren. But they can't know that yet. We need to get through this war, your ascension and anything else that comes up before we take on the councils and fight for one another. I promise the day will come when I lay my sword at your feet and everyone in the world knows you belong with me. For now, we need to keep it low key."

My lips move to argue but Keegan announces we're back at the flats in London. As we pull into the garage, my eyes are drawn to the spot where Asher was lying lifeless. Memories of his body bleeding out flood me, reminding me of what could happen if we don't follow the rules. My heart shatters in my chest. I couldn't survive anything happening to him.

"Okay," I consent and I feel his entire body relax.

He kisses my temple. "Thank you."

෧ඁ෧

"Focus, Eve. This is extremely important." Abby scolds, her face serious.

"Yeah, blood of Eden. Don't fuck this up," McKenna adds, her arms crossed.

"Fine," I grit out.

"Come on, you've got this," Abby encourages.

"*Eternal Sunshine of the Spotless Mind, Before Sunrise/Before Sunset/Before Midnight* and *Endless Love.* In that order too." I direct.

Abby slaps her hands and rubs them together. "Good movie choices for girls' time. Kenna, get the door. That's the food," she orders.

A few minutes later, McKenna strolls back into the room. The scent of pizza and French fries follows her, causing my stomach to grumble. Abby made us do manicures and pedicures then get into our pajamas and now we're all snuggled into the couch for a romantic movie marathon coupled with lots of greasy food. Her plan is to keep me busy so I won't focus on the supernatural and divine conference going on downstairs without me. I hate to admit it, but it's working.

"A little birdie told me Asher declared you," Abby says off handed.

"Would this little birdie be named Callan?" I ask.

She giggles. He's such a gossip girl.

I cock my head. "I was under the impression Asher asked them to keep it quiet."

"Nothing in this clan is a secret," McKenna counters.

"In that case, can I ask you both a question?"

"Sure," Abby answers brightly.

"If Asher's dad, Garrick, was the king of the gargoyle community, why isn't Asher king now?"

Abby swallows and shifts her focus to McKenna before turning back to me. "He has to prove himself worthy of the appointed title before he's sworn in."

"Prove himself how?" I question, not truly wanting to know the answer.

Silence.

"How?" I ask again.

"By showing his loyalty, duty and respect to our kin," Abby answers cautiously.

"And how is that accomplished?"

I put down my slice of cheese pizza.

"By agreeing to the ultimate undertaking. Protect the daughter of Heaven," McKenna answers.

I exhale loudly.

"Don't panic. It's all going to work out the way it's supposed to, Eve." Abby pats my knee.

At her words, I avert my gaze, my face paling. "That's what Aria said right before she threw herself onto Deacon's sword." My voice is hoarse.

Abby's eyes go wide. "Oh, Eve. I'm sorry. I didn't mean…" Her voice trails off.

I close my eyes and reopen them. "No, it's fine. Let's start the movies."

McKenna and Abby give one another a sharp glance then return their gazes to the flat screen before we drown our attention in love stories that have happily ever afters.

꙰

A warm mouth moves down my throat, leaving a burning sensation in its path as I arch into the chest that's making a low rumbling sound. Strong arms wrap around my waist, pulling me closer to the powerful gargoyle kneeling down in front of me, positioning his body between my legs, forcing each limb to wrap around him.

"Where are Abby and McKenna?"

My eyes are still closed.

Asher runs his nose along my jawline. "They left a little while ago. You fell asleep," he murmurs against my throat, his breath warm.

"I did?" I whimper as he nips at the dip in my collarbone. "How did the meeting go?"

"As well as can be expected." Asher flicks the tip of his tongue on the skin he just nipped. Then, only with the tip, he makes circular patterns before dragging his tongue up the middle of my throat, over my chin, and across my bottom lip, wetting it before his mouth connects with mine.

At a slow, sensual pace, he savors me. All thoughts of the summit are gone as I focus on the way his lips travel across mine. With each stroke, I fall further and further into him. My legs tighten around his body, pulling him closer.

Asher rocks his hips against me, causing my eyes to open as I release a gasp from the sensation. He holds my gaze, never breaking the kiss. My chest tightens at the intense way I'm being looked at. He pulls away, allowing each of us to catch our breath. A slow and sexy smirk appears on his face.

He leans back into me, biting my lip between his teeth and letting loose deep masculine sounds. At the release of my swollen lip, Asher pulls back again, teasing me so I'm forced to chase his mouth, which I do. Snagging it between my lips and returning the light nip before he plunges his tongue into the open slit. My hands clench the front of his t-shirt with the stirring sensation he's causing in my body. The fire ignites as the flames begin to flicker.

Dragging his body back, he stares down at me and I trace his face. Allowing my hands to roam over his eyebrows, down his sculpted cheeks, over the stubbly jawline I love so much, they land on his perfectly swollen lips. My thumb moves over them as they part. Asher's eyes close, savoring each sensation.

Without warning, he fists his hand in the bottom of my white tank top, yanking me forward harshly then devouring my mouth again. I sigh into the kiss as he begins to lift the hem of my tank at a slow pace, over my stomach, then my breasts. Once the material reaches my chin, he leans back, breaking the kiss, taking it the last little bit over my head. Throwing it on the floor next to him, his eyes appraise me. I resist the urge to squirm under his gaze. He's looking at me as if I'm something to be worshipped.

"By the grace, you're fucking beautiful, siren." His voice is thick as he swallows.

Asher places his hands on my back, caressing them up and down as he leans in and drops a kiss in the middle of my chest. My breath hitches while he moves his head to the right and kisses the swell of my breast, above my black bra, and repeats the movement on the left side.

Leaning back, he lifts his hands to the back of his shirt and pulls it over his head. My eyes travel appreciatively over his sculpted body. He takes my hands and places them on his chest, allowing me to feel his smooth skin. "Touch me," he whispers causing my eyes to lift and meet his.

Focusing on the depths of blue, I slowly move my hands, caressing him as his body shudders at the contact. My right hand finds its way to the protector tattoo. I splay my fingers over it. Gently, he positions his palm to the center of my chest, applying light pressure.

"Layback," he orders, his command firm and gentle at the same time.

I do and he presses his lips to the same spot his hand just was. Then he kisses a trail down my stomach, stopping just above where my shorts begin. Asher looks up at me through his long, sooty lashes. His hands wrap around the top of my yoga shorts, pulling them down my bare legs and throwing them next to my tank top.

He returns his attention to my stomach, planting another heart-wrenching kiss on it. He caresses the area back and forth with the tip of his tongue. I moan while he nips and sucks before tightening the grip he has on my hips.

At the sound of my contentment, he smiles against my skin.

"Ash?" I pant out.

"What do you need, siren?" The words are spoken against my stomach. The heat from his breath ignites the fire he's started.

I can't answer him, unsure of what I need. I just know my body is on fire and the flames burn. An answer in the form of his deep rumble vibrates through me, imprinting my soul.

"I have to taste you, now." His voice is deep and raw.

Without giving me a chance to change my mind, he runs his hands down my sides and hooks each thumb in the sides of my panties, pulling them down at a slow pace. I inhale sharply at the feel of his hot breath against my now very bare lower body. His right shoulder finds its way underneath my knee so my left leg is draped over his shoulder and resting on his back.

"Fuck," he gasps out as he leans forward and takes my body into his mouth.

"Oh. My. God. Asher." I breathe heavily as my head falls back into the pillows on the couch.

He growls deeply against my skin, causing the flames to rise. Just when I think I'm going to fall apart, his tongue begins to sweep the area. "You taste so fucking amazing," he says against me as the pressure begins to build inside.

My hands find his hair and clench, pulling it gently as he increases the pace of his movements. Asher's tongue moves with expert precision, greedily savoring my body.

I close my eyes and bask in the additional sensation of his fingers moving in a stroking rhythm that takes the flames higher. With a final flick of his tongue to the spot holding all my nerves, my entire body tightens. I almost pass out with its release as I scream out Asher's name.

A few moments later, when I finally compose myself enough to open my eyes, I see Asher watching me with a smugness over him. "Watching you come for me will never get old, siren." If he keeps talking like that, I might do it again from his words alone.

I just stare at him, sitting between my limp legs, shirtless. He's so striking. My heart leaps out of my chest with every inch of him that I soak in with my eyes. I push myself up with my palms and move toward him like a predator.

Asher pulls his brows together in confusion as I sink onto my knees in front of him. I lean in slowly and plant a soft kiss on his mouth.

"I want to touch you," I whisper against his lips.

He swallows, the catch in his throat evident. "You don't have to do that. It's not what this was about."

I look him directly in the eyes. "I know," I reply as the tips of my fingers skim his taut stomach and land on the button of his jeans. I wait for him to stop me, but he doesn't. Holding his gaze, I clumsily unbutton his jeans and push the sides down with both of my hands, boxers and all. He leans back with a firm grip on the sides of the table behind him.

His breath hitches and my eyes drop, taking in the impressiveness of him. That's when I see the little silver ball. My brow arches as he informs me in a deep, sexy voice, "That's an apadravya piercing."

Holy Hell, I did not see that coming. Returning my gaze to his, I run my hand over the silky skin the piercing decorates.

Asher's eyes close as he groans. "Fuck, Eve."

I smile at his reaction to my touch and move my thumb along the top silver ball in a circular motion while my other hand runs the length of him. He gasps and arches his back, white knuckling the table before grabbing me by the back of the neck and yanking me to his lips, releasing a raw growl into my mouth.

"You'll have to explain this later," I say against his mouth, my fingers brushing the piercing, causing his lips to curve into a seductive smirk.

"With pleasure, siren."

My lips brush his again, soft but firmly as I allow my hands to explore every inch of Asher in slow, steady motions.

Randi Cooley Wilson

17 Lullabye

I'm trying to control the urge to smack him. It's hard. He's driving me up the fucking wall. We've been in a staring contest for the past twenty minutes over our cereal bowls. Neither of us budges. I release a long, exaggerated breath. It doesn't even faze him. He just keeps crunching on his breakfast, loudly, to irritate me. I push my food forward with a heavy sigh.

"Asher."

"Siren."

"I can't do it."

"You can."

"What if I don't want to?"

He shrugs. "You have to."

"They're dangerous," I counter firmly.

"They're weapons. They're supposed to be dangerous," he retorts in a casual tone.

"They pierced your heart. I almost lost you because of them," I explain, hoping he'll see reason.

His face softens as he reaches for my hands. "I'm not going anywhere, siren. My death won't be at the hands of your daggers, I promise. Besides, you don't get it."

I arch my brow. "Get what?"

He cocks his head to the side, gives me his sexy smirk and uses the most annoying and cocky voice I've heard from him to date. "I'm awesome."

I narrow my eyes, rip my hands away and push off the stool. "You suck, gargoyle."

His eyes twinkle with mischief as he drops his voice. "You know I do, siren."

My body constricts at his suggestive words, reminding me of last night. "Ass." I stomp off mumbling while his light chuckle follows me down the hall.

We're in the basement. Even the flats have a training room. Three hours of weapon and hand-to-hand instruction later, I'm covered in sweat and my muscles ache. Callan launches himself at me, wielding his knife. I spin and block the thrust with a kick.

"Excellent," Keegan encourages from the corner.

Tadhg steps forward, replacing Callan. The change catches me off guard. Something flashes over Callan's face but he immediately turns to stand between Asher and Keegan. Asher's face pales. Keegan watches me with an odd focus. *What the hell?*

Tadhg smirks before lunging at me with supernatural speed. The rapid movement causes me to stumble back before catching my footing.

The large gargoyle's movements are so fast I'm having trouble absorbing them all. He produces a sword and plunges it at me, forcing me to twist away so hard I pull a back muscle in the process. Wincing, I hesitate for just a moment. It's just long enough for Tadhg to grab my throat and throw me hard against the wall before dropping the sword. It clanks at our feet.

He brings his other hand to my neck so both are squeezing tightly, cutting off the circulation of oxygen. I snap my hands up and around each of his wrists. My surprised eyes dart over his shoulder to Callan who's holding a very pissed off Asher back.

Tadhg leans into my ear and uses a low voice, his Irish brogue thick. "Ye're in a bad position, lass." He tsks, increasing his chokehold on my throat and causing my eyes to water. "How would ye get outta dis if I was a demon?" His solid body presses my back against the wall as I grunt. "I asked ye a question." Tadhg's grip tightens and my hands claw at his arms.

"Enough," Asher shouts, watching with helpless fury.

"Let him do this. She needs to be adept at defending herself," Keegan orders calmly.

I close my eyes, praying I won't pass out.

"Come on, lass, tink," Tadhg demands, urgently.

My eyes open and my hands go to my legs where my daggers would normally be sheathed.

Tadhg's eyes meet mine. "Aye, good girl." At that, he removes the hold on my neck. The release causes me to gasp in air as I slide down the wall, my ass hitting the concrete floor.

Asher doesn't take his eyes off me as he storms over, brushing past Tadhg who is backing away with caution.

"If she has bruises, I'll fucking kill you," Asher warns as he comes closer to me.

I plaster myself to the wall, still in shock. At my reaction, Asher stands at his full height and snaps around to Tadhg. His voice is a menacing bark as he points at Tadhg.

"Get the fuck away from her."

Tadhg backs up with his palms out in a show of surrender and moves closer to Callan and Keegan who are watching Asher with interest. Asher returns to me and crouches. At the sight of my neck and the water dripping from my eyes, his face became callous.

"LEAVE NOW!" Asher roars, startling me.

"Ash, you know this had to be done," Callan says, trying to pacify him.

Asher's nostrils flare and in a low snarl he says, "OUT!" At the angry order, everyone leaves in silence.

Once the room is clear, Asher sits on the floor in front of me, his face softening. He reaches out and catches my chin. "Siren, look at me." His voice is demanding.

I snap my eyes at him, fuming. "What the fuck," I croak out, stunned.

"I'm sorry," he offers in a pained apology.

"Why would you allow them to do that?" I shout but it's raspy from my scratchy throat.

He closes his eyes and releases my chin. Running his hands through his hair and rubbing the back of his neck in agitation, he says, "We thought it would help get you to understand the importance of your daggers when defending yourself. Your refusal to engage with them…we figured if we caught you off guard, you—" I cut him off.

"Tough love doesn't work on me, you asshole."

A sudden rush of tears stings my eyes.

His eyes flash a furious blue before glowing.

"I see that. I'm sorry."

I slap his hands away as he reaches for me.

"No. You don't get to touch me." I snivel.

He curses under his breath before cupping my face firmly so I can't move or fight him. "Don't," he pleads. Once I stop struggling, he plants kisses on both of my eyes. "I'm so fucking sorry, siren."

My sob finally escapes and I cling to his solid form. "You have no idea what it did to me to see you laying on the ground, bleeding out."

Asher pulls back and looks into my eyes, commanding my attention. "I do get it. There is nothing I want more than to shelter you from all this, Eve, but there's nowhere for us to hide. You're human. I need to know you can protect yourself so that at the end of this fucked up story, it's you and me left standing, together."

My body shrinks at the desperation in his plea. It's like his life force is woven within my soul. He's afraid. Not that he won't survive the war…but that I won't.

"Give them to me." I cave.

At my directive, Asher pulls me onto his lap and holds on to me like the world is on fire.

"Hold out your hands," he orders in a soothing voice.

I do and he places the smooth black onyx handles of the silver daggers into them. I look down as my thumbs brush the silver dragon symbol etched into them. They match Asher's tattoo, our bond mark.

He folds his hands over mine. "These belong to you, siren." He places a feather-light kiss across each of my knuckles before dropping one final searing kiss on my lips. "Tomorrow you'll practice with them."

Trying to block my apprehension, I feign strength.

"I've got this."

Asher calls everyone back into the training room. It looks as though he'd given them a stern warning before they returned. Tadhg walks in last. He's standing by the wall, watching me with apprehension.

My anger gets the best of me and I turn quickly to him, throwing both the daggers at him. They land in the wall, one on each side of his head, a breath away from nicking him. Tadhg's eyes widen with surprise.

I lurk toward him, stopping when we're nose-to-nose. As I pull the weapons from the wall, I narrow my eyes, lean in and whisper, "An eye for an eye, gargoyle."

"Nice to see you following gargoyle laws, cutie." Callan chuckles.

Asher's loud laugh radiates through me. "I think Tadhg might have peed his pants a little."

Tadhg raises his middle finger at Asher. "Sod off, brother." Though he does look rattled.

Internally, I high-five myself. Guess my ego got the best of me in that situation. I give Keegan a side-glance. He's smirking too.

Wow, I cracked the always stoic Keegan. I rock!

Asher's arms wrap around my waist, pulling my back to his chest before he kisses the top of my head in pride. "Come on, killer. It's late. Let's get you fed and rested."

We leave the training room, but before we completely make our way out, Keegan stops me. "You did good today." My gaze meets his and he offers me a brief smile.

꘏

I'm brushing my teeth when Asher swaggers into the bathroom. He leans his hip against the counter and just watches me. It's starting to freak me out. I squint at him before spitting.

"Can I help you?"

"Huh?" he asks.

"You're staring." I tip my toothbrush at him.

"Am I?" He tilts his head to the side, crossing his arms.

I spit one last time and start my flossing routine and gargle my mouth rinse, all while Asher just stands there, observing me. *Seriously, what's he doing?*

"Curious about dental care?"

"Curious about you," he shoots back.

"Okay."

He shrugs. "I like watching you do normal things."

I blink. "Did you get clocked in training today?"

"No." He slides his hands into the pockets of his pajama bottoms. "Want to have a sleep over?"

"Sleepover?" I repeat, less than enthused.

"Pajamas, pillow fights, gossip. You know, sleepover," he clarifies, like I'm an idiot.

I sigh. "You're freaking me out. What is going on?"

He reaches for me and grabs the hem of my tank top, pulling me towards him. I stumble a bit and have to place my hands on his shoulders for balance as he tugs me closer.

"I want you in my bed tonight. I was hoping you'd fall asleep in my arms." His eyes lock onto mine.

"Oh. That sounds." I exhale. "Blissful."

"Blissful?"

"It means—" Asher cuts me off by picking me up and throwing me over his shoulder. He smacks my ass, enjoying my squeal before I giggle.

"I know what it means, siren." He walks us to his bedroom and drops me on the large bed.

I crawl up to the pillows and get under the covers, making myself comfortable and at home while he watches me, smiling the entire time. Then he gets himself settled in before he turns a serious face to me.

"How do you know the right side of the bed isn't my usual side?" he asks with genuine bewilderment.

"Oh God. Asher, I'm sorry. I didn't even think. Is this your side?" I point to where I'm lying.

He laughs quietly. "Nope. I just wanted to fuck with you."

I narrow my eyes at him. "Mean."

That earns me his signature sexy smile before grabbing the back of my neck and bringing me in for a very long and sensual goodnight kiss.

"Mmm, cinnamony and clean. I like oral care in a human." The comment is lined with a wicked undertone.

I snort before snuggling into him and closing my eyes while he shuts off the lights. Strong arms tighten around me, keeping me safe and content, tucked into him.

"Want me to sing you a lullaby?" he asks in the darkness.

"Um, no. Thanks. I'm good. And eighteen." I laugh softly.

"Good night, siren."

"Good night, pretty boy."

The sounds of my footsteps on the marble floor echo off the tall arched ceiling surrounding me in the dark corridor. Aside from my even breathing, it's the only noise I hear.

To my left are dark gray stone castle walls with alcoves that draw your attention to huge granite gargoyle statues. On my right are several large cathedral windows that overlook the inky night sky.

My gaze lifts to the enormous, medieval double doors in front of me. Both pieces of dark wood are intricately carved with symbols I've never seen before. Each entry is flanked with two massive gargoyle statues. Both have an urn resting on the top of their heads. The fire burning in them emits the only light.

Cautiously, I approach the doors and take a deep breath then run my fingers over the beautiful carvings before dropping my hands to the iron loops. Once pulled, they allow me access to what's behind the entrance. I'm surprised to discover the double doors are actually light and effortless to open. They make no sound as I step through the archway.

I'm in what I assume is an assembly room of some sort. It's shadowy, chilled and dungeon-like with dark gray and black hued stone walls, floors and ceilings. Light discharges from thousands of lit black candles that are melting, allowing the wax to drip and run over the stone before turning solid again. Urns filled with fire line each side of an aisle that runs all the way to the front of the chamber before stopping at a raised platform.

"Well, this is a new one," I say to myself, taking the environment in. My head snaps up at the booming sound of a voice rumbling off the stones.

"Today is judgment day for you. You are here in the council chamber because of your disregard for your oath and our laws. Do you understand?" An older man's voice cascades through me, leaving chills in its wake.

I turn my focus to the front of the hall and attempt to make out what I see in the shadows. I think a man is chained, two guards on each side of him, and he seems to be kneeling in front of an extremely tall elderly man, dressed in black robes. The man in black must be at least seven feet tall. With his dark brown wings out, he seems even larger.

At the question posed, the guy kneeling just bobs his head once. I'm not sure how I'm attuned to him, but he's in a great deal of pain. I suddenly become aware they've been torturing him. His pride is strong though, which is why he is chained and being forced to kneel.

Behind the tall, robed man are two stairs that lead to a stone throne. On each side of the throne are gargoyle statues and more arched alcoves. This almost feels like a place of worship for the supernatural beings.

There are five more unnaturally tall beings on the left side of the throne and only four on the right. Each is seated on the granite stage, holding their heads high with an air of authority. There's one chair empty though at the end of the right side. Odd.

"The council is very disappointed with you," the first man says with a sigh. "We expected great restraint from a member of this council. You have tarnished the protector duties we are bound to. You have embarrassed this council and your race. But most disturbing, you have tainted your family name."

The prisoner says nothing in response.

One of the other male council members speaks from the stage. "And for what? A human girl? Pathetic."

"I love her," the captive says in a low but solid voice, which resonates in my ears as my heart rate increases.

Realization hits me as I move closer to the stage. In the light of the flames, I see the dragon tattoo on the inmate's bare back. "Oh shit."

"It is forbidden," a female retorts loudly, her long, grey hair unmoving.

The elderly man steps forward, bending so he's eye level with Asher. "Your punishment has been decided, dark prince. You shall suffer an eternity in stone. Watching her, knowing she is alive, but never allowed to touch her. Bring me the Angelic Sword," he orders with finality.

Asher positions himself straighter, as if accepting this fate. I try to run to him but am rooted in place. An unseen force holds me back as I try to fight to get to him.

The older gargoyle is handed the sword and walks slowly toward Asher. "Last words, Your Highness?" he asks coolly.

"I love you, siren. I will protect you, always," Asher says as if speaking directly to me.

My eyes widen in horror as I thrash around, trying to break free from the invisible hold keeping me in place. My ear-piercing scream ricochets off the stone as the elderly man pierces Asher's heart with the Angelic Sword.

Immediately, the granite begins to form around his body. Simultaneously, the council members all lift their heads to me.

"Impossible," the old gargoyle whispers in awe.

I keep thrashing. Something is holding me down firmly and it won't let go. My hysterical screaming isn't scaring it away. All I know is I need to get to Asher before he turns to stone.

"Eve. EVE, WAKE UP," a deep, male voice orders in a firm tone.

At the recognition of Asher's voice, I force my eyes open. The moment he comes into my watery sight, I jump on him, holding onto him for dear life. Tears stream down my face as my body shakes uncontrollably.

Asher increases his grip on me, molding me to his body as his hands cradle the back of my head, murmuring in a soothing voice, "Everything's alright. I've got you, siren. You're safe. It was just a dream." He continues to just hold, rock and whisper to me until the tears stop falling, and my body ceases trembling.

Once my breathing evens out, Asher pulls back and pushes the wet hair off my face. Gentle eyes scan mine worried about the emotional trauma I'm exhibiting. He plants a soft kiss on my lips and mumbles against them, "Be right back."

I grab at him. "Don't leave me here alone." I panic in an irrational moment of fear.

His face softens. "I'm just going to snag a washcloth. I swear. I'm not leaving." He waits for the okay.

I nod as he slides me off his lap and tries to stand beside the bed, but he can't straighten. I look up at him through wet lashes as he places his hands over my fists clutching his shirt to pry me away. Once I let go, I notice the two wrinkle spots in the material marking where I held on for dear life.

"Be right back," he assures gently then turns the bathroom light on. The water runs and a few seconds later, he's back with a warm, wet cloth that he uses to wipe the tear stains from my cheeks.

Once satisfied, he throws the towel on the floor and pulls me back into bed, holding me while I gain control over my emotions. "Talk to me."

I take in a sharp breath and relive the dream. Asher is motionless and silent the entire time. Listening intently. Once I'm done, he kisses the top of my head. "It was a just a dream. It's that simple." Though I don't miss the edge in his voice. "Just close your eyes. You're safe," he vows.

"Ash?" I whisper.

"Yeah?" he answers, speaking softly into the dark room.

"I'll take that lullaby now."

Randi Cooley Wilson

18 Shadows

I was frustrated, to say the least. The hopeless feeling that comes from having no control is starting to sink in and worm its way through my veins, affecting the way I'm thinking. I need to focus and figure out how to get out of this situation. Trapped, I take in a deep cleansing breath before releasing a lame girlie growl. Abby releases the invisible air hold she has on me.

"Sweetie, we've been at this for hours. You just can't break an invisible hold." She sighs tiredly from the crazy she's dealing with this afternoon, in the form of me.

I pin her with my stare. "I need to figure it out."

"Why?" the red head asks with her purple manicured fingers resting on her slender hips.

"I just do," I bark.

She watches me for a moment. "Does Asher know you're down here?"

I stand straight and cross my arms. "He isn't the boss of me, Abby. He doesn't need to know where I am twenty-four seven."

"Wow, you're bitchy today," she mumbles and grabs her water bottle, sucking down the last bit of liquid.

"Sorry, rough night," I apologize, not the least bit sincere about it.

"Do you want to talk about it?"

"I want to learn how to get out of an invisible hold," I bark out of frustration versus anger.

"By the grace, blood of Eden. Have you learned nothing?" McKenna's snide voice filters in.

"I'm not in the mood for your crap today, McKenna," I mutter.

"Careful, she's feisty," Abby warns and I shoot her a death glare.

"Why?" McKenna asks, already bored.

"It's really none of your business, Malibu Barbie," I retort angrily.

McKenna straightens and analyzes me, shock rushing across her perfect face.

"What?" I ask because now her face is scrunched in a weird mask.

The sides of her mouth tilt upward. "No one has ever dared call me a name before."

I squint my eyes. "Maybe not to your face."

She shrugs. "People find me frightening."

I exhale. "Well, right now you're just in the way. Move it or lose it."

She doesn't move. "I can help." Her voice is quiet but commanding.

Abby chokes on her water. My eyes dart to her then back to McKenna.

"Why?" I ask, gauging her motives.

"Why what?" she inquires with annoyance.

"Why would you help me?"

"I'm sort of obligated. You know, gargoyle oath and all." She rolls her eyes, emphasizing her lack of interest. "Fuck, do you want my help or not?"

My eyes shift again to Abby. Her mouth is hanging open, eyes wide, stunned. I sigh. She's obviously not going to be helpful in pointing out McKenna's true intentions. I turn back to the supermodel gargoyle.

"All right. I accept."

McKenna unzips her black hooded sweatshirt and peels it of her shoulders before gracefully moving her warrior body toward me. "The secret is...you can't fight your way out of the invisible hold." She motions for Abby.

I raise my voice. "Gee, thanks for your insight."

Super helpful.

The blonde goddess places her hands on her hips and throws me a stern sapphire look. "I can show you how to wield powers which will release you if you'd stop fucking running at the mouth."

"KENNA!" Abby exclaims. "He will kill you for this," she warns.

McKenna ignores her, keeping her eyes locked onto mine. "It will entail dark powers which might taint the archangel soul spirit. Are you sure you want this?"

I tilt my chin up, trying to show courage. "Yes."

She nods once. "Abby, please pull in the air energy you were using before to hold Eve."

Abby whines. "This is so going to end badly."

"Just do it," McKenna and I say at the same time, causing Abby to glare at us.

"Never thought I would see the day you two would be on the same page." She huffs.

McKenna and I catch one another's glance. I offer a small smile before the air in the room begins to whirl and I'm pulled tightly into the force.

"The key, blood of Eden, is not to panic and thrash around like a lunatic," McKenna begins. "Take in a deep cleansing breath and relax your body. Don't focus on the entrapment." She pauses before giving me a face that people who are about to drop bad news give to you. "Focus on your connection to Asher."

At that explanation, I pull my brows together and look at her in confusion. "Asher?"

She blows out her annoyance on a sharp breath. "He's already transferred his healing abilities to you. Ash also manipulates darkness and shadows."

"What does that have to do with my current predicament?" I question impatiently.

"I overheard him telling Keegan about the dream this morning," she says.

My throat constricts and I clench my teeth. I'm ticked that she knows and reeling at the image.

"The council chambers are full of both darkness and shadows," she says as if to calm me.

Abby looks me over but I don't return the glance. Instead, I nod once to McKenna in silent understanding and she continues the lesson.

"By itself, darkness is mainly used to blanket an area in total blackness. However, if you can access Asher's dark energy, you can channel it into a variety of effects such as the absence of light or a solid substance. You can also control the beings that exist in the dark and create and dispel shields, as well as teleport through massive distances via shadows."

"By the grace, McKenna. Ash is going to flip that you're not only telling her this but you're showing her how to do it." Abby exhales.

I ignore her freak out. "So, you're saying if I can pull Asher's gift, I can encase the chamber in darkness and teleport out of the hold through the shadows?" I ask, thinking I've got it.

"Bingo, blood of Eden. Well done," McKenna praises.

"Let's try it," I suggest excitedly.

"Shit," Abby answers.

"All right. How did you transfer the healing ability last time?" McKenna inquires.

I bite my bottom lip. "I don't recall. We fell asleep, realm jumped to the Kingdom of the Fae and when I woke up, I was healed."

McKenna thinks for a moment. "Let's try this. Close your eyes. Sync your mind and heart beat with Asher's as if you were planning to astral project to him." She waits a moment. "There?"

"Yep."

"Good. Now, allow yourself to feel the darkness running through his blood and the shadows he hides behind. Pull them toward you. Once you feel them flowing through your veins, picture the training room draped in blackness," McKenna instructs.

After multiple tries, the room goes dark.

"Well done, Eves," Abby encourages.

"Open your eyes and search for the shadows in the room. Once you find one, focus on it. Push all the energy you have to the shadow. Visualize your body slipping out of the force and materializing into the shadow. Allow yourself to be embraced by the dark," McKenna continues.

After a couple of solid tries, I feel myself moving and appearing in the shadow, out of the hold.

"Holy shit," I say in awe as Abby claps.

"Excellent," McKenna actually praises.

The celebration is short lived when Asher's heated voice bounces off the walls. "WHAT THE FUCK IS GOING ON?" he yells from the doorway.

"Damn. So close to getting away with it." Abby blows out.

Unexpectedly, the lights come back on as a giggle forms in my throat. I can't help it. It releases on its own accord.

Asher's head snaps to Abby. "Get away with what?"

Like a wave, Abby and then even McKenna start laughing hysterically, which only makes Asher even more upset. His anger causes us to laugh harder as tears roll down our cheeks. The more we try to stop, the funnier it becomes.

Finally, he gives up, throwing his hands up in frustration and storming off.

"Crap. Let me go talk to him," I say once the laughing fit is over.

"Good luck," Abby counters, making a glad-its-you-and-not-me face.

I turn to McKenna. "Thank you. What you showed me how to do today...well, it really means a great deal to me, Kenna."

She nods and smiles. "I know you'll protect him."

"I will, every time," I state in a firm promise before turning to face a very angry gargoyle.

To say Asher is mad would be a gross understatement. He gives me the cold shoulder and silent treatment the entire afternoon and evening. The stubborn mule has not said one word.

As a peace offering, I've decided to make him dinner. I figured it couldn't hurt. Dressing the salad, I turn my head to the left and see Asher standing in the doorway just watching me.

He has his arms over his head, leaning on the frame. The position forces his t-shirt up so I can see some of the muscles of his six-pack. His face is unreadable and his focus is locked on me, following every movement like he is memorizing me. Mouth dry, I wet my lips.

Asher steps away from the doorway without a word. The emptiness of his retreat hits me like cold water. I swallow the burn in my throat and continue with the dinner preparations.

The brooding gargoyle sits in complete silence the entire meal. Doesn't even make eye contact. After a silent dinner, he stands, places the dishes in the sink and walks to his room to mope. Buying myself some time, I do the dishes. Then, I get mad.

I've had enough of the sulking and decide to take matters into my own hands and face him, head on. I storm into his bedroom without knocking and throw my hands on my hips and narrow my eyes, ready to yell at him.

My anger is squashed the moment I see him. He's laying on the bed, ankles crossed in his jeans and a white t-shirt. The bedside task light is on and he's reading a book.

I inhale a sharp breath.

"What are you reading?" I ask with a cautious look.

He doesn't look up. "A riveting book. It's about a male protector. He's bonded to this frustrating and stubborn woman. She keeps getting herself into trouble, mainly because she acts with reckless abandon and neeeever thinks. It's going to get her killed one day." *Touché.*

I exhale and sit on the edge of the bed.

"Asher. Look at me."

He doesn't.

"Asher!" I say with more force behind his name.

At the sharpness in my tone, he snaps his eyes to me.

"I overheard you talking to Keegan this morning. You told him you believe I'm coming into seer abilities because after my dream, I explained the council chamber and members in perfect detail. If that's true, and what I saw was a premonition and not a dream, then I need to be equipped to handle things."

He closes the book with a scary calm. "I saw you wield the darkness and teleport into the shadows in the training room earlier. I felt my gifts pull to you, hence why I went down there." It was an even statement, but the implications behind his words caused me to shudder with nervousness.

"Is that the reason everyone keeps calling you the dark prince? Because you can manipulate the darkness and shadows?" I question, avoiding his accusation.

"Don't. Change. The. Subject," he warns through a tight jaw.

Our eyes remain focused on one another before I cave.

"If what I witnessed was a vision, then I need to learn how to protect you."

"I'M THE ONE WHO PROTECTS YOU!" His voice raises in exasperation.

"I won't allow the council to turn you into a stone statue," I retort, my tone unyielding.

"Stone petrifaction is the punishment for breaking my oath. I'm a gargoyle."

"I will not survive if you spend an eternity like that." I stand, clenching my fists at my sides.

Asher throws the book on the bed. "What?"

"My heart and soul would be wrecked," I yell back.

He stands slowly, his eyes wild. My hands begin to tremble at the intense way he's stalking toward me before he begins to mutter to himself.

I take in a shaky breath as he stops in front of me.

"Why?" he lowers his voice.

"Because," I mumble under my breath.

"Why, Eve?"

"Because...I LOVE YOU!" I shout.

He stills. Oh crap.

The weight of my words hangs in the air. Neither of us moves or says anything.

"Say that again," Asher requests in mere whisper.

I swallow, hard. "I. Love. You," I repeat softly, terrified he's going to bolt.

He closes his eyes, nostrils flaring and he still hasn't moved. To be honest, he isn't breathing.

"Take it back," he demands, surprising me.

"No." I hold my stance. *What the fuck?*

He opens his eyes and narrows them at me. "You have to. It's not allowed."

I tilt my head and throw my shoulders back, channeling my inner Kenna. "I don't care." I take a step to him.

Asher retreats a pace. "You can't." His voice is firm but I don't miss the hitch.

I move forward, he moves back, matching my pace.

"It's true, I do."

He moves his head from side to side, adamantly.

"Eve." My name is a warning.

The back of his legs hit the bed as I stand within a breath's reach from him. "I know it's forbidden. I realize it goes against every law you're bound to as both a protector and royalty. So you don't have to say it back. Just know, I. Love. You." I force the tears back.

Asher stands there motionless. His glowing eyes never shift from mine. My throat tightens, forcing me to gulp down the painful lump climbing up it. I nod my acceptance of the rejection and take a step back.

In an instant, he jerks his hand out and snatches my elbow, forcing me to stop. We just stand there, eyes locked. He heaves me to him, pressing my body against his as he slides his right hand behind my neck, moving me toward him.

His chin dips. "Just because I'm bound and can't say it, doesn't mean I don't feel it."

Asher's mouth descends on mine, drowning me in passion and the forbidden. His lips are forceful and violent as he deepens the kiss, fueling the fire that's always between us. Our tongues dance at a frantic pace. I moan into the kiss as desire floods through my veins. My fingers dig into his shoulders, pulling them toward me in an attempt to get even closer to him.

With our mouths fused, Asher shifts us so he can lean over me and lays me down on the bed. He pulls his mouth away, long enough to peel off both of our shirts. I scrape my fingernails down his back, over the dragon tattoo, and his body shudders in response to my touch.

I relish the sexy look of desire on his face. He watches me while he pushes the hair off my face.

"I do, you know. I fucking feel it every time I look at you," he admits.

My heart lurches at his admission. I lift my head and run my tongue over his lips, savoring the words he just spoke. In response, Asher makes a deep, masculine noise in the back of his throat, readjusting his body over mine. The erotic sound and weight of his body has me coming apart at the seams.

He moves his hands over the delicate lace of my black bra. I gasp as he presses against me, teasing the growing ache between my legs. His lips move to my neck, biting and sucking mercilessly before leaving a path of deep kisses that produce animalistic hums from my throat.

Our hips move together at an urgent pace. I sit up, forcing Asher to stand. My lips graze his skin, landing over the protector tattoo. I brush them back and forth over the scar from my dagger, causing his body to tremble in my arms at the intimate touch.

He fists his hands in my hair, holding my lips still over his heart. I look up through my dark lashes, lips still pressed to the tattooed area.

My hands drop to his jeans, unbuttoning them and pushing down the denim as the blue hue in his eyes darkens.

With his hands still tangled in my hair, he yanks my head back and then returns his lips to my mouth, kissing me hungrily. Sliding his hands behind my back and unclasping my bra, his fingers run over my shoulders and release the straps one at a time, removing the material. The caresses his fingers leave burn my skin. Asher allows his eyes to roam over me with worship.

"You're so unbelievably breathtaking." His voice is heavy with admiration.

Large expert hands glide over my breasts and stomach before unbuttoning my pants and tugging them off. Leaving me exposed in my black lace panties, he leans forward, taking my mouth again and devouring me.

"So fucking beautiful," he murmurs against my lips.

His hands caress me everywhere. I suck in an uneven breath when he thrusts his hips into my lower body.

Asher hisses in a sharp breath before planting another searing kiss on me, swallowing my whimpers as he pushes harder against me over and over at an incredible pace.

I wrap my hands around his wrists tightly and repeat his name in almost an incoherent chant. His mouth moves to my breasts, showering each one with meticulous attention and I arch into him.

"Oh. My. God, Asher." I gasp, finding my voice and grabbing his hips as we press together in an out-of-control frenzy.

He pulls his head back and looks directly in my eyes, both of us panting uncontrollably.

"I want to hear you say it again, siren," he mutters through breathy gasps.

Twisting his fingers in the edges of my panties, he settles in between my thighs, pressing directly against me in the most mind-blowing rhythm, causing a sensual friction.

Asher drops his head to my forehead and I lift my hips, urging him against my body. The hum from the protector tattoo heightens each sensation. His eyes lock on mine, piercing each layer until he hits my soul.

"I love you," I manage to whisper in between my quick breaths.

Gripping my panties tightly, so they press into my body, he grinds one last time against me in a hard, fast move as I arch my back and cry out.

Asher curses under his breath, holding me as my body quivers while the rapture floats through me.

He returns his lips to me in a slow, seductive kiss. His forehead is glued to mine. We stay like that until our breathing becomes controlled.

"Holy shit," he says, his fingers still twisted in the delicate fabric.

I inhale a lungful of air as he plants light kisses to my eyebrows. "I guess you were wrong."

He pulls his brows together in confusion.

"My virtue is safe around you." I smile as he tightens his hold of my panties.

"Make no mistake, siren. More than anything, I want to rip this delicate barrier away and bury myself in you." He pulls at my panties before releasing them and rolling onto his back, pulling me to curl into his side.

I sigh in contentment. My body is limp and my mind is vacant from the experience we just shared.

He grows quiet, lost in thought as he begins to draw random designs on my lower back with his finger. "I won't though. Not until I can say it back to you, yeah?"

I nod my agreement. "God, if it was that good with a barrier, imagine what it will be like without it."

"It's going to be so fucking amazing," he vows with a cocky smirk.

19 Wage War

My lips are starting to ache. They're swollen, bruised and have been kissed to the point that I have absolutely no feeling left in them. Asher's had me pressed against the refrigerator since I threw my full glass of orange juice at him during a rather loud screaming match.

The argument was brought on with an accusation of me 'stealing,' his word, not mine, his dark powers. After quarrelling in circles for what felt like an eternity, I was

247

done. So, in a very mature fashion, I picked up the glass and threw the citrus liquid at him.

Once the shock wore off, he grabbed me and pushed me against the stainless steel appliance, covering my body with his sticky, orange scented one in a punishing kiss that's lasted for, what I'm guessing has been about an hour now.

"Mmm. You taste sweet," I purr and lick some of the juice off his lips.

He chuckles. "I thought sweet wasn't your thing, sweatheart?"

I growl at the nickname. "Maybe it is now."

Asher grins sexily and leans in to take my lips again but stops as soon as we hear knocking at the front door. He growls and plants once last quick peck on my mouth before heading to answer it.

"Dude, what the fuck?" Callan's laugh floats into the kitchen. "Did you get in a fight with the orange juice container this morning?"

"Something like that," Asher answers in embarrassment and I bite my lip, trying not to laugh. "What's up?"

Callan sighs. "Keegan is calling a meeting. First floor. One hour. He sent me to tell you and Eves."

"All right, we'll be there," Asher responds.

The hallway is quiet for a moment before I hear Callan shout, "Morning, cutie! I like the citrus look."

His laughter is contagious as I listen to Asher pushing him out the front door.

Ash walks back into the kitchen, amusement clear on his face. "You think this is funny?" He motions to his wet and sticky body. "I'll show you funny, siren."

With a squeal, I run around the island and head to the safety of my bathroom to shower and get ready for the meeting. Through the locked door, I hear Asher laugh.

"Payback's a bitch."

Once I hear him walk away, I turn the water on and smile at myself in the mirror. Shit, I really am in love with him.

I'm attempting to blow-dry my unruly hair when Asher knocks at the door. I swing it open to see him freshly showered and looking gorgeous in his standard outfit. My outright appraisal of him with my eyes earns me a cocky brow arch.

"Like what you see, siren?" He uses his standard line while biting his lower lip.

"I've seen better." I shrug, giving him my usual answer.

He snarls and lunges for me, lifting me on the sink counter and standing between my legs. With his hands cupping my face, he murmurs against my lips.

"You're mine. Remember that."

"Forever," I promise before our lips tangle.

He moans in displeasure. "As much as I'd like to stay here all day, attached to your beautiful, pouty pink lips, we need to get down to the meeting."

I sulk. "Okay, I'll meet you down there in like five minutes."

He watches me then leans forward, placing a gentle kiss on my forehead before releasing my face and stepping back. "Five minutes, siren. I'm sending McKenna up while you finish."

"The sooner you leave, the sooner I'll be done."

He smirks and walks out the door, but turns at the last minute and smiles at me. "Say it again."

I tilt my head to the side then walk up to him, put both arms around his waist and look him in the eyes. "Asher St. Michael, you are full of gargoyle awesomeness."

He inhales and closes his eyes. "I'll never get tired of hearing that."

"What? That you're awesome?" I tease.

"Fuck yeah." He smiles before giving me one final searing kiss. "Five minutes, siren, or I'll be back to drag your cute little ass downstairs."

"Yes, sir." I salute and he walks backwards out of the room, smirking the entire time.

A few moments later, McKenna appears in the doorway. "Almost ready, blood of Eden?"

"Yep. Just give me a second."

Throwing on my vanilla-coconut gloss, I head into the living room, prepared for McKenna's wrath.

"I'm ready," I announce in a light-hearted manner, hoping she won't be bitchy.

"Is that so?" A chilling male voice rumbles through me.

I stop in my tracks at the site of the six-foot half-demon and half-gargoyle dressed in a black button down shirt and black dress pants. *Oh shit!*

Deacon turns his muscular body to face me. Brown eyes that are almost black narrow at my appearance. He rubs a hand over a snake tattoo that is mostly covered by his black buzzed hair as my eyes follow it down to his neck. The reptile wraps around his throat and continues inside the top of his shirt.

"H-how did you get in here?" I question, scanning the room for anything that might help me and wondering where McKenna is. Then I see her wrapped in an unfamiliar man's arms. Deacon's mate, Jade, has a knife pointed at her heart while she swears ferociously and profusely. *Crap.*

Deacon smirks in a sinister manner. "Unprotected again, little girl?" The question is a sneer.

A strangled laugh comes out of me. "They're all here. They can sense you," I warn.

"Not fast enough." He springs at me with such speed I can't react. His large hand roughly grasps a handful of my hair, snapping my head forward. A stinging sensation makes its way down my neck and over my spine.

He smiles at me in an evil manner one final time before we disappear, but not before my eyes lock onto a panic-stricken McKenna.

႟ႜ

With a snarl, Deacon throws me onto the cold, damp stone floor, causing me to land on my legs awkwardly. I groan as pain shoots through my body from the impact. Using my palms, I push my upper body up as I lift my head.

"You're an asshole," I spout through clenched teeth.

At my insult, Deacon raises his left hand and whips it down across my face. I cry out in pain. Blood begins to trickle down my chin from the side of my mouth. *Damn that hurt.*

"Learn. Some. Manners, little girl." He circles me like an animal.

"Fuck you," I spit out with some of the blood from my mouth.

That earns me a kick in the back with his designer shoe. Hard. I grunt and fall completely on the ground, my breath coming in shallow gasps.

Deacon squats down and grips my chin in a bruising manner. "Lucifer won't put up with your smart mouth and neither will I." With a snap of his wrist, he releases the hold as my head drops back to the ground. I close my eyes as his footsteps retreat and I hear a door close.

Once he's gone, I take in my surroundings. I'm in a square cell. Each wall is solid stonework. There are no windows and the door I heard must be hidden within the wall because I can't see it. The stone cube is empty with the exception of my body, which is lying on the floor, writhing in excruciating pain.

I suck in a breath as the tears begin to flow. Damn it, why didn't I just go with Asher? I close my eyes and picture him smiling at me as a sob escapes before I suck it back in. I refuse to let Deacon make me cry. I need to calm down and think of a way out.

Minutes become hours and hours, days. I'm not sure how long I've been here, or even where here is. Deacon has been back in the cell twice. Both times, I refused water, which led to him using my face as a punching bag.

My eyes are swollen shut. I'm sure the cuts on my face and my bruised body are infected. For some reason, I'm not able to heal myself.

I've tried astral projection and dream walking as an attempt to reach out to Asher. Neither is working. There seems to be some sort of block preventing me from using any of the abilities I've learned. The longer I sit in here, the weirder this gets. *Why hasn't Deacon just handed me over?*

I hear the door open, but can't see it because of my disfigured face. I cower and flatten myself against the wall, not able to withstand another strike to my body. I hear slow footsteps approach before someone crouches in front of me.

"Christ, love." Gage exhales roughly.

"Gage?" I whisper, stunned and my bottom lip begins to quiver.

"What the fuck happened, Eve?" he asks with a heated voice.

I let out a nasty, throaty sound. "Deacon."

Gage curses multiple times before blowing out a long, exaggerated breath. "He wasn't supposed to harm you."

"Obviously, that's not the case," I softly shout.

"I can see that. I'm going to get you out of here but you have to trust me. Can you do that Eve?"

He's silent, waiting for my answer.

Can I trust Gage? "I have no choice," I reply, defeated.

He pauses. "Understood. I just can't take you out of here though, okay? I promise you won't be in here much longer. Trust me," he urges with sincerity.

"Fine. I trust you." My voice is shaky.

Suddenly, there's another set of footsteps. "She's alive. You're done here," Deacon states coolly and I stiffen.

"But not unharmed, Deacon." Gage seethes.

"She has a mouth. I have a temper. It makes for unfriendly moments," he reasons, bored.

"Do. Not. Lay. Another. Hand. On. Her." Gage spits.

"Or what, Gallagher?" Deacon taunts.

"Or I will end you myself," Gage threatens.

The cell becomes quiet again and I release the breath I was holding. I'm not sure if I fell asleep or passed out from the pain. Or even how long it's been since Gage's visit.

The sound of loud but muffled voices grabs my interest. I attempt to push up on my palms to get a better angle to hear, but through the granite, I can't. Exhausted, I just lie back down on the damp stone and close my eyes.

"She's in here," Gage announces as the cell door opens, breaking through the fog of soreness in my head.

Immediately, I smell Asher's smoky wood and leather scent. My eyes are puffy slits, but I can faintly make out both good-looking gargoyles. Asher's eyes look wild and primal as he scans me, taking in every inch with a deadly expression.

Keegan and Callan come up and stop behind him, both wearing shocked expressions. Asher's breathing is heavy, like he can't get enough air in his lungs.

"I'm going to cut his heart out." His voice is so deep that the hatred ripples through my body.

"Secure her safety first," Gage says. "Revenge later."

Asher nods once at Gage before Gage departs with an appreciative nod from Keegan and a thank you pat on the shoulder from Callan.

The two sullen protectors stand guard while Asher makes his way to me, still trying to get a hold on his emotions.

"What the fuck," Asher exhales on a long breath before moving toward me and crouching. At his proximity, I can see the agony on his face. It's the final crack in my emotional state.

I start to shake and sob uncontrollably while he gently pulls me into his arms. "Shh. I've got you, siren," he soothes, burrowing his face in my neck. I grip him tighter.

"McKenna?" I rasp out.

"She's okay. Pissed off, but all right. Deacon and his minions flashed before they pierced her, probably sensing our arrival," Asher answers quietly.

Callan's wrecked face watches us. "Ash, we need to go before Deacon discovers we're here."

At the sound of his name, I freeze and begin to tremble in Asher's arms.

"I'm going to fucking kill that motherfucker," Asher growls out in cool detachment.

"No doubt. Let's get Eves home first," Callan answers, trying to get Asher to focus and move.

Asher scoops my injured body up and carries me out of the cell. Keegan and Callan are behind him, weapons drawn.

"Does no one else find it odd that he's letting us just walk out with her?" Callan asks.

A knowing look crosses Keegan's face. "This is a set up. Deacon's smart. He wouldn't just take her and hand her over. He wants war. In order to get it, he needs her alive and Asher out of the picture."

"I'm here, why not ambush and dispose of me now?" Asher inquires as the cold, fresh air hits my face. I can't see much, but it's dark so I'm assuming it must be night.

"He's too tactical for that. This is a game of chess to him," Callan counters, his tone solemn.

"Why even kidnap her at all?" Asher questions.

"He's playing with us. Showing you he can get to her if he wants to," Callan explains.

"Deacon is waging war, brothers," Keegan says firmly. "It's time we amass an army."

Asher's breath is at my ear. "Close your eyes, siren. We'll be home soon," he uses his sexy voice to calm.

Without warning, we're soaring through the pitch-black sky with Asher clinging to my limp form. All the tension leaves him as he holds me close. I bask in his warmth.

I'm placed gently on his stone state bed while he holds my neck so it's tipped and he can look me in the eyes. "Get me some fresh clothes, a warm wet cloth and water," he asks darkly.

My eyes are still inflamed so it's hard to see. "Why are we in Wiltshire?"

"You weren't able to heal yourself in the cell. Deacon had it spelled so you couldn't use your abilities. You should start mending now, but I'm going to help the process along in stone state by transferring my healing energy to you," Asher responds by holding a water bottle to my lips.

The cool liquid feels amazing on my dry throat.

"Drink it all, siren," Asher orders softly.

When I've had enough, I pull my lips away. His hand guides my head back to rest on the luxurious down pillows.

"Why don't ye get sum rest, lad? I'll wash and clean up da lass," Fiona's instructs.

"I will not leave her," Asher answers in a rough tone.

Feeling his eyes on me, I look over to him. I reach my hand to his cheek. The stubble scratches my palm as he leans into it, closing his eyes.

We stay like this the entire time Fiona cleans the cell grime from my body and redresses me in fresh clothing. Once she's done, she pats my hand gingerly before leaving the chamber.

Asher moves next to me on the bed, placing a cold compress over my engorged eyes. Then with great care, he cleans and bandages my cuts and bruises, kissing each one tenderly.

Once done, he scoops me up and readjusts our bodies so he can lie next to me. Never letting go of my hand, he watches me with a concerned expression. "I'm so fucking sorry, siren," he admits in a pained voice.

I want to reassure him and tell him it's not his fault. But my body isn't cooperating, my throat's too sore and I'm so tired. Instead, I just close my eyes and drift into a peaceful sleep.

My eyes open to a dark room. Forgetting where I am for a moment, I begin to panic before strong hands wrap around me, and Asher's deep voice penetrates the fear.

"You're safe. I'm here."

"How long have I been sleeping?" I ask, groggy.

"A day or so. We're keeping the room dark to help your eyes," he replies.

Feeling less sore and stiff, I turn on my side so I'm face-to-face with him. "How long was I with Deacon?" I question, noting he hasn't taken his eyes off me.

The soft glow calms my frayed nerves.

Asher picks up a loose strand of my hair and begins to play with it. "A few days." His face registers anguish.

I exhale my relief. "It felt like months."

I watch Asher, watching me.

"Aside from the exterior injuries, did..." His voice trails off before he finds it again. "Did he hurt you anywhere else?" he inquires in a soft tone, hardly breathing.

My throat squeezes at the realization of what he's asking. I begin to tremble at the thought of what Deacon could have done. "No. Would it have changed anything if he had?" I frown.

Asher's hand stills, dropping the piece of hair. "Never," he assures in a soothing and firm tone. His fingertips brush away a tear from my cheek. "I promise you there will be no mercy for him. Only death."

I gaze into his eyes. "How did he get into the flat?" My voice cracks slightly.

Asher sighs. He seems exhausted. "We don't know. Keegan and Abby are still trying to figure that out. We'll be staying here in Wiltshire until we do though. It's more secure and Fiona has offered the extra security of the Pishyakan clowder." The statement was meant to be reassuring, but I don't feel at ease. "What we do know is that McKenna was ambushed and we got there a second too late." His tone is solemn.

Having had enough of the intensity, I put on a serious face. "Can I ask you for something?"

Asher sits up and stares down at me. "I will give you anything in the world you want."

"Could I have a cheeseburger with bacon and tons of fries? I'm starving."

A small smile appears on his lips. "It's yours, siren." The answer is absolute as he places a small kiss on top of my head. "Feel up to heading to the kitchen?"

I take a quick stock of how I feel. My eyes are no longer swollen, my body isn't sore it's just slightly aching. Overall, I feel a thousand times better than I did.

"Yep, I feel much better." I force a small smile when I see doubt cross his face.

"Okay. But we'll take it slow." Asher reaches out his hand and I take it, allowing him to help me off the bed.

As soon as I stand, I feel dizzy and wobbly. It's probably just because I haven't eaten in a few days and I'm dehydrated.

Asher bends down and scoops me up. "Ash, I can walk. This is a little much."

He sighs. "Let me take care of you." I hold his gaze, and all I see is torment. He's blaming himself and I know he needs this to help him work through those feelings.

"Well, what are you waiting for then? I'm starving here," I announce as my stomach growls.

Asher chuckles. "Then let's get you fed."

Randi Cooley Wilson

20 Divine Intervention

"I don't think I've ever wanted you more than I do right this minute." Asher growls as he watches me down my second bacon cheeseburger and third helping of fries. Amusement is plastered all over his face.

I smile around my straw before swallowing my beverage. "Really? Out of all the things we've done recently, you're picking this as the number one hottest?" Disbelief lines my question.

Giving me his signature sexy smile, he drops his tone. "Well, maybe not *THE* number one, but I'm not going to lie to you, it is pretty fucking sexy, siren."

Shivers run down my spine at the sound of his voice as the butterflies take flight. He leans over the island and darts his tongue out, gently licking away some of the ketchup on the corner of my mouth before brushing his lips over mine. My body naturally leans into his and he smirks at me.

"I can't believe you didn't have a boyfriend," he throws out offhandedly as he returns to his seat across from me.

I snort. "It's not like you're the first boy I've ever kissed, Asher," I reply, watching him watch me.

He stands in one smooth, abrupt motion then moves around the room as if he's on a mission, opening and closing drawers until he finds what he's looking for. When he returns, he places a notebook and pen on the island and slides it over to me. I raise my brows in question.

"Write down the names of all the others on a piece of paper," he responds with a serious tone.

"Why?" I ask in a suspicious pitch.

Asher leans in, placing his elbows on the granite and giving me a very stern expression. "I'm going to end their existence," he explains with a shrug.

I muffle a giggle. "Seriously, you can't do that. Besides, it's not like I'm the only girl you've ever been with. You forget I've met Morgana," I retort, unsuccessful at keeping the jealousy out of my voice.

He gives me a crooked smile. "Don't be envious, siren. She was a distraction from the mundane, as were all the others. They were available to satisfy physical needs, if you will. It was uncomplicated."

I try not to cringe or throw up my burger on him. "How romantic of you," I reply with sarcasm.

His eyes lock onto mine. "You're it for me, siren."

Damn him.

I attempt to control the girlie desire to jump over the counter and plaster myself against his body. Instead, I grab a handful of fries.

"Did you get the package I left for you from Kingsley College before all this happened?" he asks, observing me shove fries into my mouth with an unhealthy fixation.

I bob my head while caressing each fry with my tongue before chewing it, just to tease him. "I did. It was basically the letter formally granting me a two-month bereavement leave for Aria." My voice drops for a moment before I catch myself. "It's conditional. I need to keep up with my spring semester classes online and physically return to class with the rest of the student body in March, after spring break."

Still watching my mouth with fascination, Asher clears his throat before flipping his eyes up to mine. "When does spring semester start?" I'll give him credit. He's making an effort to focus on what I'm saying.

"Next week," I answer, twisting my lips around my straw and sucking the liquid a little firmer than I normally would. A drop of liquid begins to slide down the straw so I decide to torture him some more and lick it with my tongue. Asher hisses in a breath.

"By the grace, don't you two ever stop?" Callan feigns annoyance as he comes in with his apron on.

This one says: *I rub my meat for two minutes.* Then in smaller type: *But enough about my grilling secrets.* A loud laugh escapes my mouth and I almost choke on my fries. He looks down at his apron and gives me a mega toothy grin.

"I couldn't sleep and when I can't sleep, I bake." He shrugs and begins pulling ingredients from the pantry.

"That's our cue, siren," Asher announces, snagging some of my fries and lacing his fingers with mine before tugging me off the chair and into his strong arms.

I go to ask Callan if he wants any help but Asher widens his eyes and shakes his head in slow motion.

"Good night, Callan," I throw over my shoulder while Asher pushes me out of the kitchen. "Are you going to tell me what that was about?" I grill him as soon as we're in the upstairs hallway.

"There's only one reason Callan can't sleep and that's from lack of relations with Abby. It's best not to get involved. One year, they got into a huge fight and it was literally three months of cookies and entering baking contests," he admits with quiet laughter.

We stop in front of our bedroom doors. "Eww, Ash, way too much information. Not to mention, I will NEVER be able to eat another one of his cookies again, at least with a serious expression. Or any of his baked goods for that matter," I add with a scrunched face and he laughs loudly.

I just watch him, soaking in his relaxed demeanor and sparkling eyes. I wish he were like this all the time, content and stress-free.

Asher just smirks and bites his lip. "Your room or mine?" he asks with a no nonsense air.

"Huh?"

He moves forward, pressing me into the wall. He leans in and drops his voice an octave. "Your room or mine tonight?"

"Mine?" It comes out more of a question than answer.

The right side of his mouth tilts up. "Good choice." He backs away and grabs my hand, steering us into my room.

Inside, he leads me straight to the bathroom. Without saying anything, Asher prepares my toothbrush and his, loading both with toothpaste. As we brush, he hands me my floss and mouthwash. I smile at each gesture pleased he remembers my routine.

Once done, he shuts off the light and directs me towards the bed, guiding me into it and tucking me into his side. Shocking but even after all the sleep I've had, I'm still exhausted.

"See you in the morning light, siren," he whispers while drawing random patterns on my lower back with the tips of his fingers.

I try not to focus on the crazy way my body stirs at his touch and close my eyes.

The brightness from the room is shining through my eyelids, forcing me to open them. I sit up and rub the sleep from my eyes to find Michael positioned at the end of the bed, looking very angry. The archangel is standing at his full height, shoulders back, arms crossed, staring down at the bed where Asher and I are, sleeping together. *Crap.*

It's at this awareness I notice the light in the room isn't just from the morning sun peeking through the curtains. It's emanating from the warrior of Heaven himself. *Crap. Crap. Crap.* The muscle in Michael's jaw is thrumming as a result of how hard he's clenching his teeth.

I shake Asher in an attempt to wake him. He moans and grabs at me to pull me back down. "If you want to touch me, siren, there is a place lower that is completely awake."

Oh. My. God.

My entire face turns crimson and I pray to God to end my misery. "Asher," I say in a deep voice and elbow him in the stomach. That gets him to sit straight up.

"What the he—" He stops as soon as he sees Michael.

"This is certainly an interesting turn of events, Mr. St. Michael. Is it standard practice for you to sleep with all of your charges after saving them from a kidnapping?" the archangel asks, staring daggers at Asher.

"Well, Michael, since all of my previous charges have been male, no. It's not typical."

I drop my head in my hands and groan. "It's not what it looks like," I attempt to explain weakly.

"I disagree, Eve. I do believe it is EXACTLY what it looks like. This is the second time I have caught you both scantily dressed and in a less than approrpiate position," Michael lectures in a paternal tone. "Allowing your entrance into the Eternal Forest was not an open invitation for continued developments. You both have fifteen minutes to make yourselves presentable and join the rest of the protectors downstairs. Once again, we will discuss your conduct when you are fit to be seen." He turns and storms out of the room.

I drop my head in my hands in humiliation and wait for Asher to freak out. He doesn't. Instead, he starts laughing hysterically.

"What's wrong with you? We just got caught in a compromising position by someone who once said, and I quote, *relations between us would have dire consequences*," I scold.

I watch him have his laughing fit. "That was before," he says, throwing his muscular legs out of the bed and standing. Amused, he begins to put on his jeans and t-shirt.

My eyes widen. "Before what?" I ask, perplexed at his sudden ease with getting caught.

He walks over to me and cups my cheeks. "Before you were mine." He plants a light kiss on my lips and moves toward the bathroom to finish freshening up. *What the hell?*

We make our way downstairs to the kitchen. Asher fuses our hands together and is pulling me along like a puppy that refuses to be leashed.

As soon as we get into the kitchen, I notice the large spread Fiona has prepared. I'm taken aback by the massive amounts of food, but then I become conscious that the counters are lined with baked goods.

The sight is my downfall and I start laughing. Asher follows my gaze and smiles before squeezing my hand in acknowledgment of Callan's all-night baking session.

The rest of the clan and Michael are already sitting at the table while Fiona fusses over them like a mother hen. She's pouring coffee, clearing plates and refilling glasses. It is all so normal, until I remember I'm watching a panther, four gargoyles and one archangel.

Kenna shoots daggers at us when she notices our clasped hands as we make our way to the table and join everyone. She snaps her eyes to Michael and then shifts them back to us in a warning. Asher ignores her and sits down directly across from the angel, forcing me to sit down in the seat next to him, never releasing my hand. It's a statement, and to be honest, I'm a bit uncomfortable.

He begins to fill a plate with all of my favorite things and places it in front of me. I squeak out a "thank you" before he plants a completely inappropriate kiss on me in front of everyone.

"By de grace." I hear Fiona exhale but I don't dare look at her expression.

Michael clears his throat to get our attention as the rest of the clan is frozen. "Am I to understand, Mr. St. Michael, that the daughter of Heaven is no longer simply a charge?" he asks with a cold, calculating stare.

Asher sits tall and looks the blond haired angel in the eyes. "Eve is not merely a charge. She is my forever."

At his statement, I chance side-glances toward Keegan and Kenna. They look like they want to cut Asher's head off. Shifting my eyes to the other side of the table, Callan and Abby are both pale. Callan looks like he's going to puke and Abby is biting her lower lip like she wants to hide under the table.

Without warning, the archangel jerks to his feet and releases his large, fluffy snow white wings, then storms around the table at us. Asher stands just as fast, pulling me up with him and then protectively behind him.

At the same time, Callan and Keegan are by our sides in a heartbeat, prepared to defend. The tension rises around us. All three gargoyles have their black wings out and are ready for battle.

Michael steps to Asher, scowling. I inhale to keep from cowering. Asher stands tall, showing no sign of weakness. The furious angel lifts his hand and Callan and Keegan pull out their weapons.

At the sound of the metal releasing, Asher holds up his free hand before throwing a look to his brothers that is clear. He is telling them to wait before striking.

The archangel rests his palm on Asher's head without permission. By the expression on his face, Michael is having a hard time with whatever visions he is experiencing. When he's finished, he yanks his hand away as if burned.

Some sort of internal discussion ensues between the prince of the gargoyles and the warrior of Heaven because the angel seems satisfied enough to retract his wings and return to his seat in a calm manner. Everyone else follows suit, but there's a great deal of unease lingering in the air.

Michael leans forward and places his folded hands on the table. "You both understand the consequences for such relations?" the warrior asks in an angry tone. I feel like a child who has been caught doing something wrong.

"Yes," Asher answers, tightening his grip on my hand and waiting for me to respond as well.

"Yes," I reply. As soon as the confirmation is out, Asher immediately relaxes.

The angel nods his head once and we sit back down before Michael speaks again. "The reason I am here is because the Angelic Council has permitted me to do some exploration into the Declan clan. We've discovered they are working with someone very close to you. That is how Deacon was able to bypass the enchantments and get access into your London flat, knowing you would be else where."

At this information, Asher tenses next to me. "Are you saying we have a traitor in our clan who's helping him?"

You could hear a pin drop, the room is so quiet.

"Perhaps not in the London clan, but yes, in a clan close to this family," Michael confirms with authority and absolution.

I wait for everyone to flip out. No one does though.

"Who?" Asher asks in a contemplative way.

"I am afraid I do not know," Michael replies, looking at me with sadness. "My intel suggests they are gargoyle though and not another supernatural."

At his answer, everyone begins to talk over everyone else. Asher shifts his focus to me and takes me in with his eyes. My hands shake as I assess what the meaning of a traitor within the clans would be.

"There is more," the angel continues, commanding our attention. "At first, I did not believe the information to be truth. However, after this morning, I cannot disbelieve. It would seem your traitor has informed the Royal Gargoyle Council of Protectors you have committed a grave crime against their oaths." His eyes are directly focused on Asher.

Asher scoffs. "What crime would that be?" The question is thrown out with an arrogant air.

"Forbidden love. You are a prince of the gargoyle race, a loyal protector, a royal member of the high council, and now a gargoyle who broke his oath to his kin and race," the archangel answers with flatness to his tone.

"Shit," Callan says with force behind it.

A low growl rumbles from Asher as he locks eyes with Michael. "I'll deal with it. Thank you for the information, warrior of Heaven."

The archangel stands and bows once to Asher and then me. "Apologies. I am being called back. I will return as soon as I can. To be clear, I will neither confirm, nor deny the accusation of unsuitable associations between the two of you at this time. Not until I know which councils and members are trustworthy. That said, if I were you both," his eyes move from me to Asher, "I would heed Priestess Arabella's warning of restraint."

Michael dips his head in respect to the rest of the room before he thanks Fiona for her hospitable efforts and then takes his leave. Everyone sits motionless, processing the information we've been provided.

Asher's voice drops to a deep, even level. "I will only ask this once of my family. Is there anything anyone at this table would like to say to me with regard to the council or Eve?" He's met with silence. "I accept your peace to be truth and acceptance then. I will not bring either up again. You have my word."

The other family members nod their acknowledgment.

"Who would betray us to the council?" Abby inquires after a moment in a confused voice.

"Gage?" Callan suggests with a scowl, laying his hands flat on the table.

"No. It would be someone who has a lot to gain from Asher being removed as Eve's protector," Keegan answers.

"Deacon?" Callan counters.

Asher doesn't comment one way or the other.

After a moment of considering Keegan's words, I stand and release Asher's hand in panic mode. "No. No. No."

Asher pushes to his feet at my sudden outburst, knowing where my mind is heading and grabs the sides of my head, preventing it from moving. My eyes widen at him with understanding. "The council will remove you as my protector and sentence you to stone petrification."

271

"Shh. Eve, stop. It's okay," he cajoles in an attempt to soothe me. "We've got this." He doesn't deny it.

"My dream," I shriek in desperation.

At this, Asher crushes me to him in a tight embrace.

Abby walks over to us. "Eve, the council would have been here the moment this was brought to their attention if they had any plans to remove Asher as your protector."

Her words are meant to pacify me, but I'm not calm. Intense fear radiates through me.

"We will need to pull together a strategy to deal with the other clans. One that will give us opportunities to extricate this traitor." Keegan tries to get everyone to focus.

"Agreed. If everyone could give Eve and I a moment before we meet," Asher requests as the other gargoyles in the room hesitate but then agree, leaving us alone. Fiona slips out with them.

Asher stands in front of me, taking both my hands in his. He dips his chin and catches my eyes with his. "I need you to listen to me, Eve. No one in my family is the traitor. Understood?" His voice is firm and strong as he speaks.

"Of course. I never thought differently. Someone, though, has tipped off the council, Asher," I remind him, pushing down the fear that rises in me at what's happening. "I agree with Keegan that it's Deacon."

He takes in a sharp breath. "I know. Despite the fact that he isn't working alone, it's their word against ours. That's what we have going for us right now. As a member of the council, I can tell you that we're strict when it comes to oaths and laws, but fair. The council will not punish me if they can't prove the accusations. I might have a plan, but you're going to hate it."

I brace myself, knowing he's about to drop something that probably is going to make me snap. "What is it?"

"We need time to see who's leaking information to Deacon. Once we figure that out, we'll know who the traitor is and this won't be hanging over our heads." He pauses before he continues in a soft tone. "It might be best if we listen to Michael and Arabella for a short time."

I can't hear anything except the pounding of my heart in my ears. "Meaning what, Asher?" I ask, my voice stern.

"I'm merely suggesting that, in public, we keep our emotions and feelings for one another in check. It's best not to give whoever is feeding the council information, fuel to hang me," Asher explains in a pacifying voice. "When we're behind closed doors, away from prying eyes, we can be open with one another." He leans into my neck and nips at it. I try to focus on his idea and not the movement of his lips against my skin.

"It makes sense. Although, I think we should try to show some self-control all the time, including behind closed doors," I suggest. He stills and pulls back, watching me. "I'm just saying, I don't want to take unnecessary chances with your life. Just until we figure out who's betraying us."

"You don't trust my family?" he questions, misunderstanding my intentions.

"Asher, I trust them with my life," I reassure with sincerity. "They're my family too, you know," I retort, keeping my need to punch him in the face at bay.

He just stares at me. "Of course they are, siren. I'm sorry. I was just taken aback at your suggestion of no touching, at all. Like possibly for months, years, cen-."

I cut him off with a soft kiss.

His hands entwine in my hair, forcing my head to tilt as he leans in and deepens the kiss. A small hum of pleasure escapes me as my hands roam over his broad shoulders, pulling him closer to me.

I breathe out, "I love you," against his mouth.

A raw, needy sound releases from him as he pulls back and says, "Forever."

I smile, understanding his meaning as he kisses each of my hands before slowly letting go. Standing a foot apart, his face meets mine with a charming grin.

"Miss Collins, let's go show some restraint."

21 | Restraint

Restlessness is crawling through my veins, making me irritated and on edge. I'm like a drug addict in need of a fix. I hate this sensation. I detest every second of this plan. Restraint sucks. It's been days since Asher has looked at or touched me. I'm starting to wonder if a person can go mentally insane from lack of physical contact. Pull it together, Eve. I scold myself.

In my anxiety-driven state, I go into the training room to attempt to burn off some nervous energy. I decide kicking the shit out of the punching bag would most likely make me feel better. Two hours later, I'm drenched head-to-toe in sweat. It drips like rain water from my hair.

I step back to catch my breath as my brain checks-in with my body. The jumpiness is still there. I step forward and start punching the bag again. My rage and frustration explodes with each connection my fists make.

"You want a spotter?" Asher asks from the doorway.

My heart clenches at the sound of his voice. I close my eyes and inhale, pushing my emotions down. I stiffen my posture and focus on the bag.

"I'm good," I reply and keep jabbing. My arms and legs are on fire but I don't trust myself near him.

In my peripheral vision, I notice he's dressed in black loose workout pants, his standard leather wristbands and a black t-shirt. The sudden urge to run into his arms becomes overwhelming, so I return my attention to the bag and beat it senseless.

"Want to talk about why you're kicking the shit out of the punching bag?" the hot gargoyle asks while coming up next to me.

Asher's eyes darken and glow as he drinks me in like a thirsty man. The muscle in his cheek is twitching like it does when he's trying to control his emotions.

"Nope," I reply and I stop, bend down and pick up my water bottle.

He's watching me while I'm gulping down my water. His gaze follows my neck with each swallow of the liquid.

Asher's hand snaps out and curls in the bottom of my black tank top, pulling me toward him inch by inch. "I like this," he says in a low, seductive voice.

He stares at me for the longest time before cockily smiling. I lock my focus onto his lips. As they get closer, our breaths intermingle and my body hums in anticipation of his touch.

"TIMES UP!" McKenna shouts from the doorway, startling both Asher and I as we jump away from one another. *Damn stealthy gargoyles.*

"By the grace, Kenna," Asher scolds her as she looks at him insolently. With a loud and long growl, he snaps up his towel from the floor and heads toward the door. "I'll work out later."

Angrily, he leaves the room and I'm left feeling empty.

McKenna's head snaps to me. "Are you willing to die for him, or have him die for you? Because I promise you, that's what will happen if the council figures out you two are shacking up." Then she lands the final crushing blow. "You've seen the vision for yourself, blood of Eden. You've seen the council's punishment for the violation of his oath."

She's right. I have and protecting him is my sole focus. Without a word, I turn and head to my room for a long, cold shower and desperate diversion.

After fighting hard to get my tunnel vision off Asher, I decide school is the perfect distraction. Spring classes begin shortly so I get organized by going online to download my eTextbooks and syllabuses then sign up with each professor via email. After, I run through each class description so I know what to expect. I haven't been this prepared for classes since freshman year of high school.

School proves to be a short-lived diversion. I decide to call my aunt to catch up. After the four hundredth time of her asking when I might be coming home, I've had enough and promise to call her later in the week.

Sitting on the window bench, I stare out onto the gardens as my eyes drift to the lake. Shivering at the memory of Saraphina, I decide to go see if Callan can show me how to bake. Sad. But true.

I pull open my door and notice across the hallway Asher's door is slightly ajar. The light is on and I hear movement. I stop, close my eyes and inhale. My heart races at the knowledge he's in there. When I have myself under control, I open my eyes only to be met with the sight of Asher's shirtless back.

Drowning in desperation and his attractiveness, I absorb every muscle and each line of the tattoo. He reaches for the waistband of his gym pants and begins to pull them down. I force my eyes away and run down to the kitchen, blushing.

Callan is leaning against the counter when I run in like a bat out of hell. His eyes widen at the sight of me before I smooth myself out and ask if he wants to make some cookies. Standing there with his coffee in his hands, he smiles knowingly over the mug.

"Let's get geared up," he answers, walking to the pantry door and throwing an apron at me.

That's what I love about Callan. He never asks questions, just jumps in when you need him. Over the next few hours, we make two dozen, different batches of cookies. This gargoyle proved to be an amazing distraction and I now fully understand his need to bake as a pastime.

The two of us are laughing hard while cleaning up the last remnants of the mess caused from our flour fight, so we don't notice Asher until he clears his throat.

We both look up and smile at him. Asher, on the other hand, looks angry, standing in the doorway with his hands in the front pockets of his jeans.

"What's going on?" His voice is tight as he eyes us.

"Eves needed to bake," Callan answers, biting back another laughing fit.

Asher pulls his brows together. "Bake?" The word rolls around his mouth like a bad taste.

"Bake," I repeat and wave my hand around the kitchen at the dozens of plates of cookies.

"You should have some. They're really good," Callan suggests and kisses my cheek. "She must get her mad cooking skills from my side of the family."

He winks and I beam at the compliment. At his statement, that little tug which warms my heart whenever one of them includes me in their family knots tighter.

"I see," Asher says with a cool, detached tone.

Callan studies Asher for a moment. "I'm going to go find Abby real quick. If I leave you two alone, remember the rules. No jumping the brooding gargoyle, cutie." Callan bear hugs me, causing me to squeal.

I swear I hear a growl come from Asher. Callan puts me back on my feet slowly and walks around Asher, guarded as he backs out the doorway. He must have heard the warning sound too.

Asher walks into the room and plucks one of the cookies from the cooling rack. "So you and Callan...baked?" His voice is off as he chomps on the dark chocolate oatmeal cookie.

Confused with his demeanor, I go to the fridge and grab the milk before pouring him a glass. "What, you don't think

I can handle a few cookies?" I ask, handing him the cup and our fingers brush. The slight touch causes the heat to rise through my body, making it tingle with energy.

Asher's breath picks up at the same time. He gives me a look that suggests the cookie isn't the only thing he wants to devour at the moment.

With his eyes never leaving mine, he roughly sets down the glass and grabs my neck, pulling me toward his mouth. He stops just before his lips meet mine. His other hand clutches my lower back, but he doesn't move closer.

Instead, he lifts me onto the counter and my legs circle around his waist. Once I'm in the position he desires, Asher's hand moves across my throat sensually.

My head falls back against the cabinet as I let out a soft whimper from his touch. Then, in a fast motion, he removes his hand and steps back.

We're both breathing hard. He just stares at me, panting and we both come to our senses. Without words, I slide off the counter and walk past him. We suck at self-control.

Over the next few weeks, we manage to avoid one another. Asher spends most of his time in strategy meetings with the visiting clans, in business meetings with Callan and Keegan, or in the training room.

I stay busy by training or focusing on school. Thank goodness classes have started and keep me pretty occupied. On rare occasions, we end up in the hallway or kitchen together and one of us has enough sense to leave.

It's been hard, to say the least.

It doesn't help that the other clans are around us more often in the house. We have to be careful about our interactions even more with prying eyes observing us with engrossed fascination. Each time I have to force a smile or interest in a clan member, it's always in the back of my head that they might be the one working with Deacon.

Marcus and Morgana are here a lot lately. It's apparent that the Manhattan clan is a close ally of the London clan. Their relationships seem so easy with one another.

Morgana's presence brings a whole different emotional roller coaster that I need to control each time I walk into the room and she's there. Though I have to admit, I've become really fond of Marcus. He's entertaining and carefree. Being around him brings a sense of normalcy back to my life.

Feeling lighter than I have in a while, I take the last step into the kitchen only to stop in my tracks at the sight of Morgana waiting for the coffee to brew, wearing one of Asher's t-shirts. *What the hell?*

Sensing my presence, she turns and offers me a phony smile. "Hi, Eve. Fiona is off today so I'm making coffee. I know how bad-tempered Asher is in the morning without his first cup."

I try to calm myself before I lunge at her and yank her extensions out. "I see," I say, my voice cracking.

The change of pitch doesn't go unnoticed by her. Morgana's bogus nice-girl-act grin grows wider, knowing she got to me.

"I wasn't expecting anyone from another clan to be here this early," I mention in an even tone.

"Our strategy meeting ran late. Deacon is one hard motherfucker to figure out," she enlightens. "Anyway, Asher and I have history so it's not uncommon for me to spend the night." She turns back to the coffee maker.

The bile in my throat rises along with my temper. I take a step toward her but stop when I hear Asher's deep voice. "Eve?" I turn and lock furious eyes with him before I brush past him at a crazy fast pace. My blood is boiling.

I hear him following, but I can't stop. I rush up the stairs and slam into my room. My breathing is completely out of control. He walks in at a slow pace and closes the door before turning to me and knitting his brows.

"What's wrong?" *Is he for real?*

The question shatters the last of my sanity and I attack him with my fists. He grabs each wrist and spins me so my back is against the door. Asher lifts my arms over my head, pinning me from another attempt at hitting him. He pushes his knee in between my legs to stop me from kneeing him.

"Whatever conclusion you've come to, it's wrong. Morgana, along with all the other clan members, stayed here last night after a late night strategy meeting. Normally, when we're in London, they stay in the guest apartment. We don't have that here, so she stayed with Marcus in one of the spare rooms. That's it, siren." He holds me in place while I process the explanation.

My heart finally stops pounding in my ears. I inhale and blow out a long breath and let go of the insane amount of irrational anger running through me.

"What the hell is wrong with me? One minute I'm fine and the next I'm ready to rip someone's face off? I can't control my temper or emotions anymore," I pant in between shallow breaths.

Asher's face softens. "It could be the ascension, or the bond might be changing. I don't know. Mated gargoyles become very possessive of one another, almost animalistic.

Perhaps that's what you're experiencing since we shared stone state," he offers while watching my eyes.

Suddenly, I'm very aware that he has me pinned against the door. My eyes close, savoring his body's proximity to me and I inhale his scent.

His voice is low and smooth as he says, "We should go back downstairs. Everyone's leaving today and we don't want to both not be present. It might seem odd."

I nod my agreement since my vocal cords don't seem to be working. Before Asher moves away, he presses into my body one time as his head drops into my neck, letting his nose run the length of my throat and over my jawline before his lips barely caress mine.

❧❧

I toss and turn for about twenty minutes. The agitation finds its way back into my body, scratching at me. I finally give up and decide I'm getting no sleep tonight. With great dramatics, I throw the blanket off my bare legs and sit up, trying to figure out how I'm going to calm myself down.

Quietly, I open the door to my bedroom. Noticing the lights are out in the house, I tip toe across the hallway to Asher's room. Just as I raise my hand to knock, the door opens and his arms dart out, pulling me into the room.

Without warning, he slams me against the wall, causing a gasp to escape my lips. "What are you doing, siren?" he asks, his voice thick.

"I-I couldn't sleep," I stutter, not able to think with him pushed against me and his breath fanning my face.

"Fuck this," he says as he roughly takes my lips with his. I melt at the taste of him as he clutches my upper thighs and picks me up, carrying me to his bed. Please don't stop touching me, I think to myself and his hand slips under my t-shirt, landing on my skin, pressing me closer to him.

At his touch, a bolt of electricity flows through me, as if the bond is content because we're reunited. I groan loudly at the warmth it causes in my veins and Asher lets out his own sound of pleasure, fueling the ache I've been feeling for him for weeks.

Gently, he lays me on the bed and covers my body with his. At a frantic rate, our hands are grabbing, touching and pulling at one another.

Faintly, I'm aware of the knock at the door and we both freeze. "Asher, it's Keegan. We need to speak, now."

Dropping his forehead to mine, he whispers, "Don't fucking move." He peels himself off me and goes to the door. He opens it the smallest amount so Keegan can't see I'm in the room.

"This just came from a messenger," Keegan states, handing him a note.

"What messenger?" Asher asks.

"A Royal Gargoyle Council of Protectors messenger." Keegan releases each word in a slow, methodic manner.

I sit up at Keegan's answer.

Asher snatches the letter and reads it as I hold my breath in fear.

"I'm requested to appear the day after tomorrow to stand trial for breaking my oath of protection of Eve Collins."

22 The Council

Sheer terror and panic flow through me as I read the letter again before placing it into my bag. I know what I have to do, but the fear floating through me is stifling. I press my lips together in trepidation as I look at the clock once more, trying to keep my breathing controlled.

"All you have to do is get to the Castle Combe Village," I whisper to myself, trying to calm my nerves.

"What are you doing?" Asher questions from the doorway. I startle. He watches me before coming over and giving me a soft kiss that rattles my soul.

Crap, how long has he been standing there?

I exhale to still my anxiety and display a fraudulent smile while focusing on the calmness he brings to me through our bond.

"A paper for class," I reply, hoping he doesn't see right through my lie.

He's quiet when he leans against the desk and takes my hands in his. Keeping his eyes trained on them, he pulls me to stand between his legs, wrapping his arms around my waist. "Hey," he says softly. "I don't want you to worry about tomorrow. I can feel the worry flowing through you. It's all going to be okay."

I nod and focus on his chest where the protector tattoo is located because my stress is more than just the tribunal. He dips his chin. "Your dream was not a premonition of things to come, siren."

My voice is just above a whisper. "What if you're wrong?" I ask with a tight throat.

He takes my chin in his hand, forcing my eyes to meet his. "I've got this. Trust me, yeah?"

I do trust him, but I will protect him. "With my life."

His eyes roam my face for any sign of hesitation. "Good girl. I'm going to let you finish your paper. I'll see you upstairs in a bit?" The question lingers, like he's worried I won't come up. *Does he know?*

I lean in, giving him my best effort at a kiss that shows how much I love him. Our lips stay fused together for a while before I pull away. Asher knits his brows as something flashes over his face, but as quickly as it was there, it is gone.

He kisses my forehead one final time before standing up and moving to the door. I hold his hands until the final moment that his fingers slip through mine. My eyes just stare at the spot that our fingers used to be joined.

"See you soon, siren," he says in a quiet voice.

With those parting words, he walks out. I look at the clock, knowing I have exactly one hour.

Somehow I manage to slip out unnoticed, which is not easy in a house full of gargoyle protectors. I meet the cab outside the gates and have the driver get me to Castle Combe in no time. It's a small village in Wiltshire, renowned for its tranquility and it's where I'm meeting my ride to County Kerry, Ireland.

The cab pulls up at the fourteenth century medieval church. I pay the driver and step out, scanning my surroundings for any danger. When I see none, I run into the cathedral, hoping I'm on time.

As I make my way into the sanctuary, I smile when I see the long, flowing red hair of the ethereal being whose help I've summoned.

Sensing my arrival, she turns to me and bows gracefully, a motion that causes her ringlets to fall over her shoulder and onto her deep emerald green Grecian dress.

I walk to her with elation. "Lady Finella, thank you so much for your help," I say sincerely.

"It is truly a great honor where you are concerned, my dear," she answers while embracing me before pulling back so she can see my face. "Did you have any difficulty using the sleeping potion I provided?" her inquiry is heavy with genuine concern.

"No. All gargoyles and panther shifters are out for a while," I reply before grabbing my cell phone and turning it off so Asher can't track me. I force away the guilt I've been feeling since lacing everyone's water at dinner. "The hardest part was watching the clock and waiting for the brew to kick in."

The beautiful fairy touches my cheek in a maternal manner. "Excellent. Well done, Eve."

I look around at the beautiful church and then back to the queen of the fae realm. "Are you sure Deacon can't get in here?" I ask with nervous energy.

She stands tall, pushes back her shoulders, placing both hands over her stomach in a regal fashion. "Do not fear. I am most confident that the demon spawn wouldn't dare come within a hundred foot circumference of holy ground."

"Good. Ready?" I question with a shaky voice.

Lady Finella just observes me before speaking. "Forgive me, however, I am obliged to inquire if you are without doubt prepared for this?"

I lift my chin and inhale. "This is the only way I can be certain he is safe." I stare at her while she considers me.

Lady Finella drops her tone to a maternal one. "Your protector will be quite irate with your actions," she elucidates, waiting for my response.

I stand straight after situating my bag over my shoulder. "At least he'll be breathing. Angry or not, Asher will continue living in this world. That's enough of an incentive for me to make this sacrifice."

She studies me thoughtfully before a warm smile graces her peach lips. "You love him." It isn't a question.

I look her directly in the eyes. "With every fiber in my body, Your Grace."

She puts her hands together. "We ought to be off then. I can take you to the door, but once there, only you will be permitted to enter. After which, I will be required to return to the fae realm."

I nod in understanding. "Thank you for helping me, Your Grace. I really appreciate it."

Lady Finella tilts her head to the side. "It is my honor, daughter of Heaven." The fairy holds out her hand, and I take it. "Are you prepared?"

I exhale a deep breath, hoping I'm doing the right thing. "Yes." At that one word, the queen flickers us out of the church, and in an instant, we materialize on a stone entryway in front of a pair of large, stained glass doors.

Lady Finella keeps my hand clasped in hers. "Welcome to Domus Gurgulio Castle," she says, motioning to the elegant doors. "It's Latin for House of Gargoyles."

Her eyes shift to mine, and the side of her mouth tilts as she leans in to whisper in a conspiratorial way. "Gargoyles are not the most creative supernatural group. We tend to leave that to the vampires." She winks.

I release a soft laugh.

The doors open and a large man stands there. His inky black hair falls midway to his neck and a bit over his slate colored eyes. He's in all black, which makes him look very intimidating, especially with his dark brown gargoyle wings revealed. The gargoyle's eyes widen when he sees Lady Finella.

"Your Highness," he greets, bowing to her. "To what do we owe this immense distinction?"

As a mark of respect, Lady Finella dips her head in a slight motion. "Rulf," she acknowledges the gargoyle. "Eve Collins, daughter of Heaven, requests an audience with Lord Falk. I entrust you will be considerate and accommodate her appeal. It is also my hope you'll offer her protection and benevolence as she is to be considered a most revered guest while under your care," she states with an air of authority that's not meant to be questioned.

He bows again. "Of course, my lady." Rulf turns to me and bends at the waist. "Daughter of Heaven, it is with enormous privilege I welcome you to Domus Gurgulio. If you'd be gracious enough to follow me, I'll take you to Lord Falk at once." He motions me into the castle.

I smile at him. "Thank you," I reply before turning to Lady Finella. "I'm so grateful to you for all your help this evening, Your Grace."

She embraces me one final time while whispering in my ear. "Good luck. I will reflect most excellent wishes to you and hope for the safety of your protector. I must take my leave now. You shall be in safe hands with Rulf."

With those parting words, she shimmers, leaving behind a wave of gold dust in the air.

I turn back to Rulf. He's waiting patiently for me to follow him. I square my shoulders and walk steadily into the castle to meet with Lord Falk, the head council member of the Royal Gargoyle Council of Protectors, prepared to plead with him for Asher's well-being.

As soon as I step into the stone building, I notice I'm in a large entryway. There are four hallways which all veer off in different directions. Not sure which one to walk through, I wait for the rather threatening dark haired creature to guide me.

"Come this way, please." The twenty-something-year-old gargoyle motions toward a long stone hallway to the right of the entry doors. I follow him blindly.

As I gaze around, I notice the walls and floors are intricate stonework. The high-vaulted, arched ceilings are

Restraint

composed of a dark wood. There are rich scarlet and gold carpets on the floors and marble and granite tables decorate each hallway. It's really beautiful in this castle.

"So you're the dark prince's charge?" Rulf makes small talk as we walk down a long corridor.

I don't trust him, so I keep my answers short. "Yes."

He snickers. "You're friends with the queen of the fae realm?" he asks, trying to get to know more about me.

I'm not interested in conversing.

I exhale a nervous breath. "I am."

Rulf stops and turns to me, a crooked smile on his amused face. "I know you don't know or trust me, but as a sworn protector of all humans, I feel obligated to warn you that whatever you did to get here without a protector is going to royally piss off Asher." He stands there looking at me. "I'm assuming the queen of the fairies assisted your dodge?"

I roll my eyes, and let out a short laugh having been caught red handed. "Have you ever tried sneaking out of a house full of gargoyle protectors? Security is tighter than a prison. So, yes, assistance in my escape from a fairy might have been in order," I respond, not making eye contact.

The gargoyle makes a face like he's really considering what I said. "Understood," he says in amusement. "Lord Falk awaits," he adds and falls in step next to me instead of ahead of me, leading us through mazes of hallways.

I give him a sideways glance. "Can I ask you a question, Rulf?"

He scans me. "Sure, Eve," he answers, testing my name.

291

I hesitate before I ask. "What are the council members like?" I inquire. "I mean, is there anything I should be prepared for?" I watch his response carefully.

He stops and touches my arm lightly. "If you've survived this long with Asher St. Michael as your protector, the rest of the council members will look like pussy cats." A smile forms on his lips before he motions to the last corridor on the left.

I inhale sharply when we enter this hallway. It's the same one from my dream with Asher. The alcoves are filled with gargoyle statues on the left, the arched windows highlight the inky night on the right and two gargoyle statues balance fire-filled urns on their head, all leading to the two carved doors in front of me.

I push back my shoulders and face the wooden entry.

"Are you all right?" Rulf asks.

I chew the inside of my cheek and nod, not trusting my voice.

"Please wait here. I'll inform the council and Lord Falk that you're here."

Rulf walks through the doors of my vision as I begin to fidget and wonder if I made the right decision by coming here. "They're ready for you," he announces near my ear. I didn't even hear him approach me.

I turn and follow him through the doors and into the dark, stone chamber that matches my recollection from my dream in perfect detail. I follow my escort down the aisle lined by urns filled with fire.

We approach the raised stage where the council sits. They're all dressed in black, five are to the left of a throne and four are to the right. Asher's seat is empty. The silver-haired, tall elder stands in his black robe with his dark brown wings extended. He looks unapproachable as he waits to greet me.

Rulf takes a knee and bends his head. "Lord Falk, I present Eve Collins, escorted by Lady Finella. She has requested haven for the daughter of Heaven, as well as an audience with you."

Unsure of what I should do, I lamely wave. "Hello," I say in a small voice. At this, the council members begin to look at one another. The elder smiles, but it's not friendly.

"Where is your assigned protector, daughter of Heaven?" he inquires.

I take a deep cleansing breath before I speak in a firm voice. "He's not here. I came alone." I'm having a difficult time looking at Lord Falk, remembering what he did to Asher in my dream. Rulf stands and moves by my side in an almost protective stance.

"Miss Collins, be assured Domus Gurgulio offers you refuge, always." Lord Falk bows to me before straightening. "May I present the Royal Gargoyle Council of Protectors?"

"Of course," I reply, trying not to sound intimidated or afraid as I look at the panel.

Lord Falk motions to two men on his far right. "Cassius and Lief." Then motions to two women. "Catrain and Ryia." He points to a male elder. "Jarin." At each one's name, they dip their head to me in acknowledgement. I follow suit.

Lord Falk shifts his focus to his direct left, motioning to a female elder. "Thea. Rowen is the only gentlemen on this side, Carac, and Sybbyl. The empty chair is for your protector, Prince Asher." He returns his gaze to me as I take in the elite council, all various ages and ethnicities.

Trying to find words, I say the only thing that comes to mind. "It's an honor. Thank you for allowing me refuge and for seeing me on short notice."

Whoa, where did that come from?

Lord Falk relaxes his wings and takes a seat on the throne after his formalities. "Why are you here, Miss Collins, and without your appointed gargoyle?"

I stand straight and look him right in the eye. "To request clemency on his behalf."

All the council's eyes are on me. Their faces morph into scowls. No one speaks. I don't wait for an answer.

"Mr. St. Michael has done nothing immoral. The accusations against him are inaccurate. It is my understanding that you are a fair council, yet you are prepared to put one of your own on trial for an erroneous charge without any evidence to support the claim," I point out, mustering up all the strength I can to sound unafraid.

Lord Falk narrows his eyes at me. "Yet here you are, Miss Collins, asking for leniency on his highnesses behalf. Why is that?" *Crap.* He makes a good point.

I hold his stare and tip my chin up. "He is my protector. We are bonded. It only makes sense that I care about what happens to him. My well-being and existence depend on his protection."

I pray they buy it.

23 Darkness

"NOT ANOTHER WORD!" A deep male voice shouts from the back of the council chambers. I don't even need to turn around to know that it's Asher. I clench my teeth. Damn fairy potion didn't last long enough. The entire council turns their interest behind me.

Rulf leans into my ear. "Do you want my protection from your gargoyle?" he asks in a serious tone. I shift my eyes to him without answering. "I'll take your silence as a yes." He stands tall again, grinning before he takes my elbow and moves us to the side to make room for Asher.

The council is now to my left and to my right I see the London clan storming up the aisle, appearing fierce. Asher just looks primal and ready to tear something, or someone, apart with his bare hands. He doesn't glance at me. The muscle in his jaw is ticking at a rapid pace.

Keegan, McKenna, Asher, Abby and Callan all stand in front of the council. Everyone but Asher takes a knee before rising. No one looks my way. They're all tense and stiff, wings out.

"Lord Falk, council members, please accept my deepest apologies for my lack of presence. I am here now, a day early, and ready to proceed with the trial. Miss Collins is incorrect. I do not require clemency," Asher explains in an even voice.

I go to step toward Asher but Rulf wraps his hands around my upper arms, preventing me from moving. I snap my head toward him, showing my displeasure. In response, he shakes his head, telling me not to intervene. His grip tightens and I give in and stay put.

Lord Falk just stares at Asher for a few moments.

"Very well, Prince. The council will grant a short break to allow you to inform Miss Collins of our tribunal rules," he says formally.

Asher tenses. "I would prefer if Miss Collins not be present during the hearing. She's human and a simple charge. There's no need for her to be in attendance," he retorts and I clench my teeth.

The elder gargoyle takes his request into consideration before responding. "Denied. She will be in chamber during the trial. After all, Your Highness, this trial is about her." His answer is final. "The rest of the London clan will remain with the council while you take a moment to discuss the process with your charge. We will send Rulf to retrieve you when we are ready to begin."

Asher's body is rigid as he dips his head. "Thank you, Lord Falk." He turns and faces me. His expression is furious. "Release your hold on her." He seethes at Rulf. At his order, Rulf lets go of my arms. Asher prowls to me before taking my elbow and guiding me out of the hall.

My protector says nothing as he drags me down several stone corridors and into a private, dark hallway that's out of sight. Without warning, he pushes me against the wall and presses his body against mine before placing a knee between my legs and dropping his forehead to mine.

Confused, I just stand frozen. I expect yelling but not this. His breath fans over my face while he closes his eyes, attempting to control his emotions.

"Are you okay?" he asks on an exhaled shaky breath.

Reveling in the feel of him, I chance moving my arms to the front of his chest.

"I'm fine," I answer in a quiet voice.

He nods his head against mine and lifts his gaze. "Fuck, I don't know whether to kiss you or strangle you, siren. What the hell were you thinking? We'll discuss the shit you pulled later. Now is not the time or place." He stares at me, his anger subsiding.

My throat tightens with nerves. "Okay," I answer weakly.

Asher's hands cup my face, tilting it back so he can get a better view of my face. "Whatever happens in that room, Eve, DO NOT REACT. Do you understand?" he asks, his tone stern.

I just watch him. "Yes." My heart lurches at the thought of what could actually happen in there.

He blows out a stressful breath, but his body doesn't relax. "I mean it, siren. You can't act in response. If I sense, even for a moment, that you're about to, I will have that dumbass Rulf yank you out of the chamber so fast, you won't know what hit you," he warns firmly.

"I understand," I reply, trying to get him to believe me.

Asher's eyes just scan mine. "You will walk out of there with me today." He holds my gaze, waiting for me to say I understand what he means.

I nod.

Asher steps away from me, releasing each part he's touching as emptiness floods my body. After a few moments of composing himself, Rulf appears.

"The council is ready for you," Rulf states from behind us in a no-nonsense tone.

We follow my guide back into the council chamber, side-by-side but not touching. The room is laced with tension as my eyes scan the clan's solemn faces. Callan offers me a wink before Asher and I stand before the assembly again.

"Miss Collins, please step to the side with Rulf," Lord Falk instructs as the good-looking gargoyle ushers me closer to Abby. At Rulf's touch, Asher's face snarls. The anger he's emitting sends shivers down my spine.

Lord Falk turns to Asher then to the council. "Asher St. Michael, elite council members, we are here today to hold tribunal on behalf of the gargoyle community. Since there is a human present, we will continue not in our native tongue of Garish, but in English for the proceedings." At his announcement, the members dip their heads in agreement.

He turns back to Asher. "Mr. St. Michael, it has been brought to the council's attention you are in violation of our laws. You have been accused of having infringed upon the oath you swore to uphold with regard to your loyalty to both the human race and your charge, Eve Collins. What say you?" The older gargoyle waits for an answer.

Asher stands tall and speaks in an authoritative tone. "As a member of this council, and next in line to the throne, I take my oath and loyalty to both my race and my charge very seriously. With respect, I ask the council what proof the accuser provided to initiate this hearing?" He waits as the council shifts their focus to Lord Falk.

The tall leader smirks. "The petitioner has provided two eye witnesses to your breach. We've interviewed both and they have validated the accuser's claims. As a member of this council, your highness, you are aware that the punishment for such forbidden defiance is stone petrifaction." My heart drops into my stomach at this reminder. Images from my vision flash into my mind and I begin to sweat.

Asher doesn't seem phased. "As you and the council are aware, the punishment is not enforceable without physical proof. You have none because none exists. The alleged accounts from two unnamed witnesses are not enough to impose the sentence. We all know that, Lord Falk," Asher counters confidently.

Lord Falk pales. "No. There is no physical proof, only verbal," he answers with annoyance.

Asher bobs his head. "Then, I think we're done here. Make no mistake though, no mercy will be bestowed to anyone who attempts to hurt Miss Collins. It is my right as her protector to eliminate anyone, human or gargoyle, who might bring her harm. Therefore, if Deacon Baptise is the accuser, I suggest you investigate him for the kidnapping and severe beating of Miss Collins instead of wasting everyone's time with a frivolous tribunal," Asher recommends with malice laced in his statement.

At this, the council turns to one another. "Do you have proof of this alleged charge against Mr. Baptise?" Lord Falk queries.

"I can provide the same amount of evidence as he has given to you of my so-called breach of my protector oath," Asher counters with sarcasm.

The elder narrows his eyes. "Fair enough. We will open an investigation into your allegation," Lord Falk agrees.

Asher motions for me to join him. I move to his side, anxious to leave. "Thank you. Then we are done," Asher states.

The older gargoyle lifts one side of his mouth. "Not quite so fast, Mr. St. Michael. The gravity of this situation is deep. As a council member and next in line to rule our race, you are aware of how seriously we take our protector oaths and laws. Therefore, we must take an accusation such as this under extreme consideration, regardless of evidence or who the petitioner is."

My stomach falls. Asher tenses next to me.

Lord Falk stands taller. "It is the council's ruling that you shall be temporarily removed as Miss Collin's protector until we can either clear you or charge you further."

Suddenly, the air is sucked out of the room and I can't breathe.

I can feel the anger radiating off Asher though he schools his face and body. "I accept the council's ruling, conditionally." The words are rushed out of his mouth, his eyes locked onto Lord Falk.

"The council agrees to hear your conditions, protector," the leader acquiesces.

Asher takes in a deep breath and closes his eyes before opening them and focusing on Lord Falk. "I would like to ask the council to remove Miss Collins from the chamber before I state my conditions." No!

Lord Falk nods. "Granted." He motions to Rulf to take me away. I turn to face Asher, panicking. He doesn't look at me. I clench my teeth as Rulf takes hold of my elbow, attempting to get me to leave the chamber.

"Wait," I bark at my escort. I don't budge because I'm heartbroken. I lower my voice to a whisper and lean into Asher. "You said we would walk out of here together. How could you?"

He doesn't acknowledge me, his jaw muscle thrumming and I am escorted out of the chamber without Asher by my side.

ޫߦ

We're surrounded by darkness as the cold, wet rain descends from the night sky, prickling my skin. My breathing is deep as my chest rises and falls quickly. Beyond the cliff's jagged drop and past the wall of stone is the Atlantic Ocean. I train my eyes straight ahead and focus on the body of water shrouded in black.

Asher stands motionless next to me. I'm not sure if he's even breathing. I slide my glance to his face. At the sight, my throat constricts. The light provided by the inky sky bounces off the ocean, reflecting in his face.

"We have five minutes before they come to escort me away," Asher says coolly.

I turn to face him. "I need you," I whisper in a pathetic voice.

His eyebrows draw together as pain crosses his face. "When I realized you were nowhere in the house, siren, I thought Deacon had you again and it almost fucking destroyed me."

A tear slides down my cheek. "I-I didn't know what to do. I just reacted."

Asher says nothing as the rain drips off his face and mine, soaking into our clothes. He just stares at the water while draped in darkness.

"All I knew was I needed to save you," I explain, my voice uneven.

"No, you didn't." His voice is low but has the same effect as if he shouted.

"Ash—" He doesn't let me finish.

His head snaps to the side, his eyes filled with distress. "Did you even stop for one second to think about how your actions affected me, or the rest of the clan for that matter? Let's not even discuss the fact that you drugged us all with fairy potion and then snuck off into the night without a protector while Deacon is God only knows where and could have done who knows what if he caught you again." His voice is eerily calm.

As the rain pelts against my skin, I shift my eyes back to the ocean because I can't stand his disenchantment with me. Instead, I try to form the right apology while the frigid droplets of water run down my face.

I let out a quick laugh. "Like you considered me when you had me removed from the chamber after promising you'd be by my side. You're always so guarded. You constantly ask me to trust in you but the truth is, Asher, you don't trust in me. If I had just been included in the strategy meetings, plans or your general thought process of attack, maybe...just maybe I wouldn't need to go off and do stupid things like tonight," I offer as a lame argument.

Asher's indigo eyes glow, illuminating the resentment and disappointment in his face. "That's your defense, Eve?" Doubt laces his every word.

I exhale. "What do you want me to say, Asher? What do you want me to do here? What can I do to make you realize this isn't about me?" I beg, my voice hysterical now.

Asher turns sharply toward me, his eyes narrow as he takes a step at me. "THIS. IS. ALL. FOR. YOU. EVERYTHING I DO IS FOR YOU!"

I take in a sharp breath. I need him to understand the depth of what I feel for him, because it's the motivation for my actions this evening. "I couldn't survive if anything happened to you. If you no longer existed in my world, it would destroy me." My voice is soft.

He contemplates my words for a moment. "By the grace, you are the most infuriating woman," Asher grounds out in exasperation. His gaze meets mine and his hand reaches out to touch my wet cheek.

In that moment, I look into his dejected eyes and my heart breaks into a million pieces. I mourn the life we had and the one we'll never have.

"I love you," I speak softly into the rain-filled night air. I hope it's enough and he'll embrace me, but I know the minute I told him how I felt, it was all over.

I don't even notice the coldness anymore because I'm empty inside. In the depths of my soul, I know any second he's going to walk away from me, this, us.

Rain pelts against his face. My body leans toward him as the tears escape my eyes, rolling down my cheeks, mixing in with the frigid rain.

Asher's eyes scan my face, memorizing every detail. I need him. I need him like I need air. He pulls away, leaving me vacant and chilled.

"I will protect you, always," he promises.

My eyes shift up and lock onto his.

"By leaving me?" The question is harsh.

He exhales a shaky breath. "If that's what it will take to keep you safe, I'll do it."

My body trembles with fear of losing him, so he grabs my upper arms to still me.

"Listen," he commands, tightening his grip around my body so I can't flee.

I shake my head in terror. "No, you can't. Who will protect me if you leave?" I sound hysterical.

I clench his wet shirt, not wanting him to go.

"The clan will protect you until I can come back, and siren, I swear I will come back to you," he vows.

"I can't do this without you," I argue, begging him.

"You won't have to. My family will watch over you. I have no choice, siren. They've made their ruling. As a member and royal figurehead, I must oblige. It's the only way until I can clear things up with the council." He exhales before speaking again. "Even if that means walking away and living the rest of my life off our memories."

I pull him closer. "No, Asher," I grit out through clenched teeth, the tears flowing.

He holds me firm as he looks into my eyes. "I don't regret one moment with you, not one second. I will always choose you over me. I will protect you, always."

"It sounds like you're leaving forever," I accuse through my tight throat.

Pain marring his face, he grabs my wrists and pries me off him, taking a step back.

I stand there wet and speechless, about to watch him walk away from me.

"Ash—" His wings snap open. "Don't do this," I plead.

"Ilem jur pri tú-tim, ew tú-tim pri pos-tim ali ide in-zen, mání, vas-wís, ew ter-ort. Esta-de ai esta Ilem de, Ilem pos-tim in-saengkt pri, tú-tim," he says in Garish.

It's the same thing he said to me the first time we went into stone state together.

My eyes beseech him to stay. "Asher…"

He watches me, his face stoic. "Forever," he whispers before he disappears into the rain-filled dark sky.

My knees buckle and I fall to the ground in shock and disbelief that he actually left.

My breath is gone.

My hand goes over my heart, trying to relieve the ache of emptiness that's forming.

Randi Cooley Wilson

He's gone.
I'm alone in the darkness.

DIALECT TRANSLATIONS

CHAPTER 7

Quí an-mání ú por lem, í ku an-in ú dur: Any harm you bring her, I will destroy you for (Garish)

Lem-de an-wís dur ú re kat ante ámo ku ulem hiúman, in-saengkt: It's unwise for you to fall in love with your human, protector (Garish)

Gres-por ku ágra-lem, rap: Leave with your protector, now (Garish)

CHAPTER 8

Cartref merch Croeso duw: Welcome home Daughter of God. (Welsh)

CHAPTER 9

Anvolde lem ansa lók, esh anten skítas de volde lem: The wingless ones cannot speak, and lack the intelligence of the winged ones (Garish)

CHAPTER 11 AND CHAPTER 22

Ilem jur pri tú-tim, ew tú-tim pri pos-tim ali ide in-zen, mání, vas-wís, ew ter-ort. Esta-de ai esta Ilem de, Ilem pos-tim in-saengkt pri, tú-tim: I promise you forever, and forever you shall have my heart, soul, mind and body. With everything that I am, I will protect you, always. (Garish)

CHAPTER 13

Dia duit (pronounced dia gwit): Hello (Irish)

Nice tae meit ye, Eve!: Nice to meet you, Eve! (Scottish)

Randi Cooley Wilson

COMING SOON

REDEMPTION
The Revelation Series

Keep reading for a sneak peek at the first chapter of
Redemption, The Revelation Series, Volume 3.

For bonus material, please visit: **randicooleywilson.com**

Excerpt from Redemption

On the morning the darkness first descended, it settled into every fiber of my existence. The emptiness materialized deep within my veins, wrapping itself around each organ. Starting with my heart, then my lungs, and finally, it crept its way into my soul.

The empty days are consumed by loneliness and the nights by endless grief. The darkness pushes me further and further into desolation and I feel as though I'm treading water, and at any moment, my body will just give up, forcing me to sink into the murky rivulet.

I'm drowning, because in spite of everything, I still belong to my gargoyle protector, Asher St. Michael. Each and every heartbeat belongs to him. Every single one of my breaths, they're all for Asher. Though I'm the one who was left behind, I know in the deepest corners of my heart, he's hurting too.

Sitting on the window bench in my room, I inhale a shaky breath, while using the back of my hands to wipe away the escaped tears. Crap. I didn't think I had any left to shed.

As my fingers brush over the surface of my cheeks, I'm reminded of the lifelessness my skin now suffers from. It used to be filled with heat and desire. Now, it's cold and unfeeling. The large organ is enveloped in an invisible armor, preventing life and warmth from penetrating it.

My gaze lifts to the dreary clouds, my only connection to my protector. Large hazel eyes reflect back at me in the glass windowpane. Mocking me, filled with sorrow. Without thought, I rub my chest, trying to relieve the emptiness his absence is causing. I keep my focus trained upward, at the heavens. "I miss you, Ash," I whisper into the empty room.

I remind myself of the last word he said to me before disappearing into the rain-filled sky. "Forever." The rest of my gargoyle sentinels, the London clan, his family, found me sitting on the wet grass, in the cold rain. Soaked and weeping. My body rocking back and forth in an attempt to comfort itself, while my mind slipped into a catatonic state. The only sound that fell from my lips was his name, spoken softly over and over again.

Each day, I go over in great detail, the last moments we shared on the rocky cliff overlooking the Atlantic Ocean. I attempt to discover a clue or inkling of something, anything, I could have said or done that would have changed his mind. Made him stay with me. Fought for us. The energy wasted. I always come up empty handed. My eyes close as I inhale while memories flood me and then float away, a daily occurrence.

"I've got you Eves. You're safe. We're all here cutie." Callan's voice was the first I'd heard before he lifted me into his protective arms.

His words weren't comforting though because he was mistaken. They weren't all there.

Asher was gone. Vanished into the inky heavens.

"Where the fuck is he?" Keegan's angry tone cut through the downpour.

"I don't know," Abby answered as her face locked onto mine filled with worry.

I only stopped saying his name long enough to utter. "He left." Then I went silent for what would be three weeks.

The night following Asher's disappearance, he reached out to Michael with instructions for the clan. The only piece of their conversation the archangel would share with me, was that Asher was safe and under the watchful eyes of the council. Then he informed me I would be returning home the next day to Massachusetts, under the protection of the London clan. That was all. No, I'm sorry. Or, I'll see you soon. Michael said nothing that would indicate my dark prince would return.

I squeeze my eyes tighter as Lord Falk, the Royal Gargoyle Council of Protectors leader's words drift through me. "Mr. St. Michael, it has been brought to the council's attention that you are in violation of our laws. You have been accused of having infringed upon the oath you swore to uphold with regard to your loyalty to both the human race and your charge, Eve Collins. What say you?" The accusation thrown out during the tribunal held at Domus Gurgulio Castle in County Kerry, Ireland.

After Asher made it clear the council didn't have any solid evidence to support the charge, the council, of which he's a member, decreed he was no longer appointed my protector while they continued to investigate the allegation of misconduct.

Due to lack of evidence, they weren't formally able to charge him with violating his protector oath, a sentence that carries a punishment of eternal stone petrifaction. For that, I'm grateful. Knowing he's somewhere breathing in the world eases the pain, a little.

I glance over at my bed with longing. It would be so easy to crawl back into it like those first few days. After removing me from the rainstorm, the clan brought me back to their home, La Gargouille manor, in Wiltshire, England.

They placed me, fully clothed, in a warm bath and coaxed me into eating and talking. I refused. Instead, I walked into Asher's room, grabbed the Property of London shirt he liked me to sleep in, changed into it, and curled up in the fetal position in the middle of his bed. Surrounded by his scent of smoky wood and leather.

My anguish was overwhelming. I cried myself to sleep for days, never moving. What was the point? I felt empty inside. I spoke to no one. Attempts were made to get me out of bed, dressed, have a meal and converse.

Finally, McKenna in a rare show of support or sympathy, stepped in and explained to the family that I needed time and space to deal with the stress Asher's and my separation was causing the blood bond.

Two days later, she stormed into the room with her mate and Asher's older brother, Keegan. At her orders, the handsome warrior snatched me out of bed and carried me into the shower while turning on the cold water. I shrieked in pain as the little prickles of water hit my skin and squirmed in Keegan's drenched powerful arms.

Once McKenna was satisfied I was clean and awake, she wrapped us each in a towel before Keegan brought me back into the room and gently placed my shivering body on the floor. Then he wordlessly took his leave.

McKenna just stood there with her hands on her perfect hips, her sapphire eyes watching my every breath. A few moments later, Abby, her cousin, walked in with fresh clothes and a plate of food. Damn gargoyles ambushed me.

"I'm not going to let you do this to yourself. You're stronger than this, blood of Eden. Get your fucking ass in gear and pull yourself out of this shithole you're creating," McKenna spit at me with her lack of bedside manner or tact. I ignored the harsh statement since it's typical McKenna.

Both girls got me dressed, with little help from me, and sat next to me on the floor in Asher's bedroom. McKenna threatened that I wasn't allowed to return to his scent-filled bed until I ate something.

After an hour stand off, I did. Pleased with their successful efforts, they continued this torment every day. Either, Keegan or Callan, Asher's young brother and Abby's mate, would snatch me up out of bed and douse me in cold water while the girls force-fed and dressed me.

After three weeks of depression, I'd had enough of their antics and feeling sorry for myself. McKenna was right; I needed to pull myself out of the shithole. Knowing I had about an hour before I was forced into an icy shower, I got up on my own, showered with warm water, dressed and made my way downstairs to the kitchen.

When I entered, the rest of the St. Michael family was eating breakfast with Fiona, the shape-shifting panther and manor's caretaker.

No one said anything. They all watched me with cautious, and stunned expressions, as I grabbed a coffee and scone then sat down with them. Without a word, I nibbled on the pastry. Once they decided I was mentally stable, everyone returned back to the table conversation.

Satisfied with my presence, Keegan announced we were leaving that afternoon for Massachusetts. And we did. A few hours later, we boarded the private jet and arrived the following morning to the estate I'd grown to love, just outside of the Kingsley College area, where I'm currently sitting, in my old room.

I inhale the rain-filled fresh spring air that floats in from the open window, overlooking the wooded area behind the house. At the same time, my right hand moves to my neck searching out the necklace Asher gave me. My fingertips brush over the feather lying on its side. The darkness creeps back in.

I choke back the sudden feeling of absolute despair. The memory of when Asher gave it to me hits me hard. The image of him causes my heart to clench. It's been so long since I've seen his indigo eyes, striking face and sexy stubble dusted jawline. I squeeze my eyes closed, holding onto the vision before it fades.

"It's beautiful, Asher." I breathe out.

"I asked your aunt to make it especially for you. It's an angel's wing, a symbol to remind you of the divine presence in your life. May I?" he asks. I nod as he brings the necklace around my neck, securing the clasp.

"I love it. Thank you." I turn to face Asher. *"But I don't need a necklace to remind me that I have a divine presence in my life. I have you."*

The emptiness fills me again as soon as my eyes open, a painful reminder he's gone. Anger and frustration begin to build and run through my veins like poison. He left me. My hand tightens around the silver chain and I yank it hard as the clasp breaks and the delicate piece of jewelry falls lifeless in my small hand.

I hate looking at it. All the trinket does is remind me of broken promises. I lift my arm to throw it out the window as a smooth, seductive, masculine voice hits me in the gut, like a punch. His unexpected presence knocks the wind out of me.

My body won't turn around. It's rooted to the spot I'm sitting, almost as if I'm being held down by a thousand weights. My heart rate picks up at the sound of his voice and his familiar scent assaults me.

"Are you sure you want to toss away something that means so much to you?" the gargoyle queries from over my right shoulder.

My hand clasps the necklace in a tight clench. Crap. He's right, I detest him for being correct, but he is. Damn him. I allow my anger to boil so that when I do finally face him, I can release it.

The striking man that I know so well moves from behind me and sits next to me on the bench, shifting his eyes out to the window's view. My breath hitches while I take in his facial features. By the grace he's good-looking.

"What are you doing here?" I ask, my tone lined with loathing and resentment.

He turns to face me and gives me a sexy smirk. A set of beautiful eyes lock onto mine. "It's nice to see they didn't have to sedate you on the plane after all," he chuckles quietly.

A short strangled laugh escapes my throat, a foreign sound. "Seriously, why are you here?" I ask with a lackadaisical attitude.

The attractive gargoyle adjusts his large body toward me.

"I'm your new protector, love," Gage says, holding my gaze.

Acknowledgements

I'd like to start by thanking my family and friends for supporting me throughout this amazing journey. Without your love and encouragement, I would never have written, and finished, this series.

Kris Kendall, I adore you. You make the editing process so easy. Thank you for putting up with my *'crazy author moments'* and giving me the best reaction to a piercing I've ever seen. You're amazing.

Kristin at Indie Solutions by Murphy Rae, thank you so much for taking these books to the next level!

Danielle at Bravebird Publishing, what can I say, lady. I'm obsessed with the cover and trailer for Restraint. To use our favorite word, you're 'swoon' worthy.

A huge debt of gratitude to the beta readers: Sara Dustin, Maureen Switalski, Terri Thomas, Meghan Tate, Kayla Clinton, Iris Cabrera, Michelle Drew, and others, for your continued dedication toward this series and these characters.

To Nichole at YA Reads, and all the amazing bloggers, who ALWAYS host my books with enthusiasiam and love, there are not enough words to show my appreciation. Thank you all for being warm and accepting of this series.

Randi's Rebels. You all ROCK! I'm grateful to you for all you do on a daily, hourly and minute basis for this series and myself. Thanks for supporting the revolution!

My little rainbow, Maddison, thank you for being patient and sharing my attention. Mommy loves you and each night will see you in the morning light.

To my hubby, Dave, I love you more than you'll probably ever know. Your support, excitement and encouragement push me through. Every. Single. Time. Thanks baby!

Finally to the readers, thank you for taking a chance on this series and embracing it as you have. It's been a journey of self-discovery, love and sacrifice for not only these characters, but me as well. Thank you for allowing me to be a part of your reading library and literary world!

About the Author

Randi Cooley Wilson is an author of paranormal, urban fantasy, and contemporary romance books for teens and adults. Randi was born and raised in Massachusetts where she attended Bridgewater State University and graduated with a degree in Communication Studies. After graduation she moved to California where she lived happily bathed in sunshine and warm weather for fifteen years.

Randi makes stuff up, devours romance books, drinks lots of wine and coffee, and has a slight addiction to bracelets. She currently resides in Massachusetts with her daughter and husband.

I love to hear from readers, please reach out to me at: **randicooleywilson.com** or via social media outlets:

Twitter: R_CooleyWilson

Facebook: www.facebook.com/authorrandicooleywilson

Goodreads: www.goodreads.com/RCooleyWilson

Rebel Group: www.facebook.com/groups/randisrebels

Made in the USA
Lexington, KY
23 December 2015